SERENE

THE HUMAN CRYSTAL

JEN PATRYN

BALBOA
PRESS

A DIVISION OF HAY HOUSE

Balboa Press books may be ordered through booksellers or by contacting:

Balboa Press
A Division of Hay House
1663 Liberty Drive
Bloomington, IN 47403
www.balboapress.com
1 (877) 407-4847

This is a work of fiction. All of the characters, names, incidents,
organizations, and dialogue in this novel are either the products
of the author's imagination or are used fictitiously.

Print information available on the last page.

ISBN: 978-1-9822-0730-4 (sc)
ISBN: 978-1-9822-0732-8 (hc)
ISBN: 978-1-9822-0731-1 (e)

Library of Congress Control Number: 2018907504

Balboa Press rev. date: 07/31/2018

My gratitude extends deeply to my Mom, Lorna and Dad, Ken, and to my family and friends. To B., thank you, from every reach of my heart.

contents

CHAPTER 1

The New York City sky was grey and moldy. The clouds were thick and low, resting atop the silver buildings by the Hudson. The air was damp, carrying unseen movements of the river, feeding the shadows that lived under the bridge. If you peered inside a wobbly glass window in Chelsea, you'd see a thin yet feminine figure. Her hair was honey with waves, her eyes were oceans with waves: interesting to look at but more so to look *into*. Her soul revealed. One could sense that all was possible in the unknown. It lived in the light that danced around her space-filled pupils.

Her legs were covered in smooth, opaque stockings; her body sleeved in a black dress. Her hand gestured toward a distorted sculpture of a dripping white owl that was two times her size. Once inside, one could hear what was coming from her lips.

"This owl was sculpted by the hands of Sheryl Ames. She lives in a remote part of Bordeaux. The earth she uses is endemic to that geography and not much is left as it has been continually harvested since the Middle Ages. Those responsible, the keepers of this clay, allow only her to sculpt from this blanc, mineral-rich soil. They see it as her birthright, as her skill has been passed down

1

for many generations. Her kiln is a giant hearth, nestled into the base of a mountain. This very combination produces layers of uniqueness impossible to recreate anywhere else in the world."

An older gentleman, dressed in a pressed dark grey cashmere suit, lifted his bushy white eyebrows up into the air and almost off his face. He responded, "Not so much, my dear."

I, being the girl you're watching and now listening to alongside said older gentleman, looked at him and took a card out of my pocket and offered it to his aged body. "Well, my name is Serene. Nice to meet you. Please take my card. I have a feeling this piece will be worth your time someday soon."

He smiled and mentioned that I was too young for him, but … if I thought differently, I could show him where this hideous owl might work in his Park Avenue apartment.

I felt fluctuating movements despite my effort to hold still. I was fighting my disgust, trying to keep it from transforming my face into my truth. I did not want to show him that he had affected me. I turned my back toward him and quietly walked away, maintaining my composure. His sense of entitlement and his insinuating that I would somehow engage with him on a level of pure use just to sell him something only confirmed that he thought he could buy some little or big part of me. From his candor, I would guess that he went through his life successfully buying many pieces of people. I had to deal with this breed of human way too often in this gallery.

My stomach was growling. I picked up a tall black umbrella, my black trench coat and walked toward the portly male figure in the office. "Be back in thirty minutes, Mr. Steinway," I said.

He never lifted his head. He just put his right hand up in the air and motioned for me to go. I then slowly and somewhat reluctantly walked out into the drizzle to eat some wet fish.

Walking down the cobblestone street I was careful to not let my heels get caught in the cracks. After several blocks, I came upon a very nice place. It had a wooden sign in the shape of a bear holding a fish in its mouth and HOKKAIDO carved and burned into the wood below. I walked through the doors.

Ahhh … peace, order and silence filled my head.

Sitting down at the bar, I breathed in the smoked-wood and earthy-tea aromas. The sushi chef bowed and greeted me. "Onegi shimase."

I placed my hands on the piece of majestic blond wood that was the bar. I then ordered two pieces of mackerel, one white tuna, one yellowtail, jalapeño and shiso maki roll with a cup of green tea. All the while, I was staring at a fat, round Japanese man.

Everything became blurry: his bulbous shape began shaking right before me. When my eyes regained focus, he was no longer a man: he was a big orange-and-white koi fish with bloated red lips that opened, spouting out seawater and a lump of kelp that plopped onto the floor. His eyes rolled around in his fish head. I blinked and then saw a fat Japanese man again.

People always said I had an overactive imagination.

I had never been alarmed by what I saw in moments like these, until I was taught that I should be. I had learned by now that maybe no one else in this room eating yummy, perfectly sliced, throbbing marine flesh on plushy beds of slightly sticky rice saw what I saw. I was guided to keep my observations of what was not made of mass and stone to myself. "We must always pay attention to the material world and ignore the ethereal."

Current civilization acknowledges the critical mass of atoms only when they come into view in the form of something we have been taught to covet. It made me feel sullen and heavy inside to think that we were constantly taught to "behave" or "act normal." Wouldn't it be nice if the world wanted our minds to see unknown things and for us to feel and communicate better with one another? Instead, I was pretty sure the message we were getting out there was to shut down, work, make money and spend money. Whatever you do, don't talk about your imagination, your dreams, the energy you feel when you walk into a room and what you know but cannot see.

I decided while eating my maki roll that I would go to a bar and secretly look for a mate. I was trying to keep this secret from myself. I did not want to admit that I was looking for love or even needed to be loved. I wanted to be strong, I wanted to be enough and I didn't want people to see my desire or—worse—risk rejection. So, I pretended to need nothing, even though it wasn't the truth. This exercise of self-deceit was very hard to do at times. I looked at my phone and noticed the time. I paid my check and walked carefully and very slowly back to the gallery.

I was cold and wet, yet instead of hurrying I took it slow. It seemed like a better use of my time then selling art, warm and dry inside the gallery.

I gingerly opened the glass doors to enter like air—unseen and undetected. My air-entering approach, however, was lost on Mr. Steinway. He did not recognize me as air or even comment on my commitment to my newfound performance art of trying to disappear by sheer will. Instead, he slammed his red and veiny fist onto the glass that covered his antique mahogany desk. I saw the condensation quickly forming on the glass around his hand. My eyes widened and I stayed silent.

"My God, Serene, where do you go for lunch? China? I hope you have a Chinese man in your bag with a black Amex. Get back on the floor and try to sell something. Oh, that reminds me. The gentleman who was in earlier today had his assistant request a time for you to show him some more sculptures for his East Hampton home. I scheduled you in for tomorrow at 1:00 p.m. So don't be late!"

I inwardly shuddered at the news. So this is what I had worked so hard for and my mom had paid so much in tuition for?

Well, I was here. I had the life that I'd dreamed of when I was a young girl back in the woods in New Hampshire. I wasn't making any money, but the carrot was there. I was chasing it every day.

And then I had a realization.

This was what I'd always dreamed my future to be. This was it. This was what it looked like. This was what it tasted like. This was what it felt like. I wasn't sure I liked any of it, but I'd picked it. Now I didn't know why. I missed the wild turkeys nesting in the moonlit tops of the ancient pines, staring at me through the window of my childhood bedroom. They used to scare me, but now they symbolized a better time. I missed the mountain air.

Growing up, I had wanted to leave and never go back. I'd never felt understood there. The nature was beautiful but cold like its people. I'd come to New York because I was in love with her. I felt life's possibilities in each inhale of breath while walking her streets. Evenings were chaotic and dangerous yet always laced with the excitement of chance meetings leading to all things golden or all things eclipsed in a moment's notice. These were only some of the ways the city spoke to me. Her voice was always clear, never warm or soft. More like "I love you" or "I hate you." I felt her confidence of pure being. I listened to her severe truth. For me, it was better than a gentle lie. I came to her because she called. Now we didn't know what to do with each other and I was stuck like a canned piece of over-sweetened fruit suspended in Jell-O staring at other pieces of strange and lifeless fruit—just waiting for that cold war mushroom cloud—for Dupont stocking-wearing women to serve our Jell-O-souls to day-drunk men.

"We should go to Death tonight." This was my best friend, Lydia. Her red glossy lips spoke as she smoked a cigarette and ashed it into her camel Hermès Birkin bag.

"Yeah, I'm down. I've never been," I said, following my trashy, beautiful friend down Fifth Street.

"Oh-my-God, it's so good. It's a dive bar, with lots of hot straight guys and always fun, crazy people. I actually can't believe any good bars are left in the city anymore and this one is *good!*"

As I listened to her high crystalline voice, I noticed all the red streetlights were shining HALT, all the taxi brake-lights screamed STOP and five signs of business on this block were ruby halogen FLAMES. *Rome was burning.* I truly do live in a beautiful hell and of course when I looked up, there was a crimson shape that read DEATH with two skulls next to it.

Lydia and I showed our identification to the burly doorman, who was dressed in a black waxed coat that hung over his combat boots and brushed the sidewalk.

"I bet he's a Brony at heart," I whispered into Lydia's ear.

We both giggled as he let us in.

Lydia grabbed my hand and led me to the bar. It was loud, dark, dirty, smoky and crowded. The lights flashed electric white and then back to black. Amid the pulsing, a guitar was being tuned. I grabbed Lydia and dragged her toward the commotion. We both flashed our lashes and stared at the same long line of a man who stood before us on that filthy stage.

The wall of music hit us at the same time. It was so loud you could feel your organs vibrate. The man had dark greasy hair that kept getting in his blackened almond-shaped eyes. He was tall, unapologetic and knew exactly what he was. His bones showed well from under his skin, their structure perfect. The space that his body was inhabiting was somehow giving appreciation to his form and presence.

This moment in time stretched into a deafening lapse of déjà vu. Those papyrus-green eyes with his dark lashes and strong nose—his features were ringing over and over in my head as I remembered him over and over again. It was a strange feeling that I'd never had before. I studied the way he moved. I watched as his hands grabbed the microphone and sang a slow, sad verse. His fingers were strong and expressive. His voice, like a drop of sepia in water, as if he came from several generations of opera singers that had all committed suicide. His skin was peachy-white with hints of luminous grey. Lydia and I both looked at each other at the same time. It was a look of shock and weakness that we shared with one another. He took a knife from his jean-jacket pocket and cut his arm. He then dipped the knife in gasoline, lit it on fire and threw it over the crowd, into the back wall. He was bleeding, sweating and shaking. I thought he was looking at me, but I knew that wasn't possible—the crowd was covered in thick darkness and he probably could not see anyone's face. Even if he saw mine, why would it matter?

When the set was over, the band came off stage and walked through the crowd. The drummer walked right up to me, grabbed my arm and kept walking with my flesh still in his hand. I quickly grabbed Lydia's arm and we were led through the crowd to a coffin door in the wall. The drummer knocked and it opened. Inside was a room with big leather chairs and one black lacquered table with a stuffed black cat sitting on top of it accompanied by a mirror with lines of good cocaine. And, yes, there is a difference between good and bad cocaine and if one is going to do cocaine at all, it might as well be the best because it was the worst.

Lydia lit a smoke and grabbed her silver straw out of her Hermès bag. She bent over, revealing her silver underwear as she snorted up two lines, sat down and ashed into her bag.

"So, I am Lydia and this is Serene," she said, looking at the wall.

The drummer got up. "Hey, my name is Greg. I am drunk and bored. Thought you two could entertain us."

"We could play a game," Lydia said, rolling her eyes.

"I like this one." A girl's voice came from around the corner.

I turned in the direction it had come from. The voice belonged to an impossibly tall girl who must have just come from cool girl heaven, beamed down on a ray of rock-and-roll light. I examined her carefully to try and learn how to be cool. She was dressed in perfectly worn-in jeans that hung on her like she didn't care about anything in the world. She wore a mix of Saint Laurent and vintage clothing appearing to have been found from long hidden culturally rich tribes that have been steeped in time. They worked well together and made me ask questions in my head. Her body was thin, in-shape and well-cut. Her skin was smooth and flawless. I wanted to know what is was like to be her and not me.

The rest of the band members started to trickle in. They carried a smell of burnt metal. My eyes wandered to the singer's arms. They were massacred. He looked at me long enough for me to look away and pretend that he did not exist. The cool model girl offered a bro handshake to the singer and the rest of the band. "Sick show, guys."

A loud thud — the coffin door of our cave swung open. A big security man was yelling at us through a deafening wall of screams. "There is a fire on the stage!"

I grabbed Lydia and we pushed through the smoke, flames, bodies and screams.

Later that night, I stumbled into my bedroom and threw myself on my bed, face-first. A tall, handsome wilderness giant with impeccable, classic, "worn-in good taste" walked into my room, picked up a coffee mug and looked inside. I couldn't cohabitate with anyone else. Like a brother, this giant was difficult at times but also my best friend. Lydia referred to him as my gayband, her play on the term "gay husband." William loved men. He was not feminine at all. He had more masculine energy than most people I knew. He was secure, calm and unwavering. He offered hard-hitting truths and worked in the medium of black and white. The word grey was not in his vocabulary and decisions were never reconsidered after deliberated on from a fact-based point of view. His mind was like a heavy, substantial gun that has been firing for one hundred years at the same target.

I buried my face and screamed into my pillow. "Ahhh, William, you wouldn't believe this guy I saw tonight."

He put the mug down. "You smell like crap! Did you smoke cigarettes by a burning building filled with asbestos all night?" he joked.

"No, I was at Death and there was a fire."

"No you're still alive. You didn't die in a fire. You are maybe a little crazy but still kicking." He laughed.

I buried my head again and couldn't help but kick my feet in the air.

DAY BREAKS

Walking along the cobblestone street, I thought to myself, *My goodness, another dreary shitshow of a day. What am I doing here?* What purpose was my life serving other than ushering large sums of money into Mr. Steinway's pockets and caging art into the confines of lonely prisons, also known as some of New York City's most prestigious penthouses, lofts and brownstones? Expressions of beautiful souls rotting in rooms for the eyes of few—the very same eyes that see many zeros in succession after another number on their banking apps. I was trying in vain to add those same zeros behind the numbers on my app as I hustled and pretended my life away. As this disturbing thought rattled about, I noticed a familiar group.

It was the homeless men who set up camp under the scaffolding next to the soup kitchen known as the Bowery Mission. They were there every day and every day I walked by the Mission on my way to the gallery. I would look in their direction, to acknowledge our shared humanity. They would stand in line waiting for rotten food. One or two would be turned up on cheap bottles of liqueur that were probably just one step up from nail polish remover and God knows what drugs. Sometimes I would see someone with actual rotting flesh, left for dead out on the street. I have seen feet that can't fit into shoes, ankles swollen, skin broken and bleeding, appendages yellow and filled with infection. Sometimes a face would be covered in sores.

There was one man, though. He had impeccable style. I would have to stop myself from taking his picture. He wore cool graphic and colorful sweatshirts in rainbow layers and had every color iPhone charger hanging from his neon yellow belt made into the likeness of a tasseled tribal skirt. I looked too long on this particular morning. He told me I should shoot myself in the face and other things I couldn't make out or, rather, was blocking out. His anger was as loud and colorful as his iPhone skirt.

The reason why I kept walking down this same street and didn't go in the other direction to avoid this heavy vista was a man named George. He was in his late seventies. He didn't appear to have been on the streets long and the world around him had not yet ravaged his sweet, open face. He always sat on an old, wooden chair leaned up against a fire hydrant. He would stand up when I came near. He would usually laugh or smile and he would always put his hand out. We would turn around on the street as he guided me to dance in the steps of his youth. Today it was the rhumba.

"*Front and back and cha cha cha,*" he sang.

After our dance, like a perfect gentleman he would say something like, "Well, it was a pleasure to dance with such a lovely young lady with such fine skills." He would always close with a laugh and pull up his pants before he sat down on his old, wooden chair again.

Before long, that loathsome glass door that led into the gallery appeared before me. My hand went to the door. My intention was to push it and walk through. Instead, I took a moment. I worked on trying to thin my oxygen intake, hoping that would also thin my need to care about anything. My heart was racing. Finally, I managed the impossible: I opened the door of the gallery and pushed down what was trying to come up and out of me.

I glided over to the owl sculpture and whispered a faint "Hello." My ears directed their attention to the *clicking and clocking* coming from a familiar sound of strong, purposeful heels on the marble floor. I turned around and saw a woman of maybe sixty-five years of age. Her hair was silvery white and fastened into a low bun at the base of her head, allowing the rest of her hair to plumage out, creating a hair beret of sorts. Her bone structure was like that of an aged Rodin dancer. She was wearing black, five-inch high-heels, encrusted with diamonds, also black. Her stockings were opaque and looked soft to the touch. Her frame was slender, encased in an impeccably tailored skirt suit. She had gloves, sunglasses and a giant new Celine handbag that looked already bent out of shape from carrying something heavy and oddly formed within its French leather innards.

Her matte, deeply creased lips parted, the smell of stale smoke and rich perfume traveled around her in a playful way. She took off one glove. A platinum owl encased her middle finger.

"May I say that I love your ring," I started the conversation.

"Thank you. This ring was just given to me by a dear friend. I rather like owls. It is a recent occurrence. Nevertheless, it is one that I don't mind."

She loosened her other glove away from her fingers one-by-one, delicately shaking them free. I nodded in silent agreement and veered toward the giant owl sculpture. Its wings were shaking and vibrating. They separated from its body, slowly slicing the air and wrapping themselves around this strange woman. The woman closed her eyes at that very same moment. It seemed like she was trying to live inside her mind so she could have an exchange with the owl.

She opened her bag. I noticed a glow coming from within.

I had to look inside. I peered my head over––not minding my manners as my curiosity had taken precedence––and upon further inspection, I saw two beautifully bold-shaped crystals. One was aquamarine and the other was a cluster of raw ametrine that was mostly a deep ruby purple with bursts of juicy amber. After moving her crystals about, she found what she was looking for. Her hand resurfaced, holding a dark grey leather-bound checkbook and a silver pen.

"To whom shall I make the check out to and for how much?" she asked.

I watched as she opened her checkbook. We both realized there were no more checks left inside. She looked up at me and said, "My name is Gertrude. I have another checkbook in my apartment. Would you mind joining me? We can have a tea. I can give you the check and arrange when my new owl friend will arrive."

"Of course," I replied, surprised.

"Perfect," she said, as she led me out.

I skipped over to Mr. Steinway's office, knocked on his door, quickly opened it and blurted out, "I have to cancel the 1:00 p.m. meeting. There is a woman who wants to buy the owl," already knowing his response.

"Oh, yes, go go! Sell the owl!" It was the third largest sum of money the gallery was asking for.

I was released from my impending doom-filled afternoon with an insecure old man with an addiction to power. I was allowed to escort Gertrude for whatever amount of time, as long as I came back with a sale. We both entered into the back seat of her black Mercedes sedan. The interior smelled of French figs and the leather was the color of a melted soft caramel. The windows were tinted a dirty rose. The driver was a young handsome man, with borderline disturbing features. Julie London played and the windshield wipers wiped. We both looked out of our window and observed the silent film of rainy New York City streets.

Once in the apartment, Gertrude motioned to a small table in the kitchen. I sat down and looked out of her bay windows. There was a gated park. I grabbed a small leather purse out of my bag that I sometimes kept my phone in.

"What a beautiful purse. May I see it?" she asked.

I handed it over and explained it was hand-painted by an Arabian artisan for a girl in the king's harem. Or at least that was the story I was told by my friend Lydia, who had given it to me. "I like the story even if it isn't true," I said, smiling and looking in her direction.

She handed my purse back to me and as she did, an image appeared in my mind. It was a large, glowing, violet crystal-cluster deep inside the earth living in a beautiful cave. I kept this to myself.

After a short, uncomfortable quiet, she broke the silence. "Yes, of course. Let me write that check." She sat at her table and took her time to execute a perfect signature and then handed it to me.

I took a sip of tea that had just been served to me by her housekeeper and looked out the window, longing to smell the magnolias blooming in the gated park.

"Would you like to join me for a walk?" she asked.

A "yes" escaped my lips a little too quickly. I definitely did not want to go back to where I had come from.

We walked down the cold, white marble stairs of Gertrude's building, where a friendly doorman opened the large, white alabaster stone doors and smiled.

Once we were at the front gates of the park, Gertrude pulled out a black wrought iron key that matched the gate. Once inside, the birds sang their songs a little sweeter. The lilacs appeared more lush. The air was thick and decadent with rainwater. We walked in comfortable silence until Gertrude broke it. "You are the oldest. Did you know that?"

I looked behind me to see if she was talking to someone else. Her steel mid-Atlantic eyes were cast directly into mine.

"I'm an only child."

"Yes, of course you are. You are the eldest soul in regards to your mother and your grandmother. Your grandmother is actually the youngest. But you are the eldest."

A shiver went down my spine. "I have always been very close to my mother and grandmother, we have always shared a special communication," I admitted.

"Yes, like the dreams."

"Oh-my-God, yes! Like our dreams, we would come to each other in our dreams. The next day, when we woke, we would call each other and share what we had dreamt.

"How do you know this?"

"I am an empath, I can feel things deeply. I get messages about people I know and do not know. It's very similar to how you communicate with your mother and grandmother."

"I could never know anything about strangers," I said.

"Maybe not now, but if you want to hone your gift, I am sure that you could know many things without spoken word. All gifts are different and like humanity, they have strengths and weakness. Also like humanity, all gifts have the ability to grow into abilities we never imagined. All possibilities are endless.

"For instance, my strength started with receiving messages about others and that was not always easy for me. When I was younger, I did not know what an empath was. I just knew that, if I looked at someone, I could take on his or her emotions and sometimes know specifics of what was going on in the person's life. It was difficult, as no one talked about experiencing what I did. So I never spoke about it either.

"I found that people who suffered drew my attention more boldly than people who seemed at peace. It was as if their souls were calling out for help and sending an SOS signal. I always paid attention. I spent a lot of my youth not honoring my gifts or my heart. I chose to have relationships solely with people in pain. I witnessed and accepted hurtful actions from others because I knew the origin of their pain and knew that they did not mean to harm me, or so I told myself. It took years for me to learn how to separate myself from the worlds pain and recognize myself as an individual. I had beautiful teachers that I have to thank for that.

"I slowly learned how to harness my energy. I learned how to protect it. It was not easy, but once I started to heal myself, the door was blown wide open. My gifts grew immensely. Part of my journey now is to help others with these gifts."

There was so much to take in. I was silent and intently listening to this strange woman. We were standing next to the magnolia tree I had been looking at from her window earlier.

"This one is my favorite. Look how purple these blooms are compared to the rest of the magnolias in the city. Just like the color of the crystal," Gertrude said.

I looked at her and thought of the amethyst cluster I had seen in my mind's eye earlier in her apartment.

"It's in your purse," she said.

I looked inside my little purse and there was the most beautiful amethyst I had ever seen. It was deep purple with waves of light lavender that undulated with delicate cellophane rainbows. "Thank you, Gertrude. This is too kind," I said in complete dumbfounded astonishment and gratitude.

"How did you get this in my purse?" I asked

"It wanted to take a ride with you," she said, laughing.

I looked at her, searching for more answers. This woman was unlike any other woman I had met.

I then closed my eyes to fully take in the scent of the regal magnolias. When I opened them again, I was looking through the black wrought iron bars of the gate. I saw a figure that looked familiar. I couldn't place it, so I kept looking. The figure slowly turned around to look behind itself. The figure's hand was on a door, about to walk into a building. Only then did I realize it was the singer from the band at Death. He was enigmatic. After a moment of staring at him, I felt lost and strange. I quickly turned my head back toward Gertrude. She was nowhere to be found.

I turned back around. He was gazing out into the street. I wasn't sure what he was looking at or waiting for. He entered the building and disappeared. I stood under the magnolia tree alone, holding my amethyst.

CHAPTER 2

Pound pound pound—the water came down. A white Bentley drove up. A man dressed in a black suit, white shirt and driving-cap exited the vehicle and walked around to the back of the car. *Pop*— the black umbrella opened with a crisp and deliberate snap of the driver's wrist. The rain's song changed as it came in contact with the taught fabric. The driver opened the door. An old woman dressed in a white pantsuit with severe shoulders walked out. Her collarbones looked ready to sever her skin. She was escorted through the gallery's front doors. As she neared, she grew taller and taller. She was maybe six foot six and she had a very "worked on" face. She was wearing soft purple eye shadow. Her plumped, poked and prodded lips were like two bloated alabaster snakes lying on top of each other.

The two snakes parted and her voice dropped to the white stone floor of the gallery. "Hello" she said simply, yet it was not simple sounding. It held a strange tonal depth and an accent that I could not place. Her driver bent his body forward slightly and in a low monotone voice, only audible to me, he announced, "The Countess de Aixurrè Saint Aire."

Mr. Steinway's portly and aged figure came hammering over.

"Hello, Countess," he greeted her as his red, wrinkly forehead began to blotch up.

"Helloo, Mr. Ssteinway. It iss nice to see you at present, as I am sure you must be very busssy. What, with owning a gallery and being that you are newly married to Sssssooo Yun." She leaned in and whispered, "Does she miss being away from the oldest profession in the world?" She then smiled with an extra breath that she left there, hanging in the air, to suggest amusement.

Mr. Steinway forced an exasperated laugh and his red blotches began to perspire. Fat, rich old men are not masters of disguise when it comes to rage.

Mr. Steinway clenched his flat bottom and began to trot over to a painting and motion with his hands. No one followed and no one cared. The Countess handed me an envelope. The minder gave Mr. Steinway a look of recognition and opened the door for the Countess. Mr. Steinway drew his flesh inward from all outside points and began a fresh turbulent trot toward me. He tried to snatch the envelope out of my hands.

"Mr. Steinway! What is wrong with you?" I asked as I pulled the letter away from him.

"Well … what did the Countess give you?" was his retort.

"I don't know, but she did give it to *me*." I unfolded the envelope and reached inside for its contents, all the while telling Mr. Steinway that he should respect other's privacy.

"Well … what is it, Serene? What *is it?*" He could hardly contain his nervous anticipation.

"An invitation to a party of some sort."

Mr. Steinway's face was now full-on red and very noticeably disturbed.

"*She invited you to her Printemps Gala?* I have known her for years *and not once …*" He was now talking to himself under his breath.

"Well you must go and return with a sale, dear girl!"

"It seems to be in France somewhere. Are you serious, Mr.

18

Steinway? I'm not sure if I should be the one to go. I'm afraid of mucking it up." Really I was just afraid to go anywhere with that giant woman. There was something off-putting about her.

"Serene, you are going and that is final! If I am to have the others cover for your time away, you will do me the favor of returning with a check. I will send you with a piece. She will purchase it no questions asked. That is how the Countess operates. You would be a fool not to go. Also, make no mistake: this is work and not a vacation. No sale and you might not have a job to come back to."

I looked down at the invitation again: "PIER 59 HELIPORT, APRIL 23, 5:00 P.M."

LATER

"William, you have to come with me! I can't go alone. I'm nervous. It's so overwhelming that I have to go to this strange woman's party in another country just to secure a sale."

"I wish I could, but I have to stay here and work my tail off. Sorry, but they aren't paying me to go with you. And I would probably have a hard time finding sandwiches I like to eat."

"Ahh, but it's France. They will have yummy sandwiches, you OCD crazy man!"

"Bring your crazy slut friend."

"Lydia?"

"Yeah, she doesn't work, right? If I didn't work, I would be a slut too!"

I picked up my phone to make the call.

From the other end of the line, I heard, "Hey, Serene. What's up?"

"Lydia! Tell me you have no important plans for a couple of days."

"I have no important plans for a couple of days. Why?"

"*Oh yay!* Meet me at Pier 59, tomorrow at 5:00 p.m. We are going somewhere near Paris for a party."

"Okay, I'll see you then."

William just looked at me with a slight look of wistful dreaminess and a dash of jealousy. "I love how she doesn't even ask another question and you know she will be there with six suitcases."

I looked at William and shook my head from side to side. "Just another day in the life of Lydia. Maybe I am better off for not owning too much of this crazy world."

5:00 P.M., APRIL 23, PIER 59

I was standing in a parking lot on the west edge of Manhattan. Wind came in off the top of the water. The chartreuse sky was moving overhead. The peripatetic pollution was painting surreal flavors of neon sorbet—melting into the horizon. The Chrysler Building and all the other silver skyscrapers, in collaboration with the Hudson, reflected what was happening above. It was as if New York had burned to the ground and all the buildings were glowing ghosts.

I heard the purr of an approaching brown Mercedes convertible. Lydia's golden blond hair was going crazy in the wind.

"Ahhh," she was shrieking. "Sooo sorry I am late."

The helicopter's propellers started. *Whip whip whip.* Lydia and her Hermès luggage were out of the vehicle and onto the tarmac in a matter of moments. She threw her pale arms around me and let out another shriek of laughter. Then she asked, "Why do you look so scared? We are not going to war! My God, you do need to get out more often. This will be good for you." Her blond hair was framing her face in a halo of golden stars that reminded me of running in fields together when we were children.

"I get out often. I usually don't have to cross oceans to do it. Also, I have this piece from the gallery to sell, so you should really try to help me do that," I said with a smile. I was half joking.

"Okay, okay, honey, where is the champers? You need at least a bottle and maybe a zanny-poo."

We were both inside the helicopter now. *Whip whip whip.*

Looking down I saw the flame on top of the Statue of Liberty's torch. I saw what looked like people in her crown and just for a flash, I thought I saw two eyes. Were those two eyes looking straight at me?

At 5:18, we landed at Teterboro, a private airport in New Jersey. From one tarmac to another. Lydia looked at me and nodded her head in acceptance and a sliver of bewilderment—which meant a lot coming from this girl. There on the tarmac stood a two-level concord jet. It seemed to have been purchased from Pan Am, their logo was still apparent under a coat of platinum paint. The plane looked as though God had plucked it out of our earthly atmosphere and dipped it into a molten platinum ocean. We both ascended the stairs and entered into the cavity of this blessed beast.

Once inside, the air was soft and clean. I couldn't believe it—it was better than the air outside. A Nordic blond woman appeared, dressed in a camel-colored pressed cashmere knee-length skirt, blazer and silk stockings. Her pale, sinuous neck was tightly surrounded by a neatly tied brown Gucci scarf. She ushered us inside, offered us a glass of rosé bubbles and set down a silver platter with two small saucers. One contained pills and the other a symphony of red and black pearl sturgeon caviar with shellfish parts amassed on a heap of lemon-scented shaved ice.

"Amazing! Champagne, Xanax, caviar and dead sea creatures. Your hostess is truly my new favorite person."

"I guess. It is all a bit strange," was all I could say in response.

As I gulped down the last sip of my champagne, I thought about how different Lydia and I were. I watched her reveling in the lap of luxury, while I couldn't seem to relax. I watched her delicate eyes flutter as her red lips opened and closed. She was telling a story to a handsome passenger. She was already making friends. Her confidence always radiated. It was one of the things that drew us together.

Lydia and I met when we were kids, not even ten years old. Little mean girls were trying to take my small bag filled with all of my prized possessions. I remember distinctly what was inside: three flavors of Bonne Bell chapstick—grape, strawberry and orange creamsicle; a sheet of sparkly, dark rainbow unicorn stickers; a Rainbow Brite pencil; and a plastic, multicolored neon charm bracelet like the one Madonna wore in the early '80s. I think it was the charm bracelet that had turned them against me and the item that they just had to have. They were trying to trade the bag of all of my prized possessions for a marble. The eldest girl, Stephanie, told me a fairy lived inside of the marble. I thought she was telling me the truth. I got really excited to meet the fairy and I gave them all of my favorite things in the world in exchange for a fairy-less white marble with mint green swirls. I kept holding the marble up to the sun under the willow tree looking for a mint-leaf fairy to appear deep inside one of the swirls. It took me a while to figure out that A) no fairy lived in the marble and B) they were laughing at me.

Lydia, just as young as me, already had a penchant for righting injustice. She didn't know who I was and I didn't know who she was, yet she walked over to Stephanie and whispered something in her ear. I watched as Stephanie and all the other girls laughed at Lydia. Despite their laughter and dismissal, something told me to keep my eye on the little blond girl. I could tell she was up to something. It was like watching a spider weave a golden web. Not even five minutes later, Lydia, my golden spider, returned to Stephanie and the other girls with the teacher's adult hand in her small child hand. Under the sun in the long grass, I watched the girls' faces turn from smart laughter and pleased-with-themselves grins to shock and then anger. The teacher and Lydia then walked over to me with my small bag of prized possessions and handed it over. I didn't know what to say. I held up the marble to give to the teacher.

Lydia smiled and introduced herself. "Hi, my name is Lydia. Do you want to be friends?"

"Yep," was my reply. And then I had to ask, "how did you do that?"

"My dad owns the school," she said through her sunshine laughter.

What kid even knows what his or her dad does at seven years old, much less how to use that power? We never talked about any details from that day. It was understood that we were sisters and not much more needed discussing aside from that. I was as fiercely loyal to her as she was to me. Nothing had wavered or changed in that department after all these years.

IN A CAR SOMEWHERE

My eyeballs were soggy and dense, yet my eyelids were like the wings of a hummingbird. I was not sure what was going on. All I knew was that Lydia and I were lying in the backseat of a town car driving in the rain. I tried to lift my head to look out the window. I thought I saw a dragon with purple and red scales slicing its long-taloned claws through the sky. Somewhere inside, I knew this image was directly related to how I felt about this event. It looked as if the inside of the car was filled with dirty smoke, but I could not smell a thing. I must have drifted off again.

When I opened my eyes, the car was driving on a sandstone-pelted driveway and to each side of the driveway were flickering lights. After about five minutes, a rather large castle estate appeared. The stones of the castle walls were engraved with the pattern of brain coral. Their color was centuries-old bone. Two black iron urns exuding fire rested upon two long stakes on either side of the main entrance. The flames were being repeatedly licked out at the wind's behest. The door was massive, fashioned in carvings and painted with a high-gloss lacquer in a sanguine red so dark and rich that it almost looked black. I tasted a drop of blood and the tartness of iron in my mouth. The glass windows possessed the color of dirty rose water, their shape was warm and wobbly, creating an illusion of romance and a constant calling of light to undulate in female form. There were no vehicles stationary in the front entrance, just a continuum of cars dropping off many people.

There was a flowing stream coming from a stoned seductress. She had three dragon-scaled tails that grew from a marble fountain. She was the crown jewel of this grand entrance. Lotuses and water lilies floated around her. Sporadically placed around the grounds were lesser sculptures of mermaids spouting salted clear milk from their bosoms. You could smell vanilla in the air.

The driver opened my door and released me into the evening.

Time screeched slowly. A knot grew within as my eyes took in the Countess emerging from her grandiose castle. It took two footmen to force the heavy doors apart before she fully appeared. She was wearing a structured gilded gold gown that was dripping with hand-embroidered brocade. Her hips were of a harsh line forming at the base of an inverted triangle. Her heeled feet acted as the point. Her eyes were lined with black charcoal and her lids were dusted in shades of purple and red glimmering metallic eye shadow that flew off the sides of her face. Her hair was stark white and perfectly coiffed. It was splayed out to one side, acting as a giant, white frothy tip of firm cream. It was styled in the best shape to frame and capture her intriguing skeletal structure. Her long sinuous neck was the perfect base to all that madness.

"Cumm in, dearrrs, let usss gut you settled in and ready for this eeevening's festivities." She spoke as her hand motioned to the interior of her palace.

Two handmaidens came to take our arms, for we both could not manage even the simple act of walking into the entrance.

"Follow me," said the maid, holding me up. I did as she suggested. Where else was I going to go?

Once we arrived at the top of the staircase, I had a moment to gather my thoughts and steady my vision. Lydia was being taken down the hallway in the opposite direction. I looked out over the balcony.

The interior was entirely made of marble and gold leaf crown moldings. Below the Countess and toward the center of the room was a little Garden of Eden. It was the focal point of the foyer. In the garden stood a vibrant pomegranate tree, beneath it were stones, moss and those amazing silver dollar plants that I loved. There was no wind. They stood still like pieces of art in a museum. Overhead was an expansive skylight and to the right of the room was a black marble fireplace. Next to it stood the longest, thinnest tusk, mounted on a wooden slab.

"What is that?" I asked a handmaiden, pointing a shaky finger in its direction.

"That is a narwhal tusk. They are sometimes referred to as the unicorns of the sea. The Countess killed the very animal whose tusk this once was."

I searched her eyes for a hint of emotion. There was nothing, not even the slightest sadness at the thought that this majestic creature's death was all for a trophy. I was hoping I could trust her, as I did not feel all that well. Her lack of empathy was a sign for me to do just the opposite. I was dreading the evening's festivities even more now. Having to break bread with a narwhal killer was not my idea of time well spent. Despite my lack of trust, I needed an ally.

"My name is Serene. What is yours?"

"Very nice to make your acquaintance. My name is Lisset. Please follow me," she continued in a controlled monotone voice.

I walked into my room. The carpet was hand loomed. The

beautiful rose-colored windows extended from ceiling to floor and opened out onto a balcony that faced the back of the property. The grand yard was covered with wild vetiver and field flowers. There were also many fragrant lilac bushes along the side of the castle walls and rows of seven-foot-tall phragmites waving in the wind before a thick blast of forest off to the right.

I threw myself onto the bed face-first and sniffed. It smelled of fire and fresh floral spring air. I looked to the left and there was a pile of wood that reached the ceiling. To the right was a fireplace with an oxidized grate. The bedding was of the finest Matteo linen, looking like it had come from a time before Christ. The worn-in but delicately soft linen rolled off the edges of the bed in large, beautiful, billowy masses onto the floor. It was abundance at its best. The pillows were made from the same fine linen. There were magnificent quilts in all different shades of white piled on top of each other. At the foot of the bed was a sinfully soft throw that was the softest thing my hand had ever touched.

I entered the bathroom. The window had an iron crisscross lattice design and was opened to allow a bird's song to enter. The bathtub was huge and filled with lightly scented water. On a small table was a decanter filled with sherry, a plate with three biscuits and an old hardbound novel. *I am in heaven.*

After an hour or so, Lisset the maid knocked on the door.

"Miss Serene, may I enter?"

I was in the tub and scrambled for a towel. "Yes, come in."

"The Countess wishes for everyone to begin to dress for the evening's events," Lisset said, while walking toward the armoire and opening its doors. Inside were the most ridiculous Alexander McQueen gold Russian fairytale gowns. They all were from a season long ago, she must have purchased the whole collection.

"She prefers all guests to wear the preselected garments. Please choose from one of these. Hair and makeup is waiting by your door. After your massage, you can call for them. When you are ready, they will escort you to the main hall where tonight's festivities will commence."

A big-boned, clean-faced woman walked in and took my towel. She said nothing but her hands were magic. The oils that she was used were very strange and even a bit bothering. When she was done with me, I felt dizzy, everything was blurry. I think it was the oils. Something felt off. *Was I drugged?*

A tall, dark man covered in tattoos entered my bedroom. He guided me to a gold wooden-framed chair with a silk-printed cushion and faced me toward the light of the open window.

After doing my face and hair, he guided my failing body into my new crust: a gold short dress that mimicked the body of an insect. The oils were seeping deeper—the haze gaining. He guided me down the stairs; through the captured garden with the pomegranate tree; and into a long, dark hallway that blossomed open into an enormous room with a table made from a family of ebony trees.

There were around two hundred place settings. I was the last to arrive—everyone was standing behind his or her chair, all eyes on me. I was escorted to my seat at the table, farther and farther away from where Lydia was. The footmen finally stopped and gestured to the last open seat.

It was him!

The guy from the band at Death! He was two seats from mine, to the right. My heart started to flutter. I did everything in my power not to stare at him.

The Countess sat at the head of the table. We were given champagne and a small gold decanter filled with black liquid. She gave a toast in a language I could not place and emptied her decanter into her glass of champagne while asking us, her guests, to do the same.

Reality diminished further. Another layer of my consciousness peeled away and evaporated into the ethos. The dinner service was beginning. Silver trays of melted Himalayan shaved ice infused with caviar were floating down to our table. Once set, grand towers of chilled sea crustaceans were placed on top. They looked like a Heironymus Bosch painting, *The Garden of Earthly Delights*.

I couldn't stop thinking, *There is only one warm body separating mine from the man I desperately want to interact with.* Although I wasn't sure if I was capable of forming a sentence.

I watched my hand quiver. I almost dropped the champagne glass as his eyes locked with mine. I couldn't look away. "You look familiar," he said, while he ran his fingers through his dark and slightly dirty hair. His brow furrowed as the trolls within him opened and shut various vaults in the hallways of his mind. I was shocked that he was talking to me. I was shocked that I could hear his voice.

My ears were on high alert, straining to learn every octave that his mouth produced while not in a thrashing, violent outpour of song. *I like his "talking" voice.*

To my elated gratitude, the servers were weaving between the seated guests once again. They seamlessly gathered the chilled dishes and put in their places even more magnanimous trays: roasted whole black truffles; beef that was fed only grass, butter and the finest red wine. *Wonderful timing.* But as soon as the servers left, I knew I would have to act normal again. A wave of shock passed through my body as I watched the person who was in-between us stand up.

The singer was standing as well ... *they switched seats.*

"You were backstage at Death the night that fire happened. Crazy."

He remembered me. "Yeah, I was. That was really insane. I have never been in a fire before."

"I wish I could say the same." I detected a silken thread of sadness in his voice.

"Oh, I'm sorry," I replied.

"Yeah it was a bad one. It got my mother," he said while looking down at his plate.

My nervousness was replaced with a deep sadness for his loss. I only had my mom, but it wasn't because my father had died. It was because he'd left. I couldn't imagine what it must feel like to lose a loving parent to sudden death. Before I could stop myself, my hand floated down on top of his. He looked at me and I could tell he was surprised. I immediately snapped my hand away and pulled it down to my side. I whispered, "Sorry."

He looked at me and said, "Thank you." *I couldn't tell if he was thanking me for placing my hand on his in compassion or thanking me for giving him back his personal space.*

The moments to come were unbearable. I ate to occupy myself, an action I thought I had mastered. Not in this moment in time. My mouth felt wobbly. I gnawed on a tender piece of meat and felt its juices release and escape the corners of my mouth. *How attractive.* My skin was on fire and tingling with discomfort. Every molecule of mine was aware of the space they were occupying near his flesh.

Hallelujah! Here were my angelic servers. They were floating down humiliation rescue clouds with things to look at, consume and save me.

I couldn't be happier to see desserts floating above our heads. That meant, hopefully, this awkward dinner would soon end and I could run away and hide.

Then, to my relief, we were all escorted to the interior rooms of the estate where people started to chatter. I could finally slip away into a dark corner to die of embarrassment in peace. The decibels of laughter rose and echoed through the rooms. Glass after glass of champagne and the small decanters of black liquid were being served and well received by the guests.

As I made my way to a dark corner, a tall couple, very tanned with exaggerated faces and makeup, stood in my way and started in.

"Helloooo, my name is George and this is Gail."

As I tried to focus on their ever-changing faces, I engaged in

29

small talk, my lizard brain taking over. "How are you connected to the Countess?" I felt confusion and the beginning of a sickness.

Everyone looked the same.

I gazed into my reflection from a glass door and got a glimpse of my skin, mouth, eyes— *I did not recognize myself.* I was meshing into the fabric of humans that danced within this room covered in the same garments. My nose, accosted by a wall of unified smell, signaled to my brain how bizarre it was that everyone smelled the same. *What's in the dark liquid?* I grabbed the closest piece of furniture to balance myself. Quickly, my focus changed from hiding to finding my friend and seeking refuge. I asked George and Gail if they had met a young lady by the name of Lydia and explained to them that she was a friend I needed to find.

Their response came from George first. "No, I do not think so. Gail, have you?"

"No, dear George and what an awful name. It has the ring of cheap American."

They both began choking from their own incessant cackling as champagne oozed from the sides of their swollen, cracked collagen lips.

I struggled through the crowd, searching for Lydia. My body went stiff. I was about to topple like a tree. *I have definitely been drugged*, I thought as I went down.

A bony yet strong hand grabbed my arm. I heard a voice call "hey!" My eyes opened again, as shot of adrenaline coursed through my body. I could say nothing in response, as it was him.

I opened my eyes large and wide and tried to focus. Through the blurriness, I saw two girls hanging on his arm, laughing and looking at me. One of the girls grabbed his face with both of her small hands. "James, don't be a bore and start conversations with anyone but us. We hate it when you talk to common girls." On the last part of her sentence she looked directly into my eyes.

So his name is James.

Lydia's voice came into the conversation. I was so relieved to have found her in this madness. I needed to get out of this strange, hazy palace, filled with insane individuals—although Lydia did not seem to share this sentiment. "My God, this party is fuckin' fabulous! I don't know what they keep putting in my champagne, but I am about to take my clothes off and *fuck everyone.* Did you see Abdul Safir? He is the crown prince of … I forgot. And those two ladies over there graduated from Harvard and are identical twins. They are psychiatrists for cats.

Did you also see all those actors and actresses at the dinner table? I thought maybe we were at the Oscars for a minute. Oh, Serene, I never want to leave!

"Ahahahha!" Lydia exclaimed in pure ecstasy.

In the midst of Lydia's titillation, I felt his hand on my arm. I knew it was him. He had touched me once and now I knew what his hand felt like on my skin. That was a strange thing to realize. That had never happened to me before—knowing someone's touch. Much less, the touch of a stranger. I looked up and saw the two girls who were hanging on him, talking and laughing, while spilling their drinks. They continued on their mission of making me feel impossibly small.

"Sorry for getting quiet at dinner. I don't really talk about my mother or that fire," he said.

I stood there in silence, really not knowing what to say or do. I noticed my feelings of scarlet embarrassment leaving and was grateful for that. I needed another moment to balance myself before I could utter any words.

Thankfully, he continued. "Do you want to sit over there?" He pointed at an ornate silk couch that was out of the way and dimly lit by the overflowing light dancing in the grand fireplace. I nodded my head yes.

"My name is James by the way. What's your name?"

"Serene."

"Why I don't talk about my mother's death is because I still can't quite understand how it happened or what I saw and I don't even know why I'm telling you this."

I just listened and found my hand floating down on his again. When our skin touched, we both looked up and into each other. He put his other hand on top of mine.

"Thank you," he said again.

"I'm here to listen, if you want to talk about it."

"I was young. I probably imagined what I saw. My mom and I lived on our own in a farmhouse in Missouri. My dad died when I was a baby. We didn't have too many neighbors. The house backed up onto a field. It was a happy house and I was a happy kid, but the fire changed everything. One moment, I was sleeping. And the next, I heard my mother screaming. I smelled horrible things. I saw so much smoke. I got up and ran down the hall to her room. I couldn't go far because the fire had already fully consumed that part of the house and her room was in flames.

"I didn't know what to do. I would have run into the fire had I seen her. I could only hear her scream and smell that smell. All I could do was cry while running down the stairs. I opened the screen door and ran into the dark toward the nearest road. That in itself was horrible. I felt like I was abandoning her. While running to find help, I felt responsible for every scream.

"What I saw next was the thing that I still can't shake. Something inside of my little kid brain kept saying. 'Look back,' *and then there was my intuition*, 'Don't do it. Don't look back.' When I did finally look back, I saw these terrible creatures. They were almost as tall as our house. There were five of them. They were making the fire grow bigger and stronger. After I looked at them, *they looked at me*.

"A red flame escaped from the top of my head. It peeled away from my hair and hovered above me, red and glowing for a moment and then it left. My red flame swam through the night air swiftly like a glowing snake of energy toward the five terrible creatures. When the flame reached these things, *it* and *they* disappeared. I continued to run but in vain. I already knew there was no way she could be alive and I thought at one point I heard the screaming stop. But I hear her still."

I was enthralled. I couldn't quite understand what he had seen. Somewhere inside, I knew what he had just told me was real. I felt his vulnerability and saw the extra water in his left eye. I felt the cool dampness in his hand.

Crystals chimed at an alarmingly loud decibel and a voice announced that everyone was meant to move to the outdoor garden for "the ceremony." James and I looked at each other as we were being moved and ushered out by footmen. I saw Lydia in the mass exodus and grabbed her arm.

"A ceremony?" I asked, wearing my expression of *this shit is nuts*.

"So she is Wiccan! She is about the most amazing hostess I have ever encountered. Like I said, you are acting cray! Have a little fun and stop worrying so much. It's not good for you." She turned her head, I watched her light blond hair disappear into the crowd.

We were all gathered in the middle of a great lawn. Before us was a stone platform that was pagan in design. I realized I was standing on a flattened black lady's slipper bloom. I soon noticed that we were all standing on a bed of beautiful black and purple lady's slippers that were now dying beneath our many person tread. Placed around a crude slab of stone were small iron bowls of fire.

The Countess started in with the same strange language as before. She shifted from English to French between sentences. She said something about the full moon and "the day of many centuries cometh the great time."

Everyone was a sloppy, drugged, swaying mess and seemed to be fine with this impossible rhetoric. This went on for quite some time. If you were one of those black or purple lady's slippers, you would have seen that we all had our eyes closed or whites showing, pupils rolled back into our heads. We were somehow connected and moving slightly to the right or to the left as if we were one being. In the middle was the Countess with a glimmer in her eyes and a slight smile on her serpentine lips. She was the only one with focus or awareness at this very poignant moment and the light from the fire gave a glow to the gold dresses we all were wearing. The moonlight touched down on the lids of the eyes that were closed and the recently placed crown on the Countess's head. All was lost on me as my awareness had faded alongside that of the others.

I was in a large room of the palace fighting for consciousness. I looked to my right and saw the lovely figure of James. His hand was on mine, he was looking straight at me. His eyes seemed to be searching for something. His dark hair was hanging into them.

A scream was heard.

The maids and butlers locked the doors and windows. A few people were trying to go outside, but they didn't make it in time.

"Oh my God."

"Did you see?"

"I think she fell from the balcony!"

Through the glass doors, we could see a woman lying face down in the dark green lawn. Her right leg was bent in a cruel unnatural way and her body was not moving.

The Countess entered the room. "There has been an accsssident. Please sstay inside where it is sssafe. We are getting help immediately."

And at that, the party revelers quickly resumed drinking the ever-flowing champagne and black liquid while laughing carelessly.

Nausea was setting in. I had a pit in my stomach and an

overwhelming feeling of sadness. I had to look for an exit from this impossible fortress. I needed air now! I was going to vomit.

Somehow, I found my escape after searching every locked door.

Once outside, I felt a moment of relief, but my knees were weak. I had to sit. I forced deep breaths. I felt so far away and was cursing Mr. Steinway for making me come here to sell a piece of artwork. I wondered what William was doing right now. I wished I could hear my mom's beautiful voice.

I heard the sound of soft footsteps coming from behind. It was probably that sneaky maid Lisset. She'd seemed to be minding me all night. I slowly rose from my position and walked into the back of the palace.

The spring air whirled up my nostrils and down the back of my throat. With every breath I became a little more clearheaded. I took slower, deeper breaths and repeated instructions in my head: *Stay focused. Look at that flower. Try to see it. Stay still for a moment. It is purple. Stay focused.* I peeked my head around a dense, tall shrub. I saw the dead, limp woman still there, face down in the cold grass. No one was coming for her.

All the drapes inside were drawn. She could not see the revelers if she were still alive and they could not see her. The Countess was walking around from the other side of the palace slowly and methodically. I watched as she approached the woman. She stared only at her, never taking her eyes away from the body in the grass. Again, I started to lose my breath. I felt drops of sweat stream down my arms. My hands and feet were numb.

I stared at the Countess from behind the bush I was holding onto. *This must be a lie!* The Countess grew taller and thinner, her eyes larger, turning into a fiery purple. Her mouth vicious, with teeth as big as a lion's, covered in dripping wet gold. Her fingernails became the same as her teeth. They sparkled in the moonlight. She then straddled the dead woman. It looked as if she were about to mount her in a gentle way. All the while her hands were moving with unearthly speed, ripping off the woman's clothes. Slowly, she was lowering her strangely angular and monstrous figure on top of her nude and lifeless corpse. A gold tentacle slipped out of the Countess's dress. *Was this her sex organ? Was the Countess an alien? What in God's name was I seeing?* I watched with terror as this tentacle found its way into the woman's lower half. The Countess was dripping drool from her mouth into the woman's mouth, while her taloned teeth simultaneously pried her lips open. I wanted to scream or just lay down and close my eyes and pray to be somewhere else. Instead, I ran to the front of the palace. My eyes were searching for a car or a road. My sight failing, my mouth turned down. I felt a hot, wet tear break away from my right eye and run down my face. I was trapped.

I heard a voice coming from the front entrance. It was Lisset's. "Serene, come in now. I have made you some tea. I will tuck you in. Just come inside now. It is time for you to get some rest."

I looked at the thick tree line and thought of what malice could be lying in the darkness. I contemplated my options. Then Lydia's and James's faces flashed through my mind. Yes, James's face too. Through the madness, I thought how odd that I cared about him so much. I didn't want to leave them behind. I walked toward the doorway as if in a trance. Most of me wanted to run, but the part that didn't want to leave Lydia and James behind was the part that was the strongest.

Just as I was about to walk up the steps to the front entrance of the palace, I gasped as the whites of two eyes appeared inches away from mine out of the darkness. It was a man standing in front of me. His one hand went directly up to my mouth and his other grabbed my hand, pried it open with his fingers and placed something cold in the center of my palm while folding my fingers into a fist.

"You will need this tonight. Do not eat or drink anything else. A car will come for you at 7:00 a.m. Stay awake until then. Lock your door. The car will take you to the airport. I will be there with two tickets for you and Lydia. It is important that you leave directly at 7:00. *Do you understand?*"

I felt another hand on my back. I turned around. It was Lisset's. I then turned to the front again and the man was gone. I felt the thing that he had just given me and thought that, if it were dust, I might make a diamond of it. My hand was already cramping. Lisset smiled a freakishly warm smile and put both of her hands on me, one at the base of my neck and the other on my shoulder—physically guiding me into the front entrance and up the staircase to my bedroom.

"The Countess would have been very disturbed had she known you were outside, Serene. You have had too much to drink. We would not want anything to happen to you—what with all the commotion of the ambulances and police."

What ambulance and police? There had been no one …

"Come inside your room and have some tea. All of your worries will melt away and you will sleep like a baby. I promise."

"Okay, Lisset. That sounds nice." I looked at her and smiled.

The moment I was inside my room, I locked the door and looked around, trying to not make a sound. I poured the tea down the sink. I felt like a mole hiding in a dark hole. I drew the curtains and sat in the middle of the bed. Only then, when I felt no one could hear or see me, did I open my hand. There was no diamond—It was the amethyst.

Oh-my-God! It was the same amethyst Gertrude had given me back in New York weeks ago. I'd left it at home. I held onto it all through the night, not moving a muscle. I was praying Lydia and James were okay. I wanted desperately to search for them now. My ears were twitching with tension, using my only sense to gain *sight*. I was drenched in my own sweat until I saw the clock strike 6:50 a.m.

I opened my door and ran down the hall to find Lydia. Thank God she was there. I saw a black car on the pebbled driveway from her bedroom window. *We had to leave.* I wanted to find James (but the man had only mentioned Lydia.) I felt torn. I heard footsteps coming down the hall. I started to run while dragging Lydia behind me. We made it to the car.

To my surprise, the tall black-as-night man was there in front of the airport. He looked much less ominous in the light of day.

"You both must go now. Your plane leaves soon. Serene, take care of Lydia. She can't stand up or walk. She needs to get on this flight with you. Don't let the airline hold her here, okay?"

"Okay. I have her. I also was wondering what would have happen if we had stayed? I have another friend there. Will he be okay?"

"He is fine. You and Lydia are not safe. I can't explain now. You just have to trust me and make this flight. Run!" he said with urgency as he looked behind him.

I took Lydia's arm and propped her up on my right hip and guided her through security. We got on the plane safe and sound. I thought of James. I kept imagining the Countess chasing him. I kept wondering about the five demons and his mother. I kept hoping he was okay.

I wondered if I would ever see him again. *Please, universe, let me see him again.*

I kept playing back what I had seen the Countess do to that dead woman, over and over in my head. *Please let him be okay.*

CHAPTER 3

BACK IN NYC

I was curled up on the worn-in leather Chesterfield couch that William had recently purchased. The massive thing practically consumed the room. I was developing a symbiotic relationship with the couch: I felt like the couch and I were two animals in the Serengeti. The couch was a rhino and I was a small bird. The couch protected me from predators, In return I never left its side and ate small bugs that would otherwise wreak havoc. In reality I hadn't been able to move from my couch-rhino since the moment I came back from France. I was convalescing as my tired mind was trying to grasp and make sense of what had happened back at the Countess's estate. William had a movie projection going and the lovely Tilda Swinton was dressed in Fendi, walking the streets of Milano, circa 1970, which I was grateful for. Anything to keep my mind from analyzing was a blessing at this point.

"So, how was the trip?" he finally asked.

Oh, William, it was dreadful and bizarre! We took a private jet to a castle in France, drank copious amounts of champagne and I saw

James—the really hot guy I was telling you about. "On paper, yes, it was great. But in reality it was the worst night ever. A woman died. She fell from the balcony. She was just left there outside while all the guests were locked in. Her dead body was ravaged by the Countess. *She is a monster!* I could have sworn I saw a strange appendage slither inside the woman." I stopped speaking, out of breath.

"So, 'shes' a man."

"Whatever it was, it wasn't human. I also didn't make a sale. Mr. Steinway is going to kill me."

William looked at me with concern. It wasn't the concern I was hoping for—like we need to save the world from the Countess concern. He looked at me like I belonged in a straightjacket. William placed one of his big hands on my forehead. "You must be ill," he said as he stared at the movie projection.

"I wish I was. I wish I had scarlet fever or was on acid and hallucinating because then all of this would not have been real and I would not be trying to make you believe what I know sounds insane," I said with a tone of somber honesty and desperation for his support.

"Well you're home and safe now. See—don't go to France. It's terrible there. I already told you that. Just stay in New York where it is safe."

I huffed into the air. I knew I wasn't going to make him understand what I had seen or was feeling. I was in a grey area and that was not William's expertise.

A WEEK LATER

I was late for work and running on the cobblestones wearing five-inch heels. My ankles almost gave out. The affronting smell of waste neatly piled up on the sidewalk in black plastic bags permeated my skin and accosted my nose. I couldn't help but look in the direction of the scaffolding where the homeless men gathered. I saw George.

"Serene, you sweet child! Ready for a twirl?" he shouted from his seat.

"George! You handsome man! I wish I could, but I'm going to get fired if I'm late again. We will dance tomorrow!"

Once I got to the gallery, I quickly swung open the doors and ran inside. Mr. Steinway's fat and troublesome body sat firmly at his desk in the back of the gallery. He only had to look at me and I knew to approach him.

"Well, Serene, where the hell have you been? You don't even show up to work without a call or an email? Were you taking an extended vacation and forgot to tell me?" he screamed, inches away from my face. His foul breath left a layer of undesirable moisture on my face. Then in a whisper, he began, "You did not do what you set out to do. Now did you?"

"Mr. Steinway, I really never had a—"

He slammed his fat, ruddy, throbbing hand down on the glass of his desk. "Shut up! This would have been the biggest sale this gallery has ever seen. I send you to France and you don't make a moment for yourself to sell this to the Countess?" He pointed at an ugly large painting behind him. Do you even care, dear girl? I am seriously questioning my judgment on hiring you.

"There are hundreds of people begging for your job!"

My eyebrows were dancing all around on my face. They were arching inward and upward as I fought back tears. Then they dropped downward as I brooded with anger. I was just fighting to keep them still and motionless. *God! I sold the owl last week.* I felt like a selling slave. I received no accolades for my accomplishments, only punishment for my shortcomings.

I went to the floor as the other gallerists looked at me and walked elsewhere. (I was obviously damaged goods and they didn't want to catch what I had. I was working very hard to maintain a certain relaxed decorum that was expected of me.)

I pulled up my stockings, tussled my hair and wiped my fingers underneath my eyes while I surveyed the room to make sure this was all done without anyone seeing.

Seconds later, I texted Lydia. *"Drink? I need one."*

We sat at a wooden bar with red lights and a small pool table. The bar sold chips for two dollars and had a famous Tijuana special, five dollars for a shot and a beer. Both were written in chalk on a blackboard. We downed our shots and drank our beers.

Lydia began. "So … did you and James talk at the Countess's party?"

I looked at her in astonishment. "Do you even remember leaving?" I asked.

"Yeah. Didn't we leave together on her jet or something? I was a bit out of it for a couple days. We partied so hard. How *amazing* was that party?"

"Amazing? You're kidding right?"

"Speaking of the Countess!" Lydia shrieked. "She has invited me back for the *Purple* magazine and Alexander Wang fashion parties! It's going to be sick. I heard she is sending private helicopters and Beyonce is performing." She said these words that horrified me while nonchalantly looking at a text thread on her phone.

"Lydia! I really, really don't think you should go. For Christ's sake, a woman died when we were there. That could have been either of us," I said, trying to get her to understand this was a *very* bad idea.

"You can be a little paranoid sometimes," she said.

"I really didn't want to have to bring this up. But you have to listen to me. The Countess killed that woman on purpose and then tore up her dead body," I replied.

"Serene, I am worried about you. First, that was an accident. No one tore up her body. She was shipped back to have an open casket and a very tasteful funeral. Life is to be lived, not feared," she said.

"I couldn't agree more, but I want to be alive to live it. How could you not notice that something was very wrong that night? Please tell me that you know we were all drugged and dragged out to be part of a ceremony. *A woman did die!* Can you even entertain the idea that it was possibly not a *fall* and maybe a *push*? There were so many things wrong about that night, Lydia. Please tell me you saw that the Countess is not like us? When she took us out for the ceremony it felt like we were in a cult. Did you not see how sinister she was? I saw her do terrible things to that woman who was dead while everyone was still sipping champagne. No authorities came. Please tell me you at least recognize that no one came for her?" I pleaded.

"It was a fun party with an unfortunate accident. That is all. I am sure the authorities just went straight out back instead of through the house. As far as what you saw, I cannot say, but it does sound really over the top. Even for you!"

I thought to myself for a moment, *maybe I am just going crazy. I know my imagination can get away from me. God, this is so confusing because, each time I say it aloud, I feel crazier and crazier.*

"You know I love fashion week. I'm not missing the *Purple* and Wang parties."

I turned her bar stool to face me, took the phone out of her hand and put it on the bar. I watched as a baby roach scurried across it. I quickly moved her phone and placed my hands on her shoulders. I looked deep into her eyes. "Promise me you won't go," I said with force.

A look of shock and silence glossed over her face in an arresting wave. "*God! Okay!* What is the big deal anyway? I promise I won't go if it means that much to you. *Jeez!* And now that I am giving up going to my two favorite fashion week parties for your crazy ass, can we please go somewhere that I don't have to stare at this poster of *The Texas Chainsaw Massacre* and worry about getting bedbugs?" she asked.

I laughed hard with very little relief. "Yeah I guess so," I said. I desperately needed a break from the constant feeling that I was spinning out of control. I knew better than to drink this sort of feeling away, but I really didn't know what else to do.

I also wanted to see if we would run into James. I know, pathetic. But I couldn't help it. Maybe it was just another escape I was seeking, but he felt more like sanity to me than my current condition of insanity.

Once inside, we went directly down into the lower level, into the bowels of Death. The stone walls and the wet smell leant themselves to the notion of being a dungeon. Lydia was dancing on an HR Geiger table in the back room in no time. She had a gold cigarette dangling from her orange lips and her bubbly boobs were bouncing along to the beat. A young guy swept in and put his hands around her hips, grinding her from behind. She smiled because that's what she wanted. I got bored after a while and especially didn't want to see the next stage of what Lydia and the stranger would get to, which would be the sloppy make-out in the mayhem of the dancing stage. I walked to the bar to get what I wanted. Immediately two guys were buying me shots. I popped a Klonopin and now was feeling nothing.

"Serene, that's your name right? Here have another." The words came as one of them handed me another shot.

I threw it back and only then did I realize all faculties were being lost. "Hey, do one of you have a bump?" I asked.

They both looked at each other and nodded, wry smiles crossing their chiseled faces. They started walking toward the bathroom. I followed. After doing a dirty bump of bad cocaine from a couple of complete douchebags, I decided to call it a night. I went and grabbed Lydia's hand and put us both in a car.

I woke up with the worst pounding headache ever. I looked on my night stand and there was only a centimeter of water in my glass. The sun was hot. I felt like I was going to puke, so I started to walk fast to the bathroom. I went to the toilet and hugged the bowl, feeling like a complete piece of shit. I puked and afterward, I just sat there for a while, shaking, curled up with a towel on the cold tiled floor, smelling the Clorox bleach that William used to clean with.

Knocking sounded on the door. "Hey, you okay?" William asked in an annoyingly together and chipper voice.

"Not so much," I said as I stared at where the base of the toilet met the floor two inches away from my eyes.

"You have a message on your phone. It just rang," he said.

I slowly got up and walked out of the bathroom.

He held up his massive rawhide and put it down again. "Isn't this a fantastic piece of leather?" He smiled inwardly, pleased with his work and the quality of the goods he had in front of him.

I grabbed my phone and saw that it was the gallery. The gallery never called me. I called right back. One of the other gallerists answered. "Oh, it's you. One moment," was all I heard before a long pause.

Mr. Steinway's voice came crashing through the silence. "Where the hell are you, Serene?" he yelled.

"Mr. Steinway, I'm not scheduled today," was all I could say in a shaky voice.

"Like hell you are not. I'm looking at the calendar and it has your lousy name on the schedule for today. And you're not here. What is wrong with you? I've had it with your little girl lost routine. *You are fired!*" he screamed into the phone and then hung up.

I sobbed and sobbed into the disconnected line. William

finally stopped his stitching and was looking at me. "Oh God. What just happened?"

I dropped my phone on the floor. "That was Mr. Steinway. I am fired ... " I gasped for air and choked on my tears as I hyperventilated a bit. "I have no job, no money. And yes, I can't pay rent and I am over this. I am over struggling and getting drunk. I am over New York, being yelled at and constantly walking on eggshells in order to sell things for people I don't like to people I don't like. I do it, all of it, in exchange for ... money: a promise of happiness and success. In reality money is just a series of numbers on a screen. It's not shelter, love, water, or food. *Something feels off.*"

"Sounds like you need a break from going out. Why don't you lie down and we can watch some movies while I work on this fantastic new leather bolster for my bed." He looked down again and neatly reorganized his tools and said, "Don't fret about money, little one. Dinner is on me tonight."

A WEEK LATER

After lots of tears, William finally convinced me to go outside. I was looking for a ray of sunshine to ease my feeling of failure and thought to take a walk. I put a little faith back in New York and let her lead me. I found myself roaming. I decide to splurge on an iced coffee. (Yes, that's how broke I was!) Iced coffee was like buying a Chanel bag right now. Walking around, I looked in the windows of my favorite shops. I couldn't shop, only look. I had $132.57 in my account. I put my sunglasses on and decide to contact a few possible prospects for new work.

Thinking about work, I realized I was near the Mission. I looked up and saw the scaffolding. I saw George's wooden chair leaning up against a brick building. I could really use that twirl I owed George right about now. My eyes searched. I saw lots of men, all homeless. It was a day like any other over here, but what registered immediately was that there was no George. I couldn't help but walk over to his chair. I stared at it for a moment before starting to walk away.

Then I heard someone shouting, "Miss, hey! Hey miss!"

I stopped and turned my head to look in the direction of the shouting. There was a man staring straight at me. I only then realized this man was addressing me. Against my better judgment, I continued to look at him and stayed still.

"You looking for George, right?" he asked.

"Yes. Do you know when he'll be back?" I asked.

"I don't think he's coming back. But he told me to tell you to keep on dancing and smiling. It seemed real important to him. So I just wanted to tell you that, from George," he said.

"Where did he go?"

"Where do any of us go?" he replied as he looked off down the wide open road of the Bowery.

"What are you trying to tell me?"

"I ain't tryin' to tell you anything except what he wanted me to."

"Well do you know when he'll be back?" I asked. I could feel my irritation grow and my anger trickling down my back like a small crab.

"Lady, George is dead. He ain't coming back. Unless he's gonna rise again, like Jesus Christ."

"What!? He was fine last week! I think you're talking about a different George," I said.

"Nope. I'm talking about the George with the bad foot. Nice guy."

"He didn't have a bad foot. We were dancing just the other day. You have the wrong George and the wrong lady." At that, I turned on my heels and started on my way again.

"The least you could do is show him a little respect," the man yelled. I could detect a level of sincere earnestness, anger and sadness.

This combination stopped me once again in my tracks.

He continued once he saw me pause. "The only time I ever saw him stand was when he was dancing with you. He could hardly walk, you know." He said this as he lit a stub of a cigar and used his free, cracked and dried up hand to block the chilly wind coming down the wide open Bowery. Little slivers of information were being tied together by my feeble mind. He had his own chair. He did only stand when I walked over to him and if I'm being honest, he favored one foot. *No, no way. I just saw him. He was fine.*

The man took a puff of his cigar and blew the smoke out through his mouth and nostrils. "Don't know why he took a liking to you, but he did. He was a real solid dude that George." He looked up at the grey clouds. A ray of thin white light pierced a pupil in one of his eyes. He closed that eye and then looked down to the human-stained concrete.

I stopped in my footsteps. I didn't want to cry again. But the hot, salty water from the well of sadness inside of me was already breached. I stared straight ahead.

"He said you always looked so sad and he loved to make you happy. We all wondered why or how he could stand on a foot so infected. He had a real bad fever the night he passed. Easy to git fixed if you have the dough. But no one calls the ambulance for our sorry asses."

I wanted to say something to him or show some emotion in regards to his own personal plight. But I couldn't. I was falling to pieces on the street and wasn't too sure what was happening … Everything went black.

Some short time later, I woke up on a piece of piss-soaked cardboard. I looked around feeling so disoriented.

"Oh, she's awake," I heard a familiar voice say. I wasn't sure what was happening.

Oh God, it all came back. I wished it was just a dream, but instead it was reality. I looked and saw that I still had my bag and the man who told me the awful truth about George was sitting next to me. I gave him all the cash I had—which was only about five dollars. I felt cheap and bad for doing so. I wanted to give him more than some government-printed paper. I wanted to help these men. I was so sorry I could no longer help George.

I picked myself up and started to walk somewhere, not sure where I was going. I just needed to go somewhere else.

A man so gentle and kind he was willing to hide his pain and dance on a mortal injury just to give a stranger a moment to laugh and smile. *I am not worthy of such kindness*, I thought. And what's worse, I had never had a chance to repay it and never would. I was unable to see what was in front of me. I couldn't help a friend.

Why was life so hard? Why was it so unfair? Why was New York such a shiny, shitty, blood diamond that we all wanted to own? So very few did. I was defiantly not one of those few. Fuck this town.

I went home to sleep and was very grateful for my bed that night. When I woke, George's death still felt like a nightmare. I had nowhere to go but public places. So I made myself a coffee. I drank it and grabbed a banana. I found a park to sit and think. *I need to find a new job.* I couldn't even afford house coffee at this point and I knew that I was getting on William's nerves always asking for money and never leaving the apartment. I hadn't reached the last resort of asking my mom for money. Yet, that humiliating day seemed to be coming very soon to a theater near me.

I found myself at Tompkins Square Park, surveying the bench situation. There was a shaded section where the chess players sat and then there were the paths of the park that had junkies and crusties. I was staring at an old junky. I got lost in thought for a moment. Strangely, my dad popped into my head. Well, the idea of him. I don't know him. The last time I saw him was when I was four years old. I had been told he was a "bad dude." I wondered if he was an old and withered junky now. Part of me hoped so.

Then I thought, *Who cares what he is doing? He doesn't deserve my thoughts. Forget him. He left me.*

I didn't bother to go over there with the junkies and crusties. Instead, I picked the open circle slightly upwind from the dog park, which was good for the olfactory system. The air was a bit cleaner and less filled with the sweetness of almost decaying plants from the city heat that had already set it in. One day of spring, then—*boom!*—hot, sticky, dirty New York City summer.

Once seated, I started to really focus on browsing the New York galleries on my phone. It wasn't that I wanted to go back to one. It's just that selling art, dressing nicely and smiling appealingly at prospective art buyers is the only skill set I seemed to have at present moment.

I wished I had some idea of what else to do with my life or where to go. I felt that familiar sense of being a toxic, pre-end-of-the-world, canned, shredded piece of fruit stuck in the gelatinous wasteland of warm cherry-flavored Jell-O again. I got a faint whiff of Nag Champa incense and heard a low roll of tribal drums. The Hare Krishnas must be near.

I looked up and saw five or six people with shaved heads wearing peach wraps with white long vaginas painted on their third eye. Awesome!

Can't think. Can't think. And now a headache was starting in from the severe heat and too much cheap coffee. I just wanted to lie here on this pigeon shit-covered bench until it all stopped. I felt something crawling on my arm. It was a molten turquoise beetle. It definitely did not seem like it would be able to live in New York City or even come from this part of the world.

The drums were starting to make sense. The bass felt good. I closed my eyes. I felt my face slightly smile as the vitamin D seeped into my skin from the sun. I was reveling in that moment until I felt a coolness replace the warmth of the sun. I swung my head up and opened my eyes. It was the man that helped me escape the Countess!

"Hello, Serene." His voice was deep and soothing.

I felt relieved to see him. "Hello. It is so nice to see you. By the way, I don't even know your name."

He smiled a beautifully warm and comforting grin. "It is Lemayian. You can call me Yema," he said.

"Wow. That is such a cool name. I have never heard of that before. Where is it from?" I asked.

"I am Maasai. It is actually a common name where I am from. I have come on your friend Gertrude's behalf. She would like to extend an invitation to visit her summer home. First, I must ask if you have the amethyst she gave you?"

I looked down and started to rummage in my bag. My hand pulled out chapstick, Band-Aids and perfume bottles. I looked at him with sad puppy eyes. "No. I don't think so," I said.

"You must keep it with you."

I thought to myself, *What is the big deal about this little amethyst?*

"Okay. I will," I replied.

"Are you sure?" He asked with a smile, but I could tell he was being serious.

"Yes. I am sure!"

I will send a car to your place in two hours so you can get the stone and pack some things."

"I am sorry, Yema. But I can't go anywhere right now. Please tell Gertrude thank you so much for the offer, but I can't go. I appreciate all of your help. I am just not in the position to be vacationing right now."

"Please do not fret. Gertrude told me of your leaving the gallery and she thought you might be pleased with the idea of getting away for a bit to relax. All accommodations will be taken care of."

Just then, a black Bentley drove up and the window rolled down. Gertrude smiled and said, "Hello dear, we would love for you to come but understand if you cannot. We are on our way to the airport now. Hope you can make it." And at that, the car sped off.

I thought for a moment. *I have no job and New York doesn't seem to be rolling out any red carpets to keep me here.* "Okay, give me two hours. I will be ready. To be honest, I would like to get away," I said.

"Perfect, the car will be waiting," Yema replied.

CHAPTER 4

COSTA RICA

We flew south like birds in winter. We arrived late at night. The house was a tall, square room made of stone and missing an entire wall.

I looked at Yema. "Are there any windows?" I asked.

"Everything here is *pura vida,* which means 'pure life.'"

"You mean there are no windows or screens anywhere on the property?" I asked while watching a colorful bug buzz by like a helicopter.

"Exactly," was Yema's reply.

Walking into my bedroom, I noticed there was a mosquito net over the bed, which I was very thankful for.

I laid down to rest but kept a light on. None of the lights were bright anyway. They all seemed to be solar-powered and gave off a soft effervescent glow.

As soon as I untensed my muscles and nodded off, I woke to a sound of horror. It sounded like demon winds. I thought of the Countess. It was low, multilayered and guttural, with no beginning and no end. The noise finally stopped when the sky started to show signs of dawn. I was white knuckling my blanket.

As soon as the sky filled with light, my grip softened and I drifted off to sleep from pure exhaustion.

It was late afternoon or early evening when I awoke again. James's face flashed before me the moment I gained consciousness. I had drifted off to sleep soaked in fear and awoke to his face. I was hoping he was okay. I was hoping I would see him again.

I was scared at how overwhelming my emotions were. I'd never felt this way about anyone before. My skin flashed hot when I thought of him and my body wanted his next to mine.

The next realization I had was that the sun was still out and that I was hungry. I threw on a colorful dress and walked down the cool stone steps to the main floor. As I made my descent, I noticed there was a terrarium climbing up the wall. It was as tall as the square home—three levels. It included a myriad of plants, frogs, bugs and geckos. There was no glass to keep them in, naturally a gecko or two would follow you around. I looked over to the right and saw Yema sitting at a table. He was looking out the back side of the house. I followed his gaze to the tall jungle grass, a tree line and about half a mile of white sand—exactly the same color as the stone floors in the house. After the sand, you could see the first break of perfect waves.

He looked at me. "Are you hungry?"

"Yes, starving."

"Meet Mrs Havershmire. She can make you whatever you like."

"Hello," I said with a big smile.

After eating, I was finding my way to the bathroom and realized there was not one door in the house except for the entrance. The entrances to the bathrooms were simply corridors and turns that led you into private alcoves with huge stone bathtubs and simple white toilets. I was pretty horrified that I was expected to relieve myself without any privacy. "Pura vida" I guess.

As I went back downstairs, I saw Gertrude's long white hair and warm smile. She was backlit from the midday sun. I started walking toward her with my arms floating upward. She began to walk toward me and we hugged. I was feeling emotional. But most importantly, I felt safe and that, in itself, made me realize all I had been through. I only now felt how much stress and shadow had been living inside of me ever since *the Countess* was a name I knew. I was happy to be here, away from her, away from New York and away from the gallery. Gertrude let me settle in and go through my myriad of emotions. I think she knew I was having a moment.

After "my moment" I had so many questions for her. I felt that Gertrude knew things I could not even begin to understand. And what's more, I knew she was helping me, I wondered why. To what gain?

"What is it, Serene?" she asked.

I only then felt my furrowed brow and realized I was twirling my hair—something I have been doing since I had hair. Whenever I was in deep thought or needed comfort, I would twirl my hair and run it on my lips. It soothed me. "I'm just trying to understand what is happening. Who is the Countess?"

"She is who she is. The question is, *what* is she?"

"What is she?"

"She is not like you or me. Not exactly. She walks with flesh and physically, she obeys the laws of science and what it is like to live on earth most of the time. However, energetically she does not obey or adhere to any laws of human existence."

"What exactly does that mean?"

"She is powerful. She can manipulate energy and use it for her gain, frighteningly so. She works in the dark, in the negative. If you work in the light and in the positive, your energy grows from within. In the negative, you must take to grow. Whenever an

55

entity or being chooses to get what he or she needs from outside sources, it becomes an addiction. The void is never fulfilled. The one who takes must always take to survive. It is a lower or shadow way to do 'energy work.' If one decides to tap into the energy within, one will always be fulfilled and the energy is endless."

Her gaze was directed at the amethyst she had given me. She walked over to it, picked it up and looked at it with a gingerly expression.

"And ... what is the deal with that amethyst?" I asked.

She laughed. "I thought you would never ask." She smiled and continued. "This is a very special amethyst indeed. I am not sure if you know how important crystals are in general for transmitting energy?" she asked.

I shook my head no as she continued.

"They are found in watches to keep time, radios and computers. They hold memory and transmit energy. The Earth, we were taught, has a molten core. Yes, there is molten rock and lava. But at the core of our planet is crystal. Scientists now know this from how the seismic waves and the earth's electromagnetic field moves across her surface.

"The only explanation scientifically is that there is a huge amount of crystal at the core. This particular amethyst came from the deepest part of her core, brought to the surface from one of the newest mountain ranges, Everest. This little amethyst was found at the top covered in snow. Legend has it that it moved up over millions of years by the earth's tectonic plates pushing together. These plates managed to escort only this one little violet crystal up from the core. This sacred amethyst is blessed by the Himalayan gods and the old souls who do their work for humanity in the temples of those mountains. It is quite special in its teaching abilities. This aptly purple in color crystal is the color of Akashic energy. This crystal is a part of Earth's Akashic energy, her soul or spirit energy," she said.

"*Wow*," I said as I held it with a newfound appreciation and watched the many rainbows within the crystal glisten and glow. Then I asked, "What is Akashic energy?"

"*Akashic* is a Sanskrit word meaning soul or life energy. Hindus believe it is the spark of life that lives in all and can be used to heal across time and space. It is the energy of all life capable of anything we imagine."

"Why is the Akashic energy purple or violet?" I asked.

"Deep purple or violet vibrates at the highest level of all the colors that we can see. Scientifically speaking, if we see purple in the cosmos we know that it is omitting the most energy possible in the physical realms."

After a while of silence and my brain digesting, she warmly asked if I would be ready for a day trip tomorrow.

"Yes, I think so," I replied.

THE NEXT DAY

Out, way past the wave breaks, into the blue Central American sea we went. I was lying on a soft linen cushion on the back deck of *Abalone*. She was Gertrude's catamaran yacht. She was a beautiful vessel. I made it my job for the day to watch the massive white sails touch the few wispy white clouds in the cobalt sky. The music sounded like light massaging glass.

Yema was pulling out snorkeling gear. "Are you ready, Serene? Have you snorkeled before?"

"Umm ... no," was my response.

"Okay, not to worry. We will take it slow, but once we are on our way, stay near me. Also, do you have the amethyst? It might be wise to bring it."

I pulled the amethyst out of my jean shorts pocket. A drip of sweat ran down my arm. I held on tight to the stone for a moment and then put it under my right foot inside of my flipper so I would not lose it. I spit in my mask as I was instructed to do. *Eww*, I said to myself as I followed Yema over to the side of the boat.

His beautiful, vibrant smile shined brightly. He looked like a happy young boy for a minute. He put his face into the water and started to swim into the deep, moving away from our vessel. I followed, but as soon as I put my face down and immersed into the water, I held my breath. The cold water was a shock. I lifted my head and started to gulp in small bouts of air. It was hard to accept that I could breathe underwater without drowning.

Finally I relaxed and allowed myself to breathe through the snorkel while my face was in the ocean. I swam right next to Yema. He looked back at me and then pointed down.

The sun was shining through the water in magisterial rays. It was coming from the middle heavens and descending into a new, magical world. Coral reefs flushed with life—so many delicate colors, including hues I could not name. The fish seemed to be the ones with clout, holding moving space, gliding over and threading through. Black and yellow tiger striped fish, rainbow parrot fish, splayed scales holographically changing colors before my eyes. We kept going. A neon green eel. It snapped its jaw and zapped away ferociously. We came to a pass. Looking down it was a thirty-foot drop.

Just then I felt heat on my back—the kind of warmth you feel when something is near. I maneuvered my body around, using my flippers as rudders. It was a spiky round ball of a thing. *Ahh yes, a puffer fish!* His mass inflated, floating along, two magnanimous round eyeballs fixated on me. I looked back and downward, feeling the cold rise from where the life was teaming. Two massive black stingrays with white stripes and spiked tails slid along the ocean's floor. In a cove, about fifteen feet down, four grouper fish—all of them bigger than me—took cover. Off to the left was a school of soft pink and hard black fish about four hundred strong, jetting back and forth in swift precision. Yema grabbed my hand and pulled me to one side. He saved my foot from almost touching a giant jellyfish's tentacles. He pushed the water toward it. We both watched as the giant jellyfish glided away.

Continuing on, Yema was swimming faster and faster. I tried to keep up and followed him to a more shallow part. He then turned around and looked intensely at me and pointed down. I just saw more beautiful coral. As I stared more intently, I saw outlines of what appeared to be tiny squid. There were five to be exact and their bodies were morphing into the exact shape, texture and color of the coral that they were hovering over. They had a keen sense of personal space. They were all in a row, with exactly the same amount of ocean between them. They were moving as if tied together with an invisible strand of gossamer. Like a dial, they pervaded the coral's immediate environment. And then, *snap*. They attacked the fish coming out of the coral and consumed them. Simultaneous to their hunting, they glowed and emanated various colors. I looked up at Yema and thought, *These must be aliens. I have never seen such interesting creatures.* As I was making this observation, I felt warmth on my back again. It was moving down my body. I was half expecting to see the puffer fish again.

When I looked down at my leg, I saw a large tentacle. *Maybe it's a giant jellyfish?* Adrenaline shot through me. Before I could comprehend what was happening, a fleshy, soft substance was suddenly all over me, gently floating into every crevice of my body. I closed my eyes for fear of pain. Yet all I felt was warmth and tingling on my skin. I allowed my eyelids to slowly open and I was right to believe I was being consumed by a grand gesture of jelly.

I was, in fact, inside of a giant glowing jelly substance. It happened so fast. I only saw points of vibrating rainbow lights moving through its expressive tentacles and two slanted eyes before I entered through what seemed like a mouth. I was inside this strange being. Yet, I could see through its fleshy jelly skin and saw Yema looking at me intently while quietly treading water. He was hovering in the same position as when I had seen him last. He signaled for me to relax and to close my eyes. At this point, I was completely submerged in water and jelly and he was telling me to relax? Yet somehow I did.

I began to hear clear, high-pitched sounds like that of a wet finger on crystal—very singular and perfectly definite. Each note created a counterpart of a perfect singular emotion that ran through me like a flash of lightning. Each sound and emotion also had a specific color that the jelly substance was radiating. It was producing more colors, sounds and emotions than I'd known existed. I felt the warmth and tingling again on my skin, but now it was going deeper into my tissue and seeping through me. Then something even stranger happened!

It felt as though my skin was melting away and I was everywhere. It was as if my skin and my senses were the whole ocean itself, wrapping around Earth with no beginning or no end. Deep inside I could feel my organs and identify them through an animalistic feeling of euphoria. It was as if my sexuality was in each organ. The feeling was so intensely pleasurable and positive. I opened my eyes and saw what I felt—a pink, purple, yellow and turquoise molten moving glow that was everywhere. I could no longer see any color without a surge of intense feeling. I now knew exactly what each gradient of color in the universe meant and what its respective messages were. The purples ring sacred and are filled with messages from deep within universal consciousness. I felt what it was like to have no body. I was everywhere, just a light being inside of another being. My mind was searching for threads of reality but there was only existence—pure, radiant light existence.

I suppose there are moments in my mind so deep where I wish for the world to be this intensely magical and beautiful. But I have always been afraid of it and maybe worried somehow that I am not worthy of experiencing the best thing I could ever imagine. Maybe I would be unable to handle something *too* good. In this moment I feel it—and I *never want it to stop.*

And then it does.

I was being pushed out of this creature. Its body was

contracting. I could still see through its skin. It was changing texture, shape and color, taking on its surroundings like a physical empath. It not only felt its surroundings, it physically became its surroundings. I was being taught this as I was still engaged in this dance of mystery, still half-inside of its womb, its child. The contraction and expanding of its form was happening more frequently and I began to feel the sense of my skin slowly return. I felt pressure from its movements and muscles. I was being massaged from my cranium to my toes. I saw a vibrating show of lights and felt warm and beautiful energy. Finally, I was ejected back into the waters of the ocean with a last uterine thrust. This magical creature had consumed me and then given me new life. I thought of my mother. It only made sense.

As fast as it came, it was leaving me now. Slowly, my head was bobbing above water and I started to breathe air once again. I felt Yema grab my hand. I looked into the water and behind me. I shuddered when I finally saw this giant creature. It looked like a massive water alien with intelligent, delicate, insectile features filled with light. It was so breathtaking and beautiful. I only focused on taking the moment into my mind. I was experiencing a state of gratitude and respect for this creature that had shared so much of itself with me. I looked again into Yema's eyes. He gave me a look of a proud father in return. He gave a slight nod up and down with his smooth shaven head, as if to say, *Yes, that did just happen.*

Back on the catamaran, I walked to the front of the vessel and sat on the right side of the net. I watched the water zoom past under me and wondered what else was in there. The moon was full and bright and there were many stars overhead. I felt completely changed and, felt somehow, that I was occupying more space in my own skin. I grabbed the net and saw everything anew. I noticed that there was a light glowing under my skin. When I clenched my fingers tightly the glow brightened and rushed to my hands. I stretched my legs and saw pink, blue and yellow points of lights flickering and traveling through my veins. Wow: *My blood was bioluminescent.*

I couldn't stop flexing and stretching my muscles so I could watch the different colors appear as my blood moved. All of a sudden, I was famished and desperately thirsty.

Yema had Mrs. Havershmire bring out coconuts for us to drink from. They soon were accompanied by bowls of fresh jackfruit covered in pink pickles and a rich, thick mother sauce. I kept seeing violet orbs of light flicker in and out of my peripheral view, as I looked out to the horizon. When I was still, they would vanish. When I moved or looked at something else, they would appear in a flash, almost too fast for my eyes to register. My hunger almost overwhelmed my new interest in examining myself and trying to catch these little flickers of light. My mouth could not seem to chew fast enough. I could not get the nutrients from the food into my bloodstream as fast as each cell in my body was screaming for it. *I felt more alive than I had ever felt before.*

That night, back at the house, we continued feasting on truffle French fries, oysters and towers of red, fleshy chilled sea crustaceans.

Gertrude came and sat next to me. "How was your swim in the ocean today?" she asked.

"I don't know if Yema told you but the most amazing thing happened."

"Oh yes, I know. Do you feel well?"

"Strangely, I feel clearheaded and filled with more energy than I could ever imagine having."

"Do you have any questions?"

I looked down at my arm and moved my fingers to watch the glow appear and asked. "What was that creature? What is happening to me?"

Gertrude laughed and smiled generously. "All good things are happening to you. You are having what some would call an 'awakening.' I can tell you, what happened to you is a very special gift. Yema and I have not experienced what you have today. We only knew that it was possible for you. The creature, I would think, is your spirit animal. It was a giant cuttlefish from Yema's description. Your guides revealed that your spirit animal would live here in these waters. We had no idea what or who it would be. Yema and I even had a going bet. I thought maybe a mantis shrimp. Yema thought maybe a dolphin," she said and laughed. "Well, we were both wrong."

"I never knew what a cuttlefish was or that it could do that."

"This was an ancient one and probably will never be seen again. It merged energy with yours and your spirit guides."

"Spirit guides?" I asked.

"We all have them, but yours are very old and very wise," she said with a smile and wink.

"Look at my skin. Am I going to be okay?" I asked as I squeezed my fist to show her the glowing.

She smiled. "This is why you are here. This is a sign. Know this. I just don't know what all of it means yet. However, I do know that the glowing will not hurt you. It is a gift. I can promise you this. More will be revealed and I will be here by your side to help you navigate."

My heart filled up with gratitude. "I am so happy that I had the chance to be here. Thank you so much for inviting me. I know that you heard about me losing my job, but it has been more than that. Something changed inside of me recently. I feel being here has given me a chance to be happy again. I know I need to get back and look for a job and pay my half of the rent."

Gertrude looked at me and said, "I know you will maybe want to fight me on this. I have given William some money to cover your rent for last month and the months to come. I would like for you to continue to gain your strength and relax here. It is not a big thing for me to do. It is a very little thing in fact. I am an old woman with a lot of money. I do not want you to feel in any way guilty or badly about it—only to be yourself and take it day by day. If you feel you must go back because you are ready, not due to logistical obligations, then by all means we will arrange for your return."

I looked at the stars twinkling in the sky while sitting on the lounge sofa. I listened to the waves and the breath of the jungle. I could not resist. I felt my bones quivering and asking me to please stay. They needed some time to warm themselves. I looked back at Gertrude with emotion welling in my gut. "Thank you. It is too kind. Yes, I think I will stay. Thank you again." I felt for the amethyst that I had put back in my jean shorts and rolled it around in the palm of my hand. *Why did I have to bring it today?*

Gertrude read my mind or saw my hand grab the amethyst in my pocket—one or the other. "This amethyst has an imprint of Earth's beginning and end. That crystal knows things we as humans cannot, energetically speaking. Because of its age and abilities, if you carry it with you, it will learn your energy. It will also teach you about Earth's energy. This is your key to not only Earth's Akashic energy but your own—a link to each other's," Gertrude said while her eyes stared into the night sky.

I heard the same guttural noises on the night I arrived. I had now learned they belonged to howler monkeys. I heard a song of a bird and saw flashes of dark rainbows and glowing insects in the sky. In a way, the jungle feels a lot like the city. There is life everywhere. You feel protected by being a part of that life, even though the bugs here are insanely big and intimidating at times. But you can't fight it. You are in their territory, not the other way around. At least they are not New York City's wildlife—cockroaches, silverfish and rats.

I greeted Yema in the kitchen. "Good morning."

He turned to me with one of his excited smiles. "Would you fancy a hike up into the mountains today?"

I answered with a smile and he went off to pack our bags.

As we started our trek up the muddy, root-infested trail, Yema warned me to be careful of a coral snake above. I looked up and there was a red, yellow and black snake dangling like an earring from a tree branch, directly north of my head. We both kept on with the climbing. We could tell that we were nearing the top, as the trees were becoming a little bit smaller. One could see the moisture in the air, if you looked into a stream of sunlight.

The trail soon opened up to a massive field and kept on in a winding sort of way. A black ferret-looking creature was running in the grass. Out of nowhere, huge turquoise wings of about six feet in length flapped over my head. I quickly ducked, for fear of being decapitated and then looked back to see what it was and where it was going. It landed on a bush near me. I whispered to Yema, "What was that?"

"It is a macaw! Probably the father of them all. He is massive!"

"How do you know that it is a male?"

"You see how beautiful and vibrant his turquoise feathers are? So intricate are the golds, reds and pinks. Look at the white designs near his eyes and beak."

"Yes, I see."

"That is how you know. In the bird kingdom, the males are always more vibrant in their colors and patterns—so they can attract the females to mate with. It is of course quite opposite for us humans," he said with a smile. "It is a sign of good luck that he flew at your head. In my village, we once had a young girl and all the birds would fly at her, just above her head."

"I never knew that was a sign of good luck."

"Oh yes it is! They were trying to tell us to crown her. She was the first child to our chief. We all knew her crown to be true because the chief's second born was a loathsome boy who caused disgrace and havoc to our way of life. But, he was the chief's son. So the crown went to him the day our chief died. Terrible things happened to the village after that sad day."

"Why didn't they make the girl chief then?"

"She was killed by the new, young chief. He knew that she was the rightful owner of his position after all of the signs and our great elders of many tribes reading it as so in the stars. No woman was ever chief before or since. Even their mother did not want her to be chief because she thought only a man should lead a village. It was a classic case of old thought patterns hindering progress. So he took his sister's life. He did not want any opposition. His ego ruled his actions. He knew as long as she was alive, he would continue to suffer the humiliation of the wise ones telling him that a woman would be better suited than him at leading his people.

"Here we are, Serene. Look out there." Yema pointed to a thick white cloud, so close that it soon enveloped his finger.

I was squinting, trying to see something. I knew we were at the top of the mountain, but there were no sudden drop-offs or cliffs. It was rounded and covered in grass, so it didn't really feel all that spectacular to me. But I did not want to let Yema down. "Yes, it is so beautiful," I said in forced elation.

Yema kept pointing. "Wait for it. Wait for it."

I went into my pack and pulled out my water bottle and started to guzzle. I only stopped when there was no water left and popped the cap back on and put it back in my pack. "Do you have any more water?" I asked.

Yema was silent. I looked up and didn't see him anywhere. I just saw the same thick whiteness thin slightly and then a hole in the white and something dark and close appeared. I started to panic. "Yema? Are you here?"

Nothing ... I didn't want to walk anywhere for fear of actually walking off the mountain. At this point, the clouds and fog were so thick I could not see in front of my two feet. I closed my eyes to regain power over my thoughts and to try to relax. I counted slowly as I inhaled my breath and held it for ten counts. I then slowly exhaled for another ten counts.

When I opened my eyes, the fog and white clouds swiftly moved away. I was almost blown over by a strong wind. There, only meters in front of me, was a huge black mountain. Now I understood. This mist was steam. I watched as the red and orange lava peacefully cracked and slowly flowed down the peak.

"Volcano Arenal!" Yema yelled finally as he jumped in front of me. He looked like that same little boy I had seen on the boat yesterday. I only saw his big beautiful eyes and wide sparkling smile. "That is Arenal. Respect her beauty," he said.

"Wow!" I exclaimed.

"We are going to the base of her tomorrow evening for a small get-together. I wanted you to see her up close first."

"Wow," I said again.

CHAPTER 5

THE NEXT EVENING

Everyone was dressed in a sea of khaki. The room was constructed of dark amber wood with a thatched roof. Some areas of the floor had glass panels instead of wood, allowing glimpses of dark black rushing water underneath. The real attraction was an illuminated, steaming waterfall that was just beyond the grounds, leading to the jungle. We were given refreshing cocktails upon our entrance. The crowd was quiet and boring. Yema and Gertrude were participating in polite conversations. They would introduce me to someone and soon after glaze over from the palatable dullness of what was being discussed. There was a small quartet consisting of Latin brass and percussion in the corner of the room. The hostess was wearing a lace dress that touched the floor and showed her back. She motioned for everyone to be seated.

A series of delicious courses came out from the kitchen. A few toasts were made, and a few quiet laughs were heard through the sounds of insects, geckos and soft bossa nova playing. After the dinner service, champagne was poured and the music became five decibels louder. The room filled with more khaki and linen-clad bodies, some candles were blown out.

I positioned myself by the edge of the room so I could have a better view of the waterfall. I felt the wood banister beneath my hands and smelled the sweet humidity of the air. There was smoke from the volcano. I felt the coolness of the night on my skin. My ears let the rush of the water fill my head. The brass section of the band started in with a sullen song. A young guy was walking over to where I was standing—he seemed not to have gotten the dress code memo. He was barefoot, wearing board shorts, a ripped Nirvana T-shirt and a long silver chain around his neck that dangled shells and a crazy pendant. His hair was bleached from sun and surf. His eyes were light blue against his smooth tanned skin.

"This is pretty beat, huh?" he said to me, while leaning against the wall and staring straight into the room.

I looked at him and scrunched up my nose. "Yeah, it really is. I guess I was expecting something else," I replied.

"Have you been to the hot springs? Me and some peeps are going soon, if you want to come? We are outside sitting at the picnic table. Bring some beer too, if you can," he said as he smiled and took a handful of ice-cold Modelo cans from a bowl on a table. He walked toward the kitchen and opened the door.

My eyes followed him. I saw the bright light of the kitchen and a few men in white chef uniforms mulling around.

As always, Yema sensed when I needed something and he was soon by my side. "He is a good kid. We are staying the night here. You should go have some fun." He gave his fatherly smile of reassurance and I almost forgot to say goodbye. I was already making my escape.

I went outside and walked around to the right of the building. There was a bright light hanging down from the thatched roof of the porch. It was swinging from side to side, covered in insects. Below, sitting at the picnic table, were some surfers and kitchen workers hanging out: drinking beer, smoking cigarettes, playing cards. All of them had smiles on their faces. Some were laughing. Some had their arms around each other in the spirit of brotherly love. One thing was definite: they were all having a lot more fun than the people inside.

The surfer kid who'd invited me stood up. "Hell yeah! Thanks for the beer!" He walked over and grabbed the sweaty cold cans from me and handed them out while motioning me to come meet everyone.

"Hey, what is your name anyway?" he asked.

"Serene," I replied.

"Killer. I'm Sammy," he said, while opening a beer with his T-shirt and offering me his elbow. He went down the line.

"This is Luke, Andreas, Thomas and Jesús. They work here." He laughed. "Yeah, right, they are wearing uniforms so you know that already. The lovebirds are Patti and Humberto," he added.

They both looked at me. Patti had tight curly blond hair and round doll eyes. Humberto was strikingly handsome, with tan skin, black hair and slanted eyes. My eyes were drawn into the shadows. It was the girl from the night of the fire at Death. She was beautiful and tanned with sun-bleached hair. She had no makeup on. She didn't need any with her impeccable bone structure and stunning features. Her hands were covered in really cool rings. One gold hoop with a small shell hung from her ear and a chain with quartz crystals from her neck. She wore cutoff ripped denim shorts, black flip-flops and an African print triangle bikini top. Her oversize shredded tank top hung off her cool model skinny body so perfectly. I wanted to drop the last beer I had in the grass and run back into the boring party and hide.

Sammy continued. "Then we have … umm, hey man, what's your name again?"

"It's James," he said, while looking up from under his thick black hair.

His brooding oceanic eyes shot through my soul for what felt like the hundredth time. I couldn't believe it was him in the flesh! I was absolutely stunned and paralyzed from shock. He was swathed in complete darkness. I barely saw his figure sitting there in that pocket of velveteen pitch-black. He was wearing black jeans and a black T-shirt.

Sammy continued. "Oh right! Your friend owns this place? Yeah, man, tight. You play shows here sometimes too?"

"Yeah, that's right," James said.

"Hey, my name is Abbey," the impossibly tall model cool-girl from cool-heaven said, toward my general direction without giving me too much of her consideration because she was too busy not giving a damn about anything.

After a minute of Sammy spacing out, a beautiful, golden goddess fairy with a singsong voice continued with the introductions. "My name is Jess and this is Andre." Her smile was so warm and beautiful she made me feel at ease immediately.

Abbey stood up. "Have to take a whiz." At that, she walked into to the kitchen.

I just stood there, not knowing what to do because James was there. To make matters worse, the only space to sit down at the table was next to him. I was trying to act cool and unavailable—a routine I learned somewhere that did what? I really didn't know, except make me act strange.

Thankfully, Jess continued the conversation. "So what brings you to Arenal?" she asked.

"A friend," I said.

"Super cool," Jess said.

Everyone was standing up and making his or her way to a dark dirt pathway. Abbey came out of the kitchen laughing heartily and then stopped when she was next to James and looked into his eyes.

Jess giggled. "It's gonna be amazing with the full moon tonight. You have to come."

We all followed the path into the jungle with flashlights in hand. I was the last one in line and kept looking back to see if anything was behind me. Jess was in front of me. She was, thankfully, keeping me company.

"Your friend is Gertrude right?"

"Yes. How do you know her?"

"I am here on a dual mission. I came with a small group of colleagues to study some insects and plant life. I am a botanist by trade. I also study the unseen metaphysical elements of the plants and their energy in connection to us. Gertrude has been teaching me about the latter part. Some plants are great teachers, as well as lifesaving medicines. They hold a plethora of secrets. I feel I am only at the tip of the iceberg of learning about their capabilities. It's been very exciting. You're very lucky to be staying with her. She has a connection to a wisdom I have not encountered before."

As Jess said this, I realized indeed how lucky I was that Gertrude had taken me under her wing. After all, I was standing in a moonlit jungle at the base of an active volcano in the middle of the night—instead of being at a dive bar getting obliterated. It was nice to feel this emotion of gratitude. I also thought to myself what a strong and intelligent woman Jess was—a scientist and a spiritualist. These were two facets that were hardly ever intertwined in one person. I got a mental vision of a twisting vine moving up the base of a tree. I was fascinated by her.

Soon, we reached the waterfall that I had been staring at all night. I could feel the heat from it. I watched as its water spray appeared and disappeared in the streams of the lights we were carrying.

Everyone started to undress and jump into the black water. They were standing underneath the wall of thermal water falling straight from Arenal herself. The palm trees and flowers were larger than I had seen before. They were gracefully bending and dipping into the fall. They looked as if they were throbbing with an extra insurgence of life. I was the last one to arrive. I slowly and nervously took off my clothes. I left my bra and underwear on.

Jess swam over and lent me a hand. "Be careful. Some of the rocks here are slippery when you get in."

My eyes began to focus. There were smooth black rocks made from Arenal's lava and worn down from her constant pounding.

Everyone lined up under the force of Arenal, their backs and heads massaged by her power, renewed and baptized by her will.

After a time, a few people got out and then the rest of us followed. Deeper into the jungle we went.

I couldn't see James or hear him. I wanted to be next to him, but I was too afraid. I knew that he was probably next to Abbey, holding her hand. The way that she looked at him made me shake a little from the inside out, dousing me in a coat of nasty anxiety and severe nausea. I knew I wasn't cool enough for him. Abbey and James looked like they belonged together. The darkness was my friend, shielding me from any view of what might be happening. This I was thankful for.

Sammy was next to me. "Oh, man, you're gonna love the next pool. It will take a while to get there, but it totally kills, man." He went into his stoned surfer laugh.

Sammy was right. When we finally got there, I saw a large sparkling pool of water in the middle of the jungle off to the right of Arenal. There was no steam and that was welcoming. Sweat was already dripping down my arms and rolling off my forehead. Again, everyone started to rip off their clothing and jump into the deep, dark volcanic water.

I swam over to a desolated spot so I could be alone. I stared at the moon and listened to the sounds of the insects. I stayed still so I could feel the breeze. *Why hadn't James even said hi to me?* I wanted to leave out of growing anxiety. But it was too beautiful not to experience. The coolness of the water and the unknown in the depths added yet another layer of nervousness. I heard everyone laughing and having fun. I thought I should try to at least act normal or be social. I could not take my eyes away from the moon or my emotions away from melancholy.

I felt two arms wrapping around my stomach from behind. A tall man's body pressed against the back of mine. I gasped. It felt too good to be real or safe. His hands went up my back to the base of my head and his fingers wrapped around my neck, still moving, holding my jaw. He turned my whole body around to face him. Those dark green eyes in the moonlight were disturbing and beautiful. "I wasn't sure I was going to ever see you again after the Countess's party. Now to find you in a jungle of all places," he said as he was still holding my face and staring intensely into my eyes.

I felt numb. I had no control of what I was about to say or do. My whole being was on sensory overload from just being next to him. Him touching me and looking into me was too much to handle.

"I don't know why we are both here at the same time, but it feels like it's for a reason," he said.

"I know. It's really strange. Why *are* you here?" I asked.

"My friends own the little hotel we were just at. I come here when New York is getting too 'real.' How about you? What brings you?"

"My friend Gertrude has a place and I am here to learn something I guess."

"Well that sounds interesting and mysterious. Although I do want to know what it is that you are learning," he said with a charming grin.

"If I knew exactly what I am supposed to learn, I would tell you. All I know is that everything is not what it once seemed. I can't work out what the end result is supposed to be or will be. I guess, I am practicing having faith—something I was not doing so well in New York."

"I want to be there when you find out," he said.

I smiled at him and we both watched the moon travel on its way down into the trees. A few people were heading back. We were tucked away under a cover of hanging wet orchids. Mist was becoming visible from the faint light of the sun that was quickly coming up from the other side of the earth. We only saw shapes through the giant leaves and heard faint talking. He slid his hands down my thighs, grabbed them and placed them around his waist.

I actually couldn't believe he was so comfortable touching me, like we had known each other for years. Then I became almost alarmed as he pressed my lower back directly into the front of his body. I could feel him for the first time. I felt waves of emotion and euphoria course through my veins. The whites of his eyes were clear and vibrant.

"I'm looking for something real. This feels like the beginning of something real.

"The night I told you everything about the fire and my mother took me by surprise. I have never felt so comfortable with anyone before. You being here right now is taking me by surprise," he said.

I felt so much heat in my lower stomach. Our bodies fit so well together. They felt unified beyond our bodies. I felt the universe stirring. He held me even tighter, almost too hard. My body quivered and something deep inside of me started to feel out of control. All of my physiology was calling to him. He took my face into his hands once again. We stared at each other for what seemed like forever. I didn't know what he was going to do next. He then placed my head on his chest and we held each other until the new dawn light appeared.

Maybe I had never felt a pure connection to another person until this moment? Our world had a slight tinge of flame to it from the mix of the sun and moonlight. There was a frog making its noise on a rock. He busied himself, licking up giant mosquitos out of the air. Only a few were able to safely buzz by. A myriad of animals created a strange yet invigorating symphony. Everything was new, alive and magical beyond imagination.

"Hi Yema! *Oh my God* last night was epic!" I said, picking up a piece of fruit and pouring a cup of dark, strong coffee.

Yema was as stoic and still as a building.

I giggled and shook his shoulders. "Yeeeeemmmaaa!" I shrieked.

"Serene, please, I need to tell you something."

He looked into my eyes. I saw a solemn sadness—a sadness that he was trying to warn me with.

"Well? Out with it, Yema. It can't be that bad."

He took my hand and placed it in his warm, large hand. "It's Lydia ... She is no longer with us."

"Well, I know that!" I laughed. "She would never come to a jungle—that's Lydia for you."

"Serene ... she is dead."

My face froze as my brain was trying to filter the information and ask two hundred questions all at once. This couldn't be true. "What?" was all I could say.

He continued as he saw that what he'd just told me was not sinking in. "They found her body on the Countess's property with deadly amounts of narcotics in her bloodstream. I am deeply sorry, Serene."

"No! That is impossible. She promised me she wouldn't go! Yema, what the *fuck!* Why would you tell me this?"

"Serene, I would not lie about such a serious matter. What I am telling you is the truth."

He left the room and returned with a *New York Times* in his hand. I began to read the headline: "Heiress Found Dead inside an Estate in the South of France." A sound of pain escaped my lungs. "Goddamn it, Lydia! Why?! Why did you go?!" I screamed into the air through tears that were running down my face into my mouth and onto the wooden floor.

After moments of shaking while gasping for air, I fell to the ground and stayed there curled up with the newspaper crumpled tightly in my hands. The ink was wet and bleeding through my skin. I stayed there for what seemed like a cruel amount of time—because the time I spent on that floor hurt so much even a second was too cruel for anyone or anything to have to suffer through.

After a long stint, I slowly got up with a sense of nothingness in my cavity. Then a wave of bitter anger unleashed into my bloodstream as I wrapped my black ink-soaked hand around a glass paperweight and threw it as hard as I could across the room. I let out another guttural animal sound, the likes of which I had never heard come from my body before.

I walked into the living room and, without looking at anyone, in a deadpan voice, I simply stated, "We have to contact the French authorities and her family. We need to hold that evil bitch accountable for this. I will kill her tomorrow if we do not do something today. Get me out of here. I need to talk to Lydia's family."

Yema went to grab my arm. I looked up with watery eyes and good amounts of fuming pain in my heart. "Don't touch me!" I yelled.

He just bowed his head. "We will get you on the phone with her family right away. I just would like you to take a day to think about going back. Gertrude and I strongly urge you not to go."

"I need to go back. I need to be at the funeral. I need to see her family. Everything has been too crazy and I really just need to have a grip on reality right now. I need to go back to New York. My best friend is dead! No more giant, crazy cuttlefish or evil Countesses."

When I woke up the next day, it was still the same. Lydia was still dead. My eyes were almost swollen shut. I ran into Gertrude's bedroom.

"Sorry to wake you, Gertrude. I need to get on a flight now. I can't wait another minute."

There was a knocking on the door.

"Come in," she said.

It was Yema. He sat down in a chair next to her window.

Gertrude began to speak. "Serene, I cannot allow you to go to New York. It simply is not safe. You, my child, have a special gift. The signs are confirmed. The Countess knows you are a threat. If you can use your gift, you will threaten her existence. The fact that Lydia is gone proves that she is in active pursuit of stopping you and what you might be able to achieve. The cuttlefish was your spiritual birth. Your journey has begun. The Countess knows this. She had everything to do with Lydia's death and we think she took her life to get to you—to weaken your spirit," Gertrude finished.

"Gertrude is right, Serene. The Countess would be wise to stop you now before you know your strength. We cannot allow you to go," Yema offered in unified support.

"I am going. I'm hearing what you both are saying. I'm just not sure that I really have this 'gift' that you speak of. And if what you are saying is true, I killed my friend. Please, I need to be there," I said, losing my breath, tears welling up. Re-remembering every minute, that Lydia was never coming back. I wanted to fall apart. Yet somehow I managed to hold it together and continue to hold my ground. "I need to go! That is final. I am getting a ticket back to New York and no one can stop me. I need to honor her life."

"We would not want you to disregard your dear friend's passing. We want you to honor her. We also want you to remain safe. I will state again that I do not support you going. However, Yema and I cannot stop you. We will go with you to support you and try to keep you from harm," Gertrude said.

"Thank you," I said with a sigh of grief stricken relief.

CHAPTER 6

NEW YORK CITY

We sat in the back seat of Gertrude's Bentley. We were one of many cars in the funeral procession, riding alongside the hearse that carried her body. It was strange to be back in New York. It was of course the emotions of Lydia's death, but there was another texture I was experiencing. I could not pinpoint what it was. I felt like I had no skin. Everything hurt. The sun was high. The day was unusually warm for this time of year. Lydia would have loved it. She was not one for the cold and always loved an Indian summer. She would always go away on a long trip somewhere in the southern hemisphere when the city froze over. She was too gentle for harsh things. She did live an extraordinary blessed and interesting life. While it may have been too short, it had been filled to the brim.

The grievers were led into Trinity church, located in the financial district. As old as the city of Manhattan. She stood in dark decay. Once red brick, she was now covered with grunge and moss. It had a very small gated cemetery with only one mausoleum that Lydia's family owned. There were only two spaces left and the family had agreed that Lydia should have one. Her untimely death seemed to make the cold hearts of her many family members grow warm again—if only for the moment.

Lydia was a loved and infamous New Yorker due to her heiress title, her fortune and her multitude of nightlife appearances. The high-profile men that she slept with and, of course, her cameos in the likes of *Vogue* and *W* magazines also added to her public allure. For these reasons, there were throngs of people she'd never met waiting outside the gated church and cemetery to pay their respects. There were about three hundred mourners. A Minister clad in heavy robes stood at the entrance of the large mausoleum. The structure itself had a female form, positioned at the right of the entrance and carved in the same alabaster stone. She was dressed in many long draping robes. Her head, in profile, tilted down, her hands, gathered together in prayer. I was behind Lydia's immediate family.

The minister was giving his death sermon. Once he finished, a close friend of the family went to the front. "Lydia was a child of light ... I remember her blond curls in the sun laughing and coming over to ask me why I was smoking. She said to me, 'Dan, why are you trying to put fire in your body? I don't want you to die, Dan.' Needless to say, she had a wonderful effect on people. She always spoke her mind and in such a playful way. I quit that day. I thought, *By God! Little Lydia is right. I keep inhaling fire into my lungs.* Her unique perspective on life will be forever missed."

I began to shake and quiver, trying to hold the tears back. Yema held my hand and I squeezed the life out of it. I was trying to keep a hold on reality. My mind started to race. I was angry and sad—more angry. Something was wrong with all of this. If Lydia had not been with me that night at the spring gala, the Countess would have never met her. Shame and guilt grew in substantial space inside of me.

When her mother looked behind and searched for my eyes

through her black veil, I just bowed my head and started to cry. It should be me in that casket, not Lydia.

Dan went on with the eulogy that was ripping my heart out and making me feel more loathsome by the moment. Then, as if the earth stopped moving, the wrought iron gates opened loudly, everyone looked to see who was entering. A large security man dressed in a black suit with sunglasses walked in. He moved over to the right to let a tall figure with a black muslin hooded cape through. How incredibly unthoughtful to interrupt a funeral!

The intruder pulled the hood back. I went numb and felt paralysis seep in. I tried to move my feet—one in front of the other. I could not. Then I tried to move my body away from this approaching figure of doom. I could not. I tried to turn my head to look for Yema or Gertrude. Yet, I could not. I couldn't even manage to blink.

From what little my senses could detect, no one but me even saw this dark cloud of a creature. The figure walked straight up to Lydia's casket directly across from her mother. Dan was still speaking. No one shed a glance in the direction of this ominous form. I watched as purple, glowing eyes dimmed from under the black tulle it had whipped all over itself. That was my only solace, dimmed eyes. I was now trying to fight and pretend in my head that this was not the Countess—that it was just a long-lost, strange relative I had never met before. All I felt was darkness and fear.

It seemed like an eternity had passed. Everyone was now moving toward the gate to exit. Finally, I felt a light thread of fluidity return to my body. I looked at Yema to try and tell him that I was scared, but I couldn't seem to get the words out. Gertrude was nowhere to be found. Yema was walking next to me, but he felt far away. It was a bit jammed and many were waiting to pass through the one-person gate.

From behind, on my neck, I felt a large, cold wet grip that slowly grew wider. The grip was forcing me to breathe only slivers of air that were sliding down my throat—like streams of horror. The figure whose grip was causing me pain came to face me. I caught a better glimpse of the Countess's eyes. They were framed from the now side-swept tulle, glowing and large. They were filled with venom and hatred. Where most people would have flecks of gold dancing around their pupils, I saw in hers little pustules of blood and small specks of dark, moldy particles resting in a sickly brown oil. My breath was completely gone, I could feel cold alabaster stone against my back—what I imagined but couldn't see to be Lydia's family's mausoleum. The Countess was stronger than me. She was larger than me and had a power over my body that I no longer possessed for myself. I didn't understand. Why was this happening? I ripped through the bleak darkness of my paralysis. While crying, I was screaming at the top of my lungs, feeling more pain than I'd thought possible. No one could hear me. *No one!* I was going to die. I saw Lydia out of the corner of my eye. She was off in the distance sobbing.

I felt my organs. My stomach was high up in my cavity, acid sloshing. My heart was wet and throbbing. My spine, like glass about to shatter. A nervous inner cramp twisted my intestines, then disappeared. I felt Lydia.

I no longer could see anything except a faint white light. I saw a few eyes in that light that I may have once known. I started to walk toward the thing that felt good. Walking away from my body, I looked back and saw my former self, writhing in pain. My body was, in fact, pressed against the white alabaster mausoleum by the force of the Countess's fingers strangling my neck.

Strangely enough, still not one person could see me. No one looked back even for a minute. No one saw anything suspicious out of the corner of his or her eyes. I was being killed before hundreds of witnesses without any acknowledgment. I was more afraid and in awe of her power than I had ever been. She was ringing my neck with her bare hands. She was sucking the soul out of my mouth into her mouth from my almost dead body while casting a spell over the masses to look away.

Just then, something snapped: my fear turned into molten anger. How dare she kill Lydia and now kill me? Who would be next? This was not right. I had to fight back. I tried to walk back to my body, but I could not.

I watched as the Countess grasped my neck even harder. Infinite death was now, just as the last of the procession of mourners left. I saw Gertrude in the crowd. Her neck was turning in a way that was not human. Her head was rotated one more inch to the right than physically possible and then more. Her eyes were painfully wide and alert with animalistic fear. I watched as her old hands and her cashmere scarf moved slowly toward the Countess and my excavated body. It was as if the winds of Everest were against her. But eventually, she made it.

Behind her, Yema came with the same terrible difficulty, fighting against the same winds.

Then it was ... *Jess and Sammy from the jungle?!* They were coming out of the crowd too. They were crawling on their hands and knees. Their eyes were clenched and their mouths open.

Gertrude made it as far as she could. She was the closest. She was staring intently at the back of the Countess's head. She opened her mouth. From the depths of her body and soul escaped a purple and pink light that surrounded the Countess. Yema then opened his mouth and tilted his head back while his neck broke and disconnected from his spine. His face glowed with yellow and green markings. Strong lines appeared from under his eyes. Circles covered his forehead and cheeks. They were the markings of a tribal design. A sound of a thunder drum banged and yellow light exploded from his chest.

Jess and Sammy were still crawling. They were trying to stand and pull the Countess down at the same time. They kept missing her ankles and could not get near enough to put a finger on her. The yellow and pink light from Gertrude and Yema surrounded the Countess and permeated her purple and black glow. Finally, the crawlers gripped her wet, slimy ankles and pulled her down to the earth.

Yema's neck and spine reconnected. He ran toward my body and picked it up. He sucked his yellow light back into his body through his nostrils and dashed into the streets.

Gertrude, still standing, continued to exude more energy as the Countess began to shriek.

REST

I woke up in a fluffy, crisp white bed, linen curtains flying in the breeze. I felt great. I must be back in Costa Rica—a huge turquoise bug flew into my window and landed on my face. I sat up quickly and let out a little yelp. I saw William's overgrown facial hair. "Are you a teddy bear?" I asked, while laughing.

I looked to my right. It was Jess! I yelped again.

I had so many questions—how had they gotten here?

"Oh my God, girl, how the hell are you? Your hair is looking a little crazy," William said while he laughed a nonchalant but uncomfortable laugh. I could sense that William was trying to cover his true feelings of worry. "It is soo humid out here," he added while he took a perfectly worn-in, navy blue American handkerchief circa 1930s out of his back pocket and wiped the sweat from his neck and forehead.

"Dude!" Jess screamed as a grasshopper landed on her. She was silently staring it down, looking into its bulbous and twitching eyes. I thought for a minute that she and the grasshopper were going to make out. But just before human and insect lines were crossed, Jess asked William if she could talk to me in private.

He rolled his eyes and left in search of some shade.

Jess and I just stared at each other for a while. I really didn't know what to make of anything at this point. I owed a huge debt to her, Sammy, Gertrude and Yema for saving my life.

"So, how are you really feeling?" she asked.

"So confused and terrified," I said.

"Sounds about right," she said, laughing gently.

"Why were you and Sammy at the funeral? How could you see the Countess?"

"Gertrude and Yema asked us to come. They were really worried about you going in the first place. I am glad we came. It took all of our strength. That was a close one." She became suddenly solemn.

"Are you okay?" I asked.

"The Countess has an energy I never knew existed, more powerful than anything I've seen before. To be honest, I'm terrified too. I'm terrified she knows any of us and has mingled with our energy. I keep having a feeling she is right behind me."

Just then, Gertrude entered and told us that dinner was ready. Jess put her buttery cocoa arm around my shoulder. I stared at all the gold rings on her fingers as we walked down the hallway together.

The dinner table was a long piece of teakwood. It was dripping with pink succulents, lilies, wildflowers, shells, candles, clear quartz crystals and big black tourmaline shards covered with silver. There were also hunks of Native American Indian turquoise in a striking shade of dark midnight green that once was a part of the Grand American West. All of these treasures commanded space on the table, in happy harmony alongside lobsters, prawns, watermelons, gooseberries and oranges. There was a full-headed red snapper covered in Indian spices and saffron threads, sturgeon caviar, Guy Larmandier rosé champagne and almost black tuna sashimi cut cleverly and splayed in a strong presence over a milky white slab of veined marble. Sitting at the head of the table was Gertrude, to her right, Yema, Jess, William and Sammy.

Before I could voice my appreciation, Gertrude chimed in.

"Please eat." She motioned for the champagne and wine to be poured for the table.

Everyone was enjoying the festive array, conversing and even laughing a little. We needed to laugh. My eyes were still puffy from constantly crying at Lydia's funeral. Her face, embalmed, painted and resembling a bejeweled Fabergé egg, rested in copious amounts of creamed satin while lifeless and utterly dead in her coffin—it was all still so fresh in my head.

I realized my moment to vocalize my gratitude as the conversation reached a lull. But again, before I could, Gertrude shifted the mood into a more serious tone. "I have gathered you here today to let you know that our worst fears have become a reality." Gertrude's eyes found mine. "As you all know, we lost Lydia and we almost Serene." She took my hand and placed it in hers.

"I saw her," I stammered. "I saw Lydia at the funeral. Her soul was there."

"I have no doubt she was trying to warn you. You are in grave danger, my lovely child."

I started to tremble from the inside out and felt my fleshy glow dim.

Gertrude took a deep breath in and on her exhale, she began. "If you look back and really look deep inside, I think you will remember why you came here," she said. At that, I instantly knew she wasn't talking about Costa Rica. There was that reminiscent tremble from deep within. It began to vibrate and there was something more. A sense of a memory and a feeling of importance. My skin flashed with waves of knowing. I felt stuck in this moment, held between space and time. I knew exactly what Gertrude was talking about deep, deep inside of myself—my truest self.

I remembered a time before I was born. I decided to come here because there was something I wanted to do. There had always been a voice inside of me saying, *There is more. This isn't it.* Now I remembered. I didn't know what it was, but I knew that I had come into this life to remember and then to do it. This memory was like coming home.

This feeling was connection to something bigger than me. I almost started to cry because I remembered I had a purpose. After my moments of elation and communion with my truest self had passed, I noticed that my breath was becoming fast and short. Moments passed with my head down in my hands. I was now trying to understand what exactly I was supposed to do, why this was all happening—why my friends had to die in the process?

"For Christ's sake, she is hyperventilating," William interrupted. He tried to rub my shoulders.

Yema put his hand on William to stop him from touching me.

William looked at Yema icily and then told me, "Keep your head between your legs and take deep slow breaths."

Gertrude looked at William with compassion and continued. "Serene, you are a conduit of a certain kind of energy that is not yet in our earthly reality.

"It has been shown to me in so many ways—dreams, visions and a sense of knowingness from my soul. You are the one. The time is now and you are the way for this energy to travel into our fabric of existence. A part of your gift is the ability to transmit, exactly like the amethyst crystal I gave you.

"The best way I can describe it is this. In your souls' energetic DNA, there is a soul song or a resonance. If we can raise your vibration to its truest song, we can unlock a channel to usher in this new energy.

The Countess wants to keep us naive and living as we are—in fear, stuck in base emotions and motives. Our failing is her success. If your potential is realized, you will starve her direct line of energy, which is the abundance of our sorrow and fear and the hunger for power over each other that we pour out of ourselves. Where does all of this energy go? How is it used? We do not think that the energy we emit can be sustenance for entities we cannot see. However, it is.

"She wants to end your life so you will not end hers. She believes you have the ability to be more powerful than her," Gertrude finished.

I threw my hands in the air in pure frustration. "Are you kidding me? She is a monster that took away control of my body and tried to kill me. I think she wins," I said.

Yema chimed in. "Serene, please listen carefully, as you will have to make a very important decision … if not tonight, then soon. The Countess wants to live and she wants to rule. Your destiny is a direct threat to her. She will stop at no end to kill you and will use those you love as pawns in her mission to end you. We do not have a lot of time. You must make a decision quickly about what you want to do."

My breathing became erratic again.

"Well, it doesn't sound like I have a choice. Either way you look at it, I am going to be hunted to death."

Gertrude looked at me hard and strong. "You do have a choice. You must decide if you want to fight her and live up to your potential—to see if you can achieve what I believe you can. Or you can hide. We can try our best to protect you and your loved ones. Of course, there will never be any guarantee. And you'll spend the rest of your life running. If you choose to continue learning about what gifts reside within you and fight her, you will have the hope of one day not having to run from her. Either way, she will not be far from this moment on. If you chose to learn to fight her, we will start preparing you tomorrow. There is a lot we must teach you. Whatever path you choose we will help you."

I thought of Lydia's soul sobbing and how easily the Countess had brought the most horrific pain and sadness into my being. I couldn't let her get away with trying to murder me after cruelly murdering my best friend. I looked up and around the table, especially at Jess, Sammy and William.

"I would like to fight her," I said.

William stood up. "Serene, I need a word with you in the kitchen please."

We walked into the kitchen. William closed the door. "We need to leave. Everyone in that room is 'lost-the-plot' crazy. We need to get out of here. I think they are trying to brainwash us or something."

Out of the darkness came Yema. "This is not a joke, this is not a hoax and we are not a cult. William, you are free to do what you please. However, if you leave us, you will be on your own and without a hopeful outcome. Your call, mate!"

I looked at William. "He is right. Trust him. I have seen things and felt things that I never thought were possible. One thing I know is that Lydia is dead and that I almost died. It doesn't get more real than that."

William caved after a long silence. "I am going to come along, but make no mistake, I think this is a terrible idea and I hate this heat."

Yema began, "Okay, everyone, we start out tomorrow!"

And then I realized what this meant. I would be dragging William along, on a journey he clearly would rather not take. We would be running away from the Countess and running away from a normal life. I would be running away from James. The night in the volcanic water felt like a ceremony that had bonded us together. I didn't want to run away from that.

I also wanted him under Gertrude's protection. I started to worry about him. *Does the Countess know my feelings for him?* I thought of him as the little boy in the field watching his yellow house burn to the ground while his mother was still inside. A shiver of panic rippled through my body.

Yema continued. "We have to do a protection ritual while we are still here in Gertrude's home."

I followed him and entered the main living room that opened out to the thick jungle grass of the backyard that led to the ocean. The breeze was wet and salty and the sound of the waves crashing was soothing. William sank into the darkness of a corner. Yema, Jess, Sammy and Gertrude all stood around a large, flattened trunk of palo santo wood that held one very large hunk of turquoise with pink crystals growing out of it. There were wild tropical flowers in various shades of white and yellow strung together and wrapped around it. An old piece of driftwood smeared with a dark oil that smelled rich with perfume was on the ground next to the trunk. Gertrude raised it into the air and Yema held out a large thick stick of gold-foiled incense that was already burning and another small stick of wood that was flaming strong and hard. He took the strong flame and the incense and, at the very same time, held them both to the black, slicked driftwood that Gertrude was now struggling to hold out.

The meeting of the three created an alarmingly large flame. I worried for Gertrude's face. She threw the stick down into an existing pit in front of the palo santo podium. Light was filling the room and being sucked out toward the ocean. The small circle of Yema, Jess, Sammy and Gertrude began to chant while holding their hands out to the sides of their bodies, their palms facing toward the heavens. Thin wisps of silver ran up the outside of their legs from the earth when they spoke the word "Pachamama."

Wisps of gold come down from a star. All of a sudden, it became quiet and still—as if the whole room was locked into a specific moment in time with no sound. Untouchable.

At this moment, Sammy looked at me. There was golden sunlight on his face; his eyes were emeralds. Gertrude had lilac solar flares dancing all around her. Jess had a burnt red-orange halo emanating from her crown. Yema had a golden yellow aura bursting away from all of his skin. Just then, all of their heads sprouted hair made of gold, dancing like threaded flames into the air. They looked like Christian angels with halos. Their hands began to gather the surrounding air and golden sun-star energy. They used their hands to move the light into the center. I watched as the light evolved into a swirling mass of glowing colors and gave birth to entities. I could see eyes and smiles.

I was watching limbs dance in the air as the Egyptian *neteru* came into the space. Amun-Ra, the sun god, was tall, rich toned, cocoa-skinned and chiseled, with catlike kohl-lined eyes. He was clad in gold and carnelian beads and a thin white piece of linen tightly and tautly wrapped around his muscles. I saw Isis, the goddess of life. She was a beautiful woman, with high cheekbones and a perfectly smoothed and sloping forehead and even more dramatic kohl-lined cat eyes. A rainbow plumage of bird feathers sprouted from both of her shoulder blades, encrusted in gold. She wore gold armbands, anklets and sandals. She was majestic alongside Nephthys, the goddess of the night and the in-between dream worlds. She was wearing sheer veils and dancing around us. Her veils floated over our heads in enchanting, slow, seductive movements.

My friends were all dripping in spiritual nectar and vibrant rainbows covered in intricate, glowing cell formations. They quickly and cunningly shape-shifted to half feline, half human. And then, in an instant, they pushed all the golden light toward me. The light soaked deep into my pores and organs. I closed my eyes to bask in the feeling of the most heavenly sunlight I had ever felt. We all slowly returned to the reality of our humanity. I wondered if anything from this point on, would ever be close to any reality I have ever known. I looked over to William. He was still half-hiding and staring. I saw even he was changed. The outline of his body was emanating a pale glow.

Gertrude looked at me. "This is to protect you through the days to come. Let our thoughts and energy stay with you. This will also help to mask your own energy from the Countess and give you power and strength." She paused for a moment and then lifted her head and said with authority, "I think it's time we start to work."

Work? Like get a job at McDonald's? What does that mean?

Gertrude gave a small laugh at my puzzled look. She simply said, "We start tomorrow."

MORNING BREAKS

I watched the geckos and butterflies moving and fluttering behind me in the terrarium underneath the travertine staircase. The large wall-like shutters were completely open. You could walk directly out to the great lawn. On this particular morning, there was a long stone table I had not seen before. Just after the table lived the jungle and the ocean.

On the table were ten large glass vessels. Inside each vessel lived a well-edited selection of exotic materials. Each one housed a specific color of objects except for two non-colors. Lined up together, they created a beautiful spectrum. I examined them— circling like a hawk so I could see all of their contents. I was trying to understand what they were exactly.

Gertrude came downstairs. "Let's begin with the Central Sun," she said while picking up the first glass vessel. She laid out its contents. They were all white in color. She handed me a feather and a stick of palo santo wood. "Go to the fire, light this stick and smudge the house. Invite white light in through your thoughts. Use the feather to invite the smoke up to the far corners of each room where energy tends to linger."

I performed these instructions and enjoyed the heavenly scent from the burning wood. After I went back to the table, I was sprayed with water from the Dead Sea.

Gertrude explained, "This cleanses your electromagnetic field. Every living entity has an electromagnetic field. It extends indefinitely throughout space. Our fields hold energy. It may be positive or negative. Energy that is not your own can cloud your unique path."

She then unrolled a small piece of white linen. There was a design of overlapping pyramids. Gertrude explained, "This is a third eye sacred geometry grid." She handed me a vial of small crystals. I put them down where they made sense to me.

"Serene, my child, close your eyes," she directed.

I did as I was asked. I felt the wind pick up and heard a few flaps of wings. Something changed in the air and the sun's warmth quickly heightened on my skin.

"Open them now," Gertrude guided.

When I did, I saw the sun so bright, full and low to the horizon it almost frightened me. It was as if the sun was going to collide with my body.

Gertrude urged me to breathe in the sun's energy and light through my crown chakra all the way into every molecule of my being. So I did. It was a magical feeling of pure light connection. My soul felt washed. This was the Central Sun, God energy. Like Reiki, we use this creation-light energy to channel through our human forms into other beings for healing benefits. I breathed in more of this golden white light from the heavens. I was starting to see this light around everything—from a rock, a tree, or even something as big as the ocean.

As directed by Gertrude, I then asked for the Central Sun's bright white, glowing aura to come to me. I covered myself with it and felt protection and the sense of a new beginning. Fear was floating away from every fiber of my soul. The poisons in my muscles from fear-based emotions were dissipating and I felt a shiver of alignment through my spine. I closed my eyes again and took in a few deep breaths to center myself.

The day went back to where it once had come from before the sun shined so bright and shone so big. Now the sun seemed like a pin drop in the sky once again.

Gertrude explained. "This energy, now that you have met

it and know it, can be used to protect yourself and others. Some people choose to take substances to open roads. Remember, those roads will no longer be available to you unless you take the substance. I am going to teach you the roads you can always travel on to find these healing energies. They will be your friends and guides to call upon at any time."

Next was the void of light vessel. Gertrude emptied its contents and explained we were going to speak to the dark energy that had been channeling through me. She also explained that my third eye was covered by the same particular energy. I asked her why this was happening.

She explained, "We all have a light. Yours has been turned on and has been getting brighter. All energy can feel or see this. Most humans choose not to acknowledge that we have energy beyond our bones and muscles. It helps them to pretend that the only goals to living in a human form are to make money and accrue power. We are taught these are the means to happiness. So, therefore, people do not think about enlightenment.

"Spirit and entities see your bright shining light and are attracted to it. The more light, sometimes the more darkness it attracts—like polar opposites. Mind you, spirit and what we do not see is only made of love and light. The darkness is not evil or demonic; it is just misplaced energy. We humans give the title "evil" when we do not understand something." Gertrude paused.

I thought of the Countess and thought she was definitely our misplaced energy. Then I asked. "Why is my third eye covered?"

"Maybe it's not a question of why but a question of how to let it be open?"

"Okay, how do I open it then?"

"Let's open up to the darkness. Shadow is one of our most powerful teachers. First, let's let the energy reveal its true nature," she said after another long pause.

African oud wood was lit. The smell was pungent, earthy and sweet. It was deep copulation in the air. A black pyramid linen grid was rolled out. I placed devils nuts, black tourmaline and skulls made of jet on it—asking in my intention to attract ancient strength. I saw goats, Wiccans, devils, bloody faces and demons—all of that which we are told is "evil." The representations came to me in perfect succession.

Gertrude handed me paper and told me to write my fears and what I did not like about myself down onto a charcoal grey piece of paper. So I did. There were more than I suspected. The darkness numbed me when I let it take over. I looked down at my paper and read the words *rejection, shame, not worthy of true love, the need to control outcomes in order to be loved*. Black smoke was filling the room. I felt things grab at me, wanting from me.

Gertrude whispered. "Negative energy must take to have power. Positive energy comes from within and radiates out. Now feel the fear. Give into it and surrender. Feel your anger and use it as power and energy to protect yourself and to gain your strength. Feel your sadness and hurt feelings; transform them into compassion and love for yourself and others. The light only gets through the cracks, where we are broken. Light can enter and heal. This is how we learn our sacred lessons. There is good in everything. The positive side of darkness is sensual, mysterious and beautiful. It demands depth and knowingness of all you do not want to see within yourself and in the world. Darkness demands strength. Let's burn your fears."

I threw them into the fire. We then anointed ourselves with a heavy, silken, oil with Arabic scrolled on the bottle.

Gertrude continued saying her words of wisdom. "Feel the power of the unknown and the excitement and mystery of what you cannot see, while keeping love in your heart and light in your mind. Know that some energy is not of this earth. These energies are only trying to communicate what they know. However, we decide what we see and feel. We may see a ghoul in a closet, only because we were told too. Next time you feel fear, gently lean into it and ask what it is you are truly experiencing. Is it simply a visual manifestation of a fear of the unknown?"

"One of the bravest commitments is to keep an open heart and mind—to decide not to decide about what you see and what gods may or may not exist. Just witness and accept, instead of trying to change outcomes we have no control over. Shifting our energy and perspective is sometimes the most powerful action we can take to change the entire world. After all, we have the ability to do so and the only power we possess is over ourselves. Why not invest the energy in ourselves and not in what we cannot control? We are co-creators, not the only creator.

"Now we will do a death mediation."

Gertrude led me through my own death. She was helping me to prepare and understand that my body, would surely cease to exist. This wasn't too hard to imagine after recent events. I worked tirelessly through deep fears of aging and helplessness— the fear that my life does not matter in any significant way, the fear that this is it, the fear that this is all for nothing. It was hard work, maybe the hardest thing I'd ever had to do. I had been pushing away the fact that I would die from the moment I understood what death was.

We went through the rainbow of vessels. I learned so much and so quickly. Most importantly, I think, I learned vibrations or bands of energy exist at all times on all planes. This is so important because we are these energies and therefore, we exist at all times, on all planes.

The green vessel was the vibration of the water goddesses of the Orishas, an African based religion. One Orisha is Jemenja, the goddess of the seas and oceans. She has an uncanny connection to the same energy as the Christian Mother Mary. I could feel that they were one in the same band of vibrational energy. We humans created both of them through our consciousness and prayers. We attributed to them both very similar energies from different "tribes" of humanity—both in different places on Earth. The thread of connection was our universal need for a compassionate motherly love. They even bore the same hue of blue.

Just as my soul was in my body at this moment, it also had the ability to simultaneously exist on different planes—creating on Earth and the farthest part of the cosmos.

"One" I said out loud while looking at the sunrise.

I only now realized we had worked throughout the night and into the dawn of the next day.

CHAPTER 7

RIO DE JANEIRO

We boarded Gertrude's plane at 11:00 a.m., en route to Rio de Janeiro. Once we landed, we walked out onto the steaming tarmac. A large pearlescent-white 1984 Cadillac and a chauffeur dressed in casual whites, framed by the not-too-far-off airport palm trees and lush jungle flora was awaiting our arrival. We piled in and off we went.

As we entered the city, I looked to the right and left of the main highway. I saw a myriad of cement blocks and shanty shacks. Some had tin roofs painted in bright colors and some had nothing to shelter them from the elements. None, from what I could tell, seemed to have glass windows.

Our car was driving fast and everything was a blur. But for a moment, my eyes locked in on one particular cement block. I saw a deeply cocoa-skinned man and a young girl standing in their square, cement one-room home. A single light bulb hung from a wire. They were looking out and I was looking in. Our eyes met. The man was bare chested. The girl wore a grease-soaked pair of red corduroy boys underwear. *If that were my lot in life, I would not survive long.*

Soon enough, the car began to navigate through city streets, behind which lived the massive sprawling beach of Ipanema. Very soon, fantastic jutting vertical hills were all around us, coming straight out of her crust.

The car stopped in front of a grand white house, with a huge veranda. There were large white pillars, long windows and many levels. It looked like a plantation house. It probably once was, when the Portuguese first came to this part of the world. Gertrude just then started to explain that we were, indeed, in the "Old Portuguese Rio." As we exited the car, two men with machine guns came out. They manually closed two gates behind us and locked them. William looked at me and gave me that all-knowing look of, *I told you so. We are going to get killed and they are in a cult.*

As we entered the front entrance, an elderly woman came down a white staircase dressed in a colorful printed caftan that was brushing the floor. She had on a large gold hand-hammered necklace and earrings that were of an interesting and captivating design. She also wore many sculptural rings. I took particular notice of a big raw crystal stone jetting out from her index finger. She had so many on you could only see the tops of each finger. The room was filled with a sweet, almost rotting floral scent. There were six-foot tall vases on each side of the marble mantle, holding flowering trumpet tree blossoms as well as huge orchids. A handsome young gentleman dressed in an olive-green, button-down Prada T-shirt, Hermès-orange tailored trousers and deep chesterfield-brown loafers entered. He was carrying a silver tray of sweet sun tea. The woman and Gertrude smiled and hugged one another.

"Gertrude! It has been ages!" her friend said.

"Dear Beatriz is the founder of the School of Uban Flora. We met during our younger years," Gertrude said.

Soon after their embrace, Beatriz hugged and kissed each of

us warmly and invited us to stay in her home for as long as we wished. Looking at me, she exclaimed. "You must be Serene! Gertrude has told me about you. You have the look of 'the work.'"

"Have you been working with the vessels?"

"Yes. How did you know?"

"I got an image in my mind. I see the dark one has resonated with you."

"If 'resonated' means scared me, then yes."

She looked at Gertrude. "Gertrude created the black vessel's ritual because we all must face our fears and realize our own death. After all, to be alive, is to one day die." She said this, with a big, warm, loving smile and walked away.

That evening, I lay down to sleep in an old, wooden sleigh bed—thinking about my own very real death. Beatriz was right. It was surely coming for us all. Why did we not talk about it or accept it? I didn't want to accept that I would face the end of my body, life and youth. Yet I knew I would have to accept them all, if I was lucky enough to live a long life.

My room was high up on the fourth floor. I watched frames and figurines tremble on the ledge of my fireplace. I walked out onto my veranda past the whitewashed shutter doors that were beginning to gyrate like a woman's hips. I hung my head over the railing. Looking down, I saw many people talking, laughing and moving about on the first floor veranda. I heard a tribal drumbeat and then the sound of a woman's voice rang out. The people below screamed, *"Ahh. Oohhh. Oppo, oop!"*

Most went inside and the drums continued their beating. My heart began to beat faster, along with the drums. The whites of my eyes grew large and clear. I put my usual cat eyeliner on and threw on my vintage grey and stone linen sundress. I opened the door to my bedroom and saw a beautifully bronzed couple walking up the staircase. I could tell they were looking for a quiet place. I could also tell that they had never been here before by the way they were looking around. Yet they were comfortable enough with themselves and each other to venture out into this strange house as if they owned it. They owned the world with their ease, compatible beauty and lust. No one would deny them anything. I went downward and onward into the pit of this plantation house, following the strength and volume of the drums. As each roll of them sounded and the rhythm played, I felt a pull from my chest that I followed.

I wanted to dance.

I was on the second floor of the house and saw a door that seemed like it was "the one." I opened it and saw an old ballroom. It was here, in this room that the party was happening. I went to the middle of the dance floor. I felt very self-conscious and even a little embarrassed. Everyone seemed to be dancing in pairs. So I just started to move a little and look around. I was making small gestures with my body that alluded to dancing. It felt dangerous to be surrounded by people I did not know or could not even speak to. Soon, I realized no one cared what I was doing. The drums were rolling in heavy over the crowd; the woman's voice began to sing again.

Everyone was screaming, clapping and stomping his or her feet on the wooden floorboards. The singer was dressed in a leopard print costume with long gold and black feathers flying into the air off of her shapely behind. Her skin was rich, buttery and glittering with gold shimmer. Diamonds, gold jewels, smoky eyes and feathers danced all over her face. She was a big beautiful, magnificent samba bird. Her hair was brownish blond and spiraled with excitement down the curvature of her back. Her smile was so big and bright it allowed her overt sexuality to be approachable and fun. Someone in the crowd yelled, "Quenia!" Her feathers fanned and shaked from the movements of her fast samba. Her hips were like a quake moving Earth—her diamond encrusted heels grinding into the old floorboards. That was her name, Quenia.

I was taken aback by how she was doing everything *soo* right.

I almost did not notice the handsome man in front of me with his black hair and his beautiful angular nose, wearing a big smile, putting his arms around my waist while grabbing my right hand. We started dancing together. I just let my hips and feet follow his. There was no other way really. I got lost in the drums, the smoke from the cigars and marijuana and the sweat from all of our bodies dancing in the sticky night air. I was completely drenched in sweat.

This was not a place to come and be seen. This was a place to dance and be alive. The music lulled and everyone started to leave the ballroom and go out toward the deck. I followed my dance partner. Looking up, I heard a loud thundercloud crash. The drums and the samba queen's voice elevated. Everyone screamed again and began to dance out on the wooden veranda. The sky cracked opened, the rain came down like Arenal's waterfalls washing over us. Everyone continued to dance and hold one another.

My wild and handsome partner led me down a staircase. An old woman was sitting in a closet, caged in chicken wire. A few big brown bottles of warm and dust-covered Brugal beer stood lifeless behind her on a shelf. My dance partner said something to her in Portuguese that I did not understand. She said something back and I thought, *How odd.* This seemed like a conversation and not a sale of beer. She turned her back toward us and then kept rotating as she turned back around. Her face was covered in oil. She was holding a chicken in her hands. She looked deep into my eyes. *This was happening so fast.*

Before I could turn to walk away from disgust, one of my dance partner's hands clasped swiftly around my two wrists, while his other hand held the back of my neck, forcing my face toward the woman. When I struggled to break free, his grasp began to tighten and hurt.

She continued in her tongue, cracked the chicken's neck, took a knife and slit its throat. She held the chicken over her head and twisted its neck, letting its hot, just living blood cascade into her mouth. She gulped, threw something into the air, shouted in my face and spat the horrid mixture directly into my eyes, nose and mouth. I was struggling and sweating, trying to break free from this accosting bio-filth and hot death.

Finally, when they were both done, she turned back around. He shoved me away and said, "This is a gift from her." His eyes were menacing. I knew instantly, even before he had said anything more, *her* was the Countess.

I started to run as fast as I could while frantically wiping away the chicken blood and the old woman spit from my skin. It smelled of tin and decomposing trash. I ran all the way to the entrance of the massive colonial castle. I was in shock and now in full flight. I must have managed to wipe most of the fowl blood away from my face because no one seemed to care or take notice. The young, sweaty, party goers were talking, laughing, smoking and hanging out. At the front door, there were a few trans-gendered women covered in gold chains and one tall man covered in layers of gold. He also had an AK-47 leaning on his right hip and a pretty trans girl leaning on the other side of him. They all seemed very relaxed and no one was alarmed by the automatic machine guns in their presence.

All of their gold jewelry made me realize no one else here had any jewelry on or was wearing any designer clothes. I immediately understood who was in charge and that maybe it was best not to look like you had too much or it would go on the neck of the guy with the gun. Pretty cut and dry. I guessed, since everyone knew what was up, there seemed to be no need for questions or uneasiness. Everyone knew his or her place and kept things as they were. My place was clearly not here. Not where *she* could find me. Like *she* just had. *What the hell was that spell?*

I was trying to put my dance partner and the evil old woman out of my head. I felt embarrassed that I had put myself in a position of vulnerability like that.

Gertrude and Yema came down to join us and explained that we would be going on an outing. William and Sammy were ready to go. Jess and I ran up to get dressed. When we came down the stairs to leave, Beatriz looked at Jess and said, "I think you should leave your earrings here. Do you have any sneakers?"

"Um, no," Jess replied.

Beatriz went into her closet and pulled out some ruby red and royal blue pumas circa 1978. She said, "Trust me. You will be glad your toes are covered."

Jess laughed her fun, sensuous laugh and replied, "Well, thank you, B." She bent over to tie up her new kicks and all of her long, thin chains dangling crystals fell out of her tank top. I watched as one of them made a rainbow on the warm stucco wall.

We were driving to the one place in Brazil that I did not want to go—one of the shanty villages, also known as favelas, near the airport. And of course the car could not navigate through the maze of mud roads because some were too narrow. It was not the best car to have in the favelas anyway—maybe a beat-up 1960 Pinto but not a shiny white Cadillac. We were already going to look out of place as it was.

When the car stopped, we were on the outskirts of the favela looking in. I was terrified to go any farther. The sun was setting. The walkways were pungent with reek and slick with bile, some parts almost flooded. Jess was silently thanking Beatriz for her sneakers right now.

A boy, who looked to be about four years old, was unclothed and crouched down holding a small tin bucket, filling it with dark putrid water. I couldn't believe my eyes when he brought the bucket to his mouth and began to drink from it. I wanted to run and grab it out of his hands. I then saw an older man walk over and do the same with his bucket so he could have a drink. The child wasn't drinking dirty water because he didn't know any better. He was drinking it because that was the only water to drink. My heart sank.

There were one-room "homes," if you will, all on top of one another. Some had tarps to keep the rain out and some were just cement blocks with no paint. Others were painted in happy island hues but covered in dirt or graffiti. Lights began to flicker on and off in some of the abodes as the darkness seeped in—which happens pretty fast around here. There were no plants to be seen, yet we were standing in "jungle terrain." I was hurdling through trash. Every small square structure was more depressing than the last. There were little bodegas or grocery stores, covered in cages, offering very little. Mainly it was just canned goods and small things like butter and eggs. Fluorescent lights usually hung from their ceilings, swinging back and forth, casting strange shadows that made what little bits the store had to sell look even more apocalyptic.

A little girl came up to me, pulling on my shirt and asking for money. I felt so badly for her. Then in the next split second, I wanted her to not touch me. She had some sort of rash on her face, along with blisters and open sores on her arms. I quickly pulled my arm away. I felt so ashamed for reacting this way. I looked at her in pure fear and horror. I could see how my doing so, hurt her. I could see in her eyes that she was scared by my swift recoil and the disgust on my face. I looked in my pocket to give her all the money I had on me.

Yema looked back to me and said, "No, you can't do that here. If you give her money, we will never get to where we are going or maybe never leave."

Gertrude kept walking at a fast pace while chiming in. "He is right and that goes for everyone. Do not give anyone anything. These streets are a maze that these children know well. Word travels fast and if they hear we are giving *free* money away in the streets, it won't be a good outcome for anyone."

I felt so terrible that I could not help this little girl. I couldn't look back. I kept my hand in my pocket, listening to her small voice as I walked away.

A tall, thin young woman, maybe seventeen or so, with glistening bronzed skin and a dark yellow, ruffled dress walked assuredly up to Yema. She grabbed his arm with her strong and expressive hand. She wore many necklaces made of colorful beads. She spoke in Portuguese to Yema. He motioned for us to follow. I was in awe of her muscular yet elongated form and symmetrical yet severe bone structure. She had perfectly shaped, big eyebrows that framed her mysterious eyes. We scurried through more twists and turns.

I looked down at my feet and saw that they were covered in mud and there was a paper wrapper stuck to the side of my shoe. A door opened. The tall young woman pushed us in one by one, still talking in Portuguese while looking out into the street to take account of who was looking at us. The feeling in the air was that we had a very limited window of time that we were working with and even that short amount of time seemed borrowed.

The moment I stepped inside, I gagged, for the stench was even more putrid than that outside. My eyes were adjusting to the lack of light in the room. It took a couple of seconds before I could see. Once I could, I wished I could not again. Each wall was smeared in feces and what appeared to be spoiled, rancid blood. In the center of this square room was a thin, cocoa-skinned and very handsome man sitting on his knees. Surrounding him were a myriad of objects—red carnations; bottles of liquid in unmarked containers; long, white feathers the size of a human; a black horn; a worn-in, green stone; and a dead, lifeless, grass-green snake. He looked at me. "My name is Dondi. Please sit," he said, pointing at a rolled-up square of worn-in, dirty red carpet.

So I did.

He lit a green, white, black and red candle. He began to pray in Portuguese to statues of Christian saints and mirrors standing in the right corner of the room.

"I am calling in your spirit guides," he explained.

"Who are my spirit guides?" I asked.

"I think you will meet one today. Patience."

He then grabbed my left hand and examined it very closely. He folded my hand together and then splayed my fingers out and then folded my hand again. He studied each finger and then turned my hand around. He took the side of my pinky and pointed at it. "You see there? That is the star of conductivity."

I looked and to my amazement, there was a little star. Little lines on the side of my left pinky finger were all moving out of a single point.

"You are a transmitter. And because of this, she can feel you and you will soon be able to feel her." He then looked around the room. "She is darker than you think and I know how scared you are now. If you are having a hard time blocking her out, you can rub this on your forehead. He pushed forth a horrible effluent of half liquid and half mire. "This is the rancid blood of a fowl and its manure. She cannot see herself, mind you and this is what she smells like. This is some of what she is. I know it is malo, but it will save you from her."

I thought, *Great. More sludge for my face.*

"Okay, what else can I tell you? Ahh, yes. The amethyst is very important. It is the color of your aura and the sign of magic. It not only comes from the middle. It comes from the beginning and your female bloodline. All the women before you and around you who are blood were born through the amethyst."

I thought, *This is true. My mother, my grandmother and all of my aunts were born in February. Their birthstones are all amethyst.*

"You must sit within yourself. Be honest. No more self-perpetuated lies. Really feel what you're feeling. Really see what happened. If you were hurt, go back and take a look. Start to learn your own thoughts and feel your energy. This will give you strength and open doors."

I knew what he was talking about. My fears, my coping mechanisms, my lack of ability to take care of myself emotionally—these were truths that I didn't like to face.

"Also, do not let the brujas, the witches, get to you. Like the crone last night. 'She' will send as many as she can. She is their temporary God. They serve her as one. You are no longer safe in the world. Know this. Fear her. Stay with your tribe. Take care."

As all of this was being said, his tall, thin counterpart was pouring oil over my head—one bowl after another. It was the only thing that saved me from vomiting from the other smells in the room. The oil seemed sweet and musky. There was a slight scent in there that my nose was trying to decipher. I could not get enough of it. I wanted to smell it more and to try and understand it.

After the last bowl was poured over me, Dondi paused. I questioned whether I felt hands over the crown of my head. Heat was moving down to the front of my neck, onto my sternum and over each of my breasts. I couldn't see because of the oil in my eyes. I could only hear the girl sit down behind me. She twisted my arms into her hers and pulled them directly back, almost out of my sockets. Then my vision returned.

To my surprise, I saw a giant, white tiger in front of me. His massive head was inches from mine. His eyes were brooding. I could see and feel him purring. It was almost deafening. He was radiating pure majesty, in contrast to this rotting, cement room. I sat there wondering how he could be so clean without a single mark of grime on his perfect, silvery white-and-black-striped fur.

I heard Dondi's voice, although I could not see him due to this massive tiger standing in front of me. "Do you see anything? They have told me something is here."

"Yes, there is a huge tiger staring at me right now, as a matter of fact."

"Ask him if he is your teacher. Always ask Spirit this. They cannot say yes if they are trying to trick you."

"Are you kidding?"

"Just do it."

"Are you my teacher?"

"What did he say?"

"He nodded his head up and down once. I took that as a yes."

"Okay, good. Ask him if he will help you."

I looked into the tiger's eyes. "Will you help me?" I asked, feeling really stupid.

He started to open his mouth and show his teeth.

Dondi chimed in. "You have to ask him from your heart and really mean it. Don't waste time."

I swallowed, closed my eyes, took a deep breath and tried to summon a sense of well-being and connection with myself. I focused on really feeling his energy in front of me.

I saw in my mind's eye all of his stripes, dancing as flames on his fur. His eyes were closed and so I closed mine. I tried to unite our minds' eyes together somewhere in the middle of our two physical forms and show him who I truly am.

Defenseless, confused, flawed and scared. I was still. Only then, at the moment when I felt the most calm and certain that I was getting through to him, did I really ask him for his help. I was dragged away from my quiet meditation into a new harsh reality. My body was sweating and adrenaline was pumping through my glands. He was above me. His eyes were so angry and slanted— beautiful really—and his teeth were all over my face, about to crash through my skull.

At that moment, everything in my body screamed *stop!* Instead of fighting him or shielding myself, I became more still. I tried to evoke a place of calm.

He backed off and then walked around me. He was growling and panting. His claws showed through his thick paws every so often when the soft pads of his feet hit the dirt ground. Then he stopped—not where I would have wanted him to stop, but where he wanted to stop, which was directly behind me. I admit the fear of what he could or was about to do crept back.

A voice from somewhere inside was telling me what to do. So I listened. I slowly put my two hands down on the ground and knelt—one knee at a time. And very slowly I bent over and placed my forehead on the ground. I then lay down to show him true submission and my ultimate trust in him that he would not harm me or take my life. He then nudged his massive fur-covered head directly into mine. He swept up like a bird taking flight.

His fur was hard and soft at the same time. I could see specks of silver and gold out of the corner of my eyes. I smelled the rich, thick, sweet oil that had just been poured on me moments ago. A growing rumbling came from the back of his throat. *PUDDDDDDddeeerrrrrr. Puddddddeeerrrrrr.* He was purring. We lay together in the dirt for a minute as he flopped down next to me, pushing his body into mine. The next minute, he jumped up and sauntered off into a sunset horizon that manifested out of nowhere in the dark and dank room in which we sat. He never looked back. His body disappeared into that new, just formed horizon. I saw a golden glow where he'd last stood before he was no longer there.

Dondi came over to me and looked into my eyes. "I think he is on our side now. He is one of your guides, but he can be difficult and very stubborn. Know that, at all times, he has a purpose. He is a great energy. I also received a message from him for you. He said meditation will help you to be honest with yourself and learn what you need. He also said it will greatly help you in unseen ways. His wish is that you meditate every day.

"I wasn't sure what he wanted for you and your path. I wasn't sure he would even talk to me. He wants you to be truthful with yourself, to center yourself and allow your feelings to be known. Always carry the truth he demanded of you in your heart and protect yourself."

He smiled and put a thick, hand-rolled mapacho cigar to his mouth, his nostrils widening as he inhaled. He held the smoke in for a few seconds. When he exhaled, the smoke exploded from his mouth. His big, perfect, yellow teeth shined bright. A contagious laugh kept pouring out of him as his stomach heaved in and out. I just stood there staring at him. I guess I didn't think it was that funny. He seemed suddenly mentally unbalanced in that moment. It caused me great uneasiness, making me feel that maybe all of this was just an illusion and not really happening. I felt dragged back to "reality" fast.

The mood was changing. I felt a cold dampness usher into the room and rest on the top of my skin. Yema had a look of counting time on his face.

Gertrude said, "It is indeed time. We need to get back soon."

"The most important protection from evil is to keep happy. Consciousness cannot see what it does not know exists." As he said this, his eyes got big and crazy, before he, again, lost himself in the fabric of his own manic cackles.

I gave him a hug and held on a second or two after he let go of me. His beautiful, young counterpart darted into the shadows, away from our goodbyes. Yema and Gertrude grabbed my hands as they started to walk as fast as they could out the door. Back into the labyrinth of the favela we went. We did not have a guide this time and full night was upon us. This did not make me feel very safe. My fears and anxieties exploded in my chest as I remembered the black vessel and sitting with my mortality.

If you think about your death, do you call to it? Do you attract it to meet you sooner than if you do not think about it? As I mulled this troubling thought over, I began to pay attention again to where I was and what I was doing. The streets of the favela already looked different. I instantly knew that we were not going to get out as easy as we had gotten in. I could hear Jess's crystals and chains clink together as she started to pick up the pace. We made a right.

I saw a lone eye. It belonged to an old man, straddled by a

girl wearing a beer- and sweat- drenched lace orange bra and green terrycloth shorts. They both were sitting on a blue plastic chair in front of a bar. Her skin glistened from the humidity. We picked up the pace. Yema was directing, but I knew that there was no direct path and we were just trying to go in the direction of where we had last left the car and our driver. Yema kept looking in his pocket. I saw the glow of his phone. He mumbled, "Still no reception."

I heard something in Portuguese. It was a boy's voice. I then saw a few shadows coming toward us. Six young teenagers were rapidly surrounding us. Five wore neon-colored handkerchiefs wrapped around their faces right under their eyes. The leader of the pack, who was maybe thirteen years old or so, wore nothing but a thick gold chain and his Tommy Hilfiger jeans midway down his rear end. They were all carrying semiautomatics and although I couldn't understand what they were saying, their shiny, big guns in our faces spoke volumes and told me all that I needed to know. Violence, sadly, is a universal language.

Gertrude started talking to one of the boys in Portuguese. "Tranquillo, Hector." She looked deep into the eyes of the boy with the neon pink and green handkerchief. "Seu pai não passou muito tempo atrás. Foi uma morte trágica. Eu vejo sangue"

Hector looked at her, eyes fuming. "Shut up. Do not talk about my father, you puta velha." He cocked his gun and pointed it directly at her head. His arm extended, his little veins throbbing. Gertrude did not flinch.

"He tells me to tell you that your son is with him." Gertrude put her arms together and she motions like she was cradling a child. She pointed to Hector's neck. "You have that scar there from the old coffee table. The day 'it' happened. He also says ... he let you. He did not want to fight you. Do you understand, Hector?"

The boy's arm was visibly weak. The gun had gotten heavier

for him and his aim had moved down a couple of inches. His face was less harsh. I could tell he was listening.

She is speaking the truth. You can see it in the hard, angry, hurt eyes of the gang members surrounding us.

Hector asked Gertrude something in Portuguese. She replied with a smile and laughed while throwing her hand into the air. We were all silent as we watched Hector's reaction.

There was a long pause.

He let out a laugh of relief—the kind of laugh when you have been crying all day and just need to break away from the sheer pain of it all so as not to go completely insane; that laugh that takes you off the edge, while throwing you over at the same time.

The other gang members wore looks of disbelief on their faces. Some even looked scared.

All of their guns, now pointing down.

Hector picked up his jeans with his free hand and motioned to a dirt pathway with his gun. Gertrude began to walk down the path. We followed her.

The gang members stood still and did not follow. We were granted passage, at least on this corner.

After about twenty minutes or so of walking fast, almost at a running speed, I saw the white Cadillac. I was surprised that the driver was still alive and the car was still there.

CHAPTER 8

After returning for a night of rest, we continued on. We were heading to Manaus, where the Rio Negro becomes the Amazon River. We were traveling deep into the sacred Amazon Jungle, where hopefully the Countess could not find us. It felt like she was getting closer by the minute. She had dangled an enticing carrot in front of me at the samba club in Beatriz's home and I had taken it. I knew I needed to be strong. I was in constant fear that her eyes were everywhere. The only moment I forgot she was looking for us was when I was thinking of James. Even then, I suspected that my subconscious guided her prying finger into my head. Relaxation was not an option.

We boarded our vessel, *O Golfinho de Rio* (*The River Dolphin*). She reminded me of a New Orleans riverboat that had the architectural fashioning of an old plantation home from the Deep South's past. She had two levels and a captain's hull.

The O Golfinho de Rio moved through the pitch-black darkness with only the light of the stars. I missed the moon.

Its hard to keep track of such a strange thing as time while on a river. I was beginning to think like the Mayans. Time no longer seemed linear. Instead, I felt it speeding up and slowing down. In the pockets where time slowed, my heart had time to feel—to feel James. *Will I ever see him again?* I was aching for him. Everything reminded me of him. I replayed the moments of us holding each other in the volcanic water at Arenal. The idea of never being able to see him again made me feel like I was falling off a cliff screaming. My soul was calling to him. My body wanted his. The thought of us being together was the only thing that kept me going. Yet, the idea of it finally happening was too much for me to handle. It felt like love and death were two vines intertwining, growing around me like a cage.

I had been focusing my energies on regular activity in order to lessen the madness of my mind. Thank God we had some of those. My only solace had been taking day treks into the jungle.

We anchored our vessel and used a small rowboat to meet the jungle's edge. We always started at dawn. The movement re-shifted my concentration from the fear of death to which branch I needed to clear in order not to get whacked in the face. I very much looked forward to this part of the journey on O *Golfinho de Rio*. It felt good to stretch my legs. It also felt like we were the only humans on Earth. We had gone some days now without seeing faces other than our own.

The jungle was thick and the sounds were varied and alarming—like a wall of unfamiliar noise. My mind hurriedly tried to figure out what each sound in the wall was and what deadly creature could possibly be responsible for making it. The birds' plumage were all in stunning colors of molten turquoise or fire red with neon accents. I had only seen birds like this in museums. I observed drops of dew in-between their feathers that sparkled in the sunlight. Each movement gave birth to a kaleidoscope of color.

I had never seen colors like this. I definitely had never breathed air quite like this. The only way I can describe it was that it was like breathing water. It was like being an unborn child in the womb of Mother Earth, taking in oxygen through her embryonic fluid. The jungle possessed an unprecedented depth of sensitivity. If you stayed still, everything around you stayed still. If you moved, everything moved. She read us and knew us.

Gertrude walked over to me and put her arm around my shoulder. We looked out into the stars from the lower deck. She looked at me with her soft, silvery eyes. "So, what do you think?"

"I think I never want to live in a city again. It is magical out here," I replied. At the same time, I was thinking, *I am scared of the jungle and of you.*

Gertrude laughed. "Well, we are seeking out a special man tonight to protect you. You should be more scared of him right now!"

She read my thoughts again! I looked at her, searching for a smile or a hint that she was joking. I could see no sign of levity. Now I was really scared. I was starting to see how clear and easy it was for her to read my mind.

We will work on that my child. We will work on making you mentally strong. She said this in thought, without words. She squeezed my hand to let me know everything was going as planned. That little squeeze gave me some small level of comfort.

My world and what I had once known was continually being shattered into pieces. *How am I going to be able to learn everything these people told me I was capable of?*

Just beyond my nose out in the darkness came many sounds and strange noises from animals and insects. They were living, hunting, eating and moving in the velveteen, black brush. The river was moving along smoothly. At least we weren't moving too quickly to the jungle's edge. A calming fact that I held onto.

That didn't last for long. Soon enough, my righteous fear set in. I watched the jungle rush up on us.

This was the first time we were walking into the jungle at night. Gertrude, Yema, William, Jess, Sammy and I all wore headlamps, hiking gear and small backpacks with some clothes. I thought to myself, *Why do we have to go in here at night? Why couldn't we be doing this in the light of day?* My nerves were twisting in agony.

My first step onto land was not flat. Rather, I stepped onto a giant bump and my foot was sliding all over it. My flashlight shone onto a tree root covered in wet moss. I soon realized that nothing was flat and with that realization, I heard a crunch and felt a lump under my right foot. Oh man, it was an exoskeleton of a large insect. I looked down and saw a *huge* crushed beetle. Its yellowy glowing guts were stuck to the jungle floor and my boot. I heard a screeching noise and rustling movement. I pointed my head in that direction. An armadillo was moving along hurriedly. I looked directly up and saw five small monkeys moving from treetop to treetop. One had a small baby on its back. Her eyes were red in the glare of my headlamp. I didn't think she liked the light at all. She screeched at us, showing her teeth while propelling herself aggressively into the darkness.

At this point, Yema was in front making the pathway with his machete. I wondered how anyone could know where we were going. I heard running water and it clammed my nerves. In that moment of reprieve, I got a sense that there may be fewer trees ahead because the air was feeling a little lighter—it might open up and give me some space to breathe. Hopefully, I wouldn't have to worry about as many insects attacking me.

At the end of that thought, I felt a quick procession of pricks moving up the back of my spine. I turned around and for a second, I saw the Countess right in front of me, standing eight feet tall. I screamed and William started hitting my back. As I flailed my arms into the air, I felt something drop off of me. Then I heard what sounded like a thousand pairs of high heels hitting a stone floor. I looked in horror: a huge black millipede was scurrying up a tree.

William's eyes were big and I could tell he was freaked out. Jess started to laugh a nervous laugh. Sammy exclaimed, "Dude!"

Yema looked back at us. All I could see were two thin halos of bright white light around his enlarged pupils dancing in the darkness.

"Hurry everyone," he said in a loud whisper.

Gertrude looked back. I saw fear on her face.

"Serene! Run!" she shouted.

I didn't know what was going on. I just did what Gertrude told me. I picked up my feet and ran toward Yema. As soon as I got close enough to him, he grabbed my arm to pull me along. While we were both running side by side, he screamed into the clearing of the jungle "Paddamouth!"

I saw something coming toward us—feathers, bones, skulls and … a man's face. He was chanting and holding a giant stick that had an ember glowing at its tip. Smoke was pouring from it. His eyes went moon wide. He threw his head back, only to throw it forward again into mine. He spat in my face and a fireball ignited all around me. I was wearing a fire aura. I saw a purple smoke that appeared and started to surround me.

"She's here!" yelled Yema.

The birdman who gave me the fire suit continued to chant, only louder now. As I sensed earlier, a giant clearing appeared. There were little huts and around thirty people wearing beautifully hand-stitched clothing. They formed a circle and the feathered man pointed to the center. I entered the circle. Yema, Gertrude, William, Jess and Sammy all did the same. A woman with geometric tattoos on her face scooped out a healthy amount of a strange brown mixture. She poured it into a halved hollowed-out nut and gave it to me. Flames still licked all around me and this purple smoke was still there. Yet somehow I could grab the nut and drink from it. The chanting grew louder and more like a droning, powerful harmony. I heard the shaking of the seeds and bunches of champaca leaves shaking over and over again. The mixture went around and everyone drank from the same hollowed-out nut.

I was staring at the man in front of me. He was wearing a rainbow halo of feathers. He had a bone through his nose and many explosions of colorful beads around his head, hands, neck and feet. He was a walking rainbow. His eyes and teeth started to glow. I knew there were others, but at this moment it was just me and him. He smiled, a wide-open mouth full of light and pointed up to the sky.

The clouds were moving fast and the moon was full and bright. *How did that happen? Where did the moon come from?* It had not been out earlier this evening. I could see all the stars as if I was charting the universe. I could see clouds of space gas and nebulas. Every point in the sky was aglow.

I looked to the people standing in the circle. They were beautiful. Everyone appeared to be dressed in his or her own individual pattern. I could see that the embroidered patterns were messages to the jungle. They were magic. I could see how the stitches had been laid on the fabric in time—the stitches showing themselves to me in order of appearance as they were originally woven, first, second and so on until the last stitch. I could see and feel their intentions. I also saw the air, the jungle and the universe reading them at this very moment. I was blown away that I could see human intention with my eyes. At that moment I knew that intentions are as concrete as the materials that go into building a city, if not more so. I looked to my clan.

Gertrude whispered, "It's the Shipibo tribe. We are in a Shipibo village."

I could sense the excitement in her voice. She was young, yet her hair was still white. Her eyes were glowing bluish pink with silver points of light dancing around them. She was clad in neon-pink: the embroidered flowers on her dress vibrating beautifully.

Yema, William, Jess and Sammy all looked like themselves, but better. Their faces were in a moment of perfect symmetry. Youth, power, beauty and sexuality emanated from them. The Shipibo's patterned dresses were reaching out to me. I saw the patterns in front of me in the air and in the bark of the trees. The patterns were protecting and asking the jungle for help with the vibrations that they were creating.

Once again, I could see the intentions with which they had been created by the Shipibo women. They used the piri piri eye drops to help them see where to lay the stitches. When the women connected with the jungle and they looked at the designs with their eyes, they moved and vibrated, unlocking messages that traveled through the threads that help to co-create the fabric of existence on their specific vibrations. The women themselves were unlocking their deep-seated intentions on so many levels that I could not comprehend. They were so powerful and so in tune with the jungle and the universe. *I am so proud to stand here with these people.*

Then, as if on cue, the fire around me was growing and turning hot white. Like pure molten energy, the purple smoke was gathering into a concentrated ball in front of me. It was growing and shaping into a form.

It was the Countess in all her wickedness, now standing ten feet tall in front of me. She was stranger and more grotesque than I had remembered. Her feverish, wispy white hair was in constant movement, swirling around her face like a vicious storm cloud. She opened her palms and faced them to the earth's floor. An expression of concentration overcame her. Out of the ground hopped wet, shiny frogs sporting an array of magnificent colors. Yellow, black, green, red. The birdman stepped out of their way as they hopped over to him. He motioned to me to stay away.

I received a message from Paddamouth in my head. *These are arrow frogs. One frog's poison can kill one hundred humans.* He looked at me. His grin became that of an excited child going toward a Christmas tree filled with gifts. He pointed to the jungle behind me. I looked and in the darkness, I saw glowing eyes in the trees and bush—all different shapes and sizes, some blinking and others staring steady. I heard the low, guttural sounds of the howler monkeys. It was a battalion of grumbling sound that hit your stomach and inner ear with aggressive force. I felt something slithering up my leg. I looked down. The birdman and I were standing in a pile of orange and black snakes. I shuddered: my fear was overwhelming. He again grinned that same excited smile back toward me and closed his eyes. I watched as he tilted his head back. It looked like he was basking in an unseen sunlight.

He let the snakes slither up and all around him.

I thought I might pass out, what I was witnessing him go through was also happening to me. I was covered in black-and-orange undulating scaled armor—armor that was made of a grotesque amount of serpents. *I can't take this.* I looked down one last time to make sure that this was all, in fact, still happening. I saw that the poisonous arrow toads were slowly being consumed by the snakes that now occupied my body, acting as a second layer of skin. They were protecting me. My feelings of horror quickly changed from confusion to gratitude.

Huge turquoise wings were flapping overhead, coming from behind. I looked and saw that they belonged to a massive macaw. Those very same wings began to attack the Countess. Behind the Countess, I saw crocodiles charging towards us. Some were even standing on their hind legs, running at full force. They were grabbing the macaws out of the sky with their massive jaws and clamping down on them like vices. I looked over to the right and saw an explosion of feathers in the air. I knew another one was lost.

All the while, the birdman and I were still covered in our armor of serpentine protection. The toads continued jumping up onto us, resulting in their death as they became new bumps in our snakes' bodies. I stood in awe. More animals from either side of the jungle's edge joined the fight. Panthers and cheetahs were running and performing amazing feats of speed and acrobatic feline agility. Scorpions and praying mantises were fencing with their angular appendages. Howler monkeys and flying squirrels came catapulting from treetops and vines to entangle. It was the essence of life at the height of performance creating a visual symphony of greatness. I watched the birdman revel in pure delight. The Shipibo and my friends wove their fingers together like a protective quilt. They threw their energy into the cosmos. It was like the aurora borealis dancing in the sky.

I realized Jess and Sammy were on the ground, lying in the dirt. Gertrude had a look of fear plastered on her face. Yema was being attacked by a swarmy crocodile that had come out of nowhere. Where was William?

The birdman turned to me and called to the sky. A black panther was circling Jess. A family of angry howler monkeys began biting her and screaming their howling winds into her face. I noticed with horror that she was bleeding. I ran toward her, flinging away the toads and snakes that covered my body.

The Countess took speed and gathered in toward Jess. The birdman ran toward the Countess and reached out his bare hands, placing them on her flesh. He was trying to stop her from moving any closer to Jess. It was nothing for her to have a full-grown man try to drag her down to the ground. The birdman looked like a fly, causing her no concern. This was not a good sign. I watched as Jess's face twisted in torment.

I couldn't believe what was happening again in front of my eyes. "*No!*" I screamed as I watched the panther dart in at her. The monkeys were tearing the hair out of her scalp as their innocent faces changed from furry animals to gruesome killers. I was still running toward her, unable to cover ground fast enough. The jungle kept growing between us. Sammy was still lying there.

I searched again for the faces of my friends. Yema was nowhere to be seen. Gertrude had joined forces with the birdman to try and hold the Countess down. It was a battle royal of energy between the three, creating a pyramid of light and dark. When I finally reached Jess, the panther lashed out at me. I threw a rock at it. I watched as the last remaining snakes and toads that surrounded my body detached themselves from me completely and began to attack the panther. I screamed and threw my arms in the air, running directly at the monkeys. I ripped each one off of my friend until I had Jess in my arms.

I saw the Countess's eyes inches away from me. I felt her slimy, taloned hands ripping at my face. Tears were forming hot wet pools that began screaming down my cheekbones. I was absorbing her hatred and fear, it was ripping through my soul. It was so palatable that it alone felt like it could kill me. She twisted her head and recoiled her hand and snapped it down on my forehead. At that moment, my skin flashed violet and emanated a bright light.

The Countess snarled with a look of disgust as she took a moment, that felt like a year, then recoiled her hand again and let her fingers crash down onto Jess's forehead. Jess screamed. It wasn't a scream of fear, but a scream of death—a scream that sounded as if it had come from her last moment of life. I held her in my arms. I hugged her and cried as I pushed with all my strength and will to get the Countess off of her.

The Countess was drooling blood. I thought, *Oh God! No! Please don't do that terrible thing to my friend.* I couldn't allow her to do what she had done to that woman's dead body that night at her castle. I was praying as I was shaking—still trying to push her away. I could feel her reveling in our pain and fear, suckling on our life force. The glow on my skin was fading. I knew there was no more time.

Just then, I saw the birdman's face appear like a rising sun from behind her back. He was climbing on top of her, riding her like the dragon she was. His face was bleeding and I could hear

Gertrude's voice in my head. *Hang on, Serene! Hang on! Please hang on.*

This gave me another ounce of energy to fight and I did. I dug deep inside and fought for my friend and for my life. The birdman was chanting. I saw the patterns of the Shipibo on the Countess's face. *Oh please,* I thought. *Please help us, patterns. Hell yes! Shipibo, help us.*

I felt the Countess slightly shudder and her hand went to close over my face. I watched her face contort with pure hatred and power. *This is it. This is how I die.* I saw a branch at her throat and noticed that there was enough pressure to asphyxiate her. The patterns on her face started to vibrate stronger and the trees were growing taller.

The Countess started to convulse and shake over and over. Each convulsion gave me hope. Her grip loosened and I fell with relief on top of Jess. I watched as the Shipibo surrounded us. They shot their viortes, spiritual flaming arrows of intention, into the Countess. They were pelting her in the back with great speed and power. The Countess's form slowly shrank. She became more humanlike. She hissed in a language that I did not understand and backed away into the jungle, never turning her face away from ours. The thick darkness of the dense jungle ate her up and she was gone. I could tell she was weakened which gave no relief in light of her seething anger.

I knew we had not won by any means. We had barely gotten her to leave and at a great cost. I looked down at my beautiful, intelligent, strong friend. She was limp and weak. I searched for her breath.

The birdman and Yema gently pulled me away from her as Yema spoke. "He is a great healer. We are going to try everything in our power to save her. You can come and stay near. We have to start now if she will have a chance."

I agreed and dragged my body alongside them. I needed to be with her.

CHAPTER 9

The sky was still dark but softening. Yema, Gertrude, William, Sammy and I had been sitting in a circle around Jess's body for hours. She was sprawled out on the floor of a hut. Paddamouth, the birdman, was chanting and blowing smoke over her. She was still. It didn't look like she had any breath left in her. I felt responsible. Her beautiful face was riddled with bite marks and scratches and covered in dirt. I brushed away flies that were trying to get into her wounds.

After some time, we heard the words of Paddamouth. "I must leave. I have work ahead. My people and I must clear the space. We need to call in great energy to save her." He turned back on his heels and walked toward the sun, which was now on the horizon.

I was praying these great healers could help her. I had faith in their power, but I was so frightened that the Countess's power was stronger. The thick, lush jungle was capturing some solar rays. There was a heavy fog that hung in our clearing, clinging to the tops of the huts. A sickening sweetness was hanging in the air. The birds were singing songs alongside the insects. I heard clicking, chirps, squawks, constant hitting on hollowed wood, screeches and screams. The animals of the sun were making their first excited sounds of the day.

Out of the corner of my eye, I saw a villager who did not look like the others. He was tall yet muscular in a healthy, slender way. His features were sharp and his hair was disheveled. He was looking off into space and laughing uncontrollably, making some sort of stirring motion that I guess was a dance.

"How did the Countess find us?" I asked Gertrude.

"She is always near. It's not a question of how she will find us, it is, rather, a question of when will she find us. You have to keep moving. The Countess is wounded, but she is angry and she is near. Sammy and I will stay with Jess. Where you have to go my body cannot."

"I won't leave her. The Countess will finish her once she has the strength to come back. I can't have another friend die because of me," I pleaded.

"She will be safer away from you. She will have a chance to heal here. The Countess will not waste her time with Jess now, not when she is this angry. She will be going wherever you go. She wants you, Serene. There is still much for you to learn. We have to keep you safe and on your path. It's the only way. I will have to say goodbye for now." She leaned in and gave me a kiss on each of my cheeks. She planted a third one between my eyes as both of her soft hands held my head.

Yema walked over and gave me a pat on the back. "Okay, little one, we must move."

We said our goodbyes to the villagers, Gertrude and Sammy. I visited Jess again and promised her that I would see her soon. It was just Yema, William and me that would be moving forward on this part of the journey. I walked over to my brave and powerful rainbow birdman. I hugged him. He stared into my eyes for a long time, a smile across his face. He took off one of his multicolored necklaces. It had crystals, nuts, dried seeds, pieces of select wood and feathers tied into it. It smelled of rich palo santo wood and piri piri. He looked at it, held it up to the sky, kissed it and then placed it around my neck.

Afterward, he stepped to the left to reveal another person standing behind him. It was as if he was offering this person as some sort of gift. The man's gaze was aimed at Yema. It was the same man from earlier who looked as if he was completely and utterly insane doing a dance by himself. He wore a big grin. His white teeth, almost perfect, except for a few jagged ones and two smallish fangs, shone. They looked like the teeth of a fox or a wolf. Yema could not contain his excitement and joy at seeing this man. They both cracked up laughing and gave each other a rugged man hug.

Yema exclaimed, "You old crazy goat! How the hell have you been?"

"Good, mate. And how's about yourself? Days been good to ya?"

They exchanged a few more casualties and then Yema introduced us.

"This is my good friend, Van."

"What are you all up to?" Van asked.

Yema explained that we were going on a mountain trek.

Van quickly cut Yema off. "All right, let's go then! Give me five minutes to grab my sack." Van ran off with the excitement of a little boy to a hut in the village. He came back with a pack on his back and a smile plastered on his face.

Yema quickly added, "This is not like old times—not a fun trek. Get my meaning?"

Van smiled again. "You all look miserable. I'm coming to entertain." He punched Yema on the shoulder and quickly ran ahead of us and continued on without looking back.

We started through the jungle. Yema and his wildly wielding machete were leading. We walked for hours and hours. We found out that Van was in the village working with Paddamouth. He said he'd had a vision that this was what he was meant to do—to take this trek with us.

I saw William roll his eyes at the phrase "I had a vision."

We kept on for hours. "Oh my God! The humidity is killing me," William complained.

"Don't worry. We have about five more hours and then we will be at the base of the mountain," Yema said as he powered through the green vines and tangled wood with his blade.

A couple of days passed. Not one of us felt these were good or short days. We knew the Countess was on our heels. We could feel her darkness. We trekked incredible distances each day. My toes had blisters and William's complaints about the heat were relentless. Other than that, no one was talking and the tension was like another person walking alongside us.

Van was the only one not tense. It was nice to have him along. He added much-needed levity to our group. The fear and stress from Yema, William and me ate up the little crumbs of happiness he left on his way.

My mind was filling with doubt. I prayed Jess would be okay. I thought of James and I hoped the Countess would not find a way to get to him. Then I pushed the thought out. I did not want her to know my fears.

I was desperate to learn what I was meant to—if only to stop this pain and this running, to stop my friends from getting hurt and to stop this perpetual fear of losing my life to her will. I felt weak and sad. My legs were tired from days and days of hiking.

After each short night's rest, we were all happy to start again, expend our nervous energy and keep our feet moving. It was a cycle of sleepless nights filled with anxiety and body-aching days.

"So how many more days do you think until we reach the top?" William asked.

Yema just laughed. "You mean how many more weeks, right, William?" And that was the end of that conversation.

Van was nonchalantly picking a berry off a tree to eat while talking to a lizard.

"So, Van, how did you and Yema meet?" I asked, trying to pass the time.

He called to Yema. "You want to take this one, mate?"

Yema began. "Her name was Dinka and she was so very beautiful. Her eyes were big, round and mysterious. Her cheekbones were high and well, her backside was glorious and like no other woman's." He laughed. "She looked like a queen and acted with the kindness and grace you'd expect from one. She was not too serious either, a quality that always drew me in.

"In the early mornings when I was not out on a hunt or herding with the other men, I always seemed to find myself crouched down with my face smashed into a warm, thick belly of a goat. I would get my hands and feet stepped on by many nervous hooves. I endured this discomfort so I could sneak up on her. She would let out a short, high scream once she saw my body instead of one of her family's goats. Her short scream would quickly roll into the most beautiful laugh I have ever heard. I would take advantage of catching her off guard. I would run over and give her a kiss on the cheek. I would leave, walking fast, out behind the fence using the mass herd of goats once again to hide me from any onlookers. These were our stolen moments of courtship, without being recognized by our families. During this time, I was not sure if I would ever have more than these moments with my Dinka. My family was not as high ranked in the tribes as other young men of my age. We both knew somewhere deep inside that maybe this was 'too good to be true,' as the Western saying goes. Every morning, I thought of her and every night, I saw her when I closed my eyes.

"Soon it was the time of year when all the young men get dressed in robes of maroon and blue. We put on our necklaces and totems made in our tradition. The young women wear colorful dresses and robes with many beads and paint their exquisite features to tantalize our eyes. While the sun starts its journey into the earth and just as the first hint of dreaminess and haze set in, we sing for the women and start our poll-hopping dance. They sing for us and dance as well. During the ritual, came the highly anticipated telltale time to be matched in the eyes of our friends and family.

"We were so close. We shared the same tribe, the same age, the same time on this earth. But it did not happen for us. Alas, the elders chose Dinka and another man. They met in the middle and danced, as was the tradition. It was done and they were bound for life. In a moment, our future lives were decided. The look in her eyes made me feel so ashamed that the tribe did not think my family or myself was worthy of her. I felt that I had let her down and, in some strange way, that it was my fault that we were not matched.

"Otherwise, the wisdom of our elders and the guidance of our ancestors would have let this story be a different one. The next day, I passed by her and whispered, 'Meet me by the big tree at the edge of the village when you're done with your chores.'

"I waited for two hours until she came to the tree. I explained to her that I had a plan. I wanted to take her and a couple goats from my father and go out into the land and have a life with her. I could see her eyes drinking in and paying close attention to every word that came out of my naive mouth. I was filled with nervous excitement to think maybe we would still have a chance at our love. Of course, we both knew that, if we left, there would be no coming back to the lives we had once known—for an act like this would result, perhaps, in my death. Dinka would never be allowed to marry or to be happy if we wanted to come back. I was ready to risk it all. It would just be us and the animals, living side by side together until we died.

"I had all the confidence of a young man rushing with testosterone, having never fully touched a woman. My energy was a force to be reckoned with. I told her I would wait again by the tree at 2:00 a.m. the next morning. I would take my goats and everything that we would need to survive. I promised her that her life would always come before my own—that I would obey her every wish once we began this life together. I knew even then, filled with stupor and blind ignorance that she would be sacrificing more. Women need their families and they need comfort and this life would have neither.

"So again, I waited and waited under the tree in the true darkness of night. I kept feeding the goats to keep any noise from them to a minimum. I had my satchels filled with some food, blankets, hides and hunting gear strapped to their sides. I saw the moon was moving and that the time was right. As the moon moved, my confidence followed. I started to doubt everything. Yet I stayed and waited until the sun came up into the sky. There was no sign of my beloved.

"I was dejected, I could only stand next to the tree as if I was tethered to it. I knew I could not look into her eyes ever again without feeling this pain. I saw her sister walking over to me. She seemed very careful and when she saw me, she motioned for me to stay and wait. She went back to the village and like a fool about to make love or get himself killed, I just waited. I waited until I could almost not bear the emotion or the idea that my family would soon start to look for me. Even if I did walk those couple hundred feet back into the village, I would have to be chastised for not going on a hunt or doing my part.

"And then I saw her. She was walking to me from the open land and not from the village. She asked with a cheeky tone and smile, 'Why have you been standing here all morning?'

"I looked at her with bewilderment and she just smiled.

'Come, I have my animals ahead, but the lions might have them soon.' She made a sound of a big cat and laughed as she turned on her heels and walked into the wild open away from our village."

"Oh my God, Yema! You lived off the land in the Serengeti with her? What happened? Where is she now?" I asked.

"Well, I actually never got to that part. We were fierce hunters and brave. We lived out there just us two, holding each other under the stars at night, killing and eating anything that would dare to rip us from this life or each other. She saved my life on many occasions, as I did hers. We were true equals—although I knew she was more powerful than me. One day, we met a strange young lad out in our great wilderness. He was with a film crew. He hired us to help them with the lay of the land that we knew so well. We showed him where the giraffe, zebras, cheetahs and elephants roamed. We brought him into our world. What we didn't realize was that he was bringing us into his. He grew up in Johannesburg, South Africa, but knew our language. We all three became friends from working together so closely for two years," Yema finished.

"Yeah, mate, those were the days, eh?" Van said with a nostalgic smile.

William chimed in. "How many days has it been for us now?" He was looking at me.

I tried to think and figure it out. My mind drew a blank. "Yema, do you think we are close?" I asked.

Yema turned his head away from the upward path and simply said, "It's been eleven days."

"What about Dinka?" I asked, trying to keep the conversation going in a more positive direction. "What happened to her?"

Van stared off into the distance at this question and Yema was quiet for a while. Finally he broke the silence and in a low but audible voice, "I'll tell you some other time."

No one else pried or asked any more questions. I could sense his loss and wanted to respect his privacy. I put a pinch of coca leaves in my mouth that Yema and Van had found for us. I focused on keeping my pace, only allowing myself to look back every so often.

NIGHT FALLS

We awoke the next morning. I felt like we were birds hanging off the side of a cliff. It didn't really feel like we were standing vertically on the earth anymore. Rather, we seemed to be slanted to the side. My head was pounding and I didn't want to move. I saw Van approach. I rolled over and pulled the sleeping bag over my head.

"Hey, dawl. Sleep well? Come on. We need to get up and moving," he said.

William was already boiling some water for coca tea. I saw Yema stretching not too far off.

"Awe, man, I can't move," I said as I started to wonder if I would ever be able to move my body again. *Okay*, I told myself, *get up and get on with it.* I started to roll up my sleeping bag. As I did, I looked out onto the horizon. It was stunning. The sun was out and the sounds of the jungle were uplifting. I went to take a sip of tea as I rolled my amethyst back and forth in my hand. Dondi's voice came into my head. I remembered the message from my white tiger about mediating every day. *There is no time like the present*, I thought.

I took a seat to begin a meditation. As I took in deep breaths, I examined my life. I was astonished at what was playing back to me.

There were white-faced monkeys that lived and slept on the sides of the cliff. It was almost like a cave system, way up here, etched out of the side of this high dark, russet-colored rock. We were coexisting with them—sleeping when they did and waking when they did. Just now, I heard a loud crescendo of flapping

133

wings belonging to brightly colored parrots that were taking off by the thousands under my feet. I looked down onto the tops of the highest trees and watched the mist and clouds roll in. They wove in and out through the spaces in-between all the throbbing greenery. There defiantly seemed to be less moisture in the thin layers of the earth's atmosphere up here. I wondered how many miles there were from my exact location to the darkness and outer space up above. *Is this my life?*

This was not me wearing heels in a New York City gallery selling artwork and sipping cocktails with "successful" people wearing articulated clothing that all screamed "I am amazing!" I let my spine reach into the earth and the crown of my head into the cosmos. I worked on connecting my breath. My mind kept wandering and dancing around. *James, James, James, Lydia, Jess, the Countess, James.* Their faces, names and eyes alchemized, becoming molten gold pouring into my thoughts. Again I reached into my mind and told it to "let go." I felt free for some moments, but I returned with speed to where I sat. I felt better than I had before this practice. However, I still felt I wasn't going where I should and that I wasn't able to let myself go where my soul wanted to. I was scared to go too far.

We started out again, back into the thickness of green plant life. We went on for hours. It seemed like we were walking to nowhere at this point. *Will we ever get to this mysterious place? Does Yema even know where we are going? After all, he probably hasn't made this trek more than a few times in his life. Who knows how long ago that was? We could all be lost.*

I heard something. *Ahhh, water!* "Yema do you hear that?"

"Yes," he said, looking back with a smile.

We climbed up some more rocks. I heard things falling. Yema quickly took his arm and pushed me back against a giant rock. I gasped. He pointed to my right. I saw vines and rocks. He pushed and cut the vines away with his machete and motioned for all of us to step back. Like simply opening a curtain, Yema took his smooth right forearm and moved a massive amount of jungle vines to the left. By doing so, he revealed a wall of sound, followed moments later by a wall of water rushing with great speed and mass. He looked at us and said, "Okay, here is where it starts to get hard."

"Oh no! Hell no!" I screamed. I was looking down a cliff whose depth I couldn't even measure because I couldn't see the bottom. I was staring at a never-ending drop. It was drawing me in and calling for my body.

I looked up at Van because, through my fear, I heard his voice. It was smooth and calming. "I got you, dawl." He guided my body. *I feel safe.*

William was, of course, turning back on his heels to abort this whole crazy mission. With a very tense expression on his face, he looked at us and started. "Serene, if you want, you should come with me now. There is another way down and another way home without being killed or, worse, eaten by cliff monkeys. Yema and Van, you both are crazy. I'm not sure why you like to play with death, but two years in the Serengeti should be enough for one lifetime, don't you think?" William said this with force and confidence as he was beginning to walk away from us.

At that moment, I became distracted by my surroundings, in spite of William's futile efforts to escape. Wet, shiny, almost plastic-looking purple flowers were dancing and glowing like fairies—each with its own face and personality. The waterfall was massive, but there seemed to be a stone corridor behind it and to the right. Maybe it was made thousands of years ago when there was not as much water?

I started to walk down the stone hallway. I saw some sort of tiny muskrat scurry forth. I followed his path into a world of pleasure. I could not stop looking at all of the various species of orchids that were glowing and moving. After witnessing one lash out and eat an insect from thin air, I realized these were not just orchids.

Upon closer inspection, I discovered that inside each one lived an alien-like fairy. Every flower had an even more immersive and intricate orchid mantis living inside it. One was milky, white with ombre pink legs. They were impossibly bent up into the shape of an orchid's petal. His eyes were vibrant turquoise with flecks of neon yellow and bright sherbet. I looked at another species of orchid and to my utter delight and interest, I found a more ominous variety of mantis inside.

This one was standing upright on its four stick legs. His arms stretched upward, saluting the air above. I again saw the shape of the orchid's petals. They were attached to his neck, creating an open cape movement. His head looked like a helmet, painted in green and vibrant golden yellow tiger stripes. His eyes were maroon red. His antenna, also maroon red, stood straight up, looking like a Spartan Mohawk. His bravado cape was black and red at the tips, while whites and blues moved down to the core of his body. His wings looked like they were made of cabbage leaves. All in all, he looked like a warrior with an intense stare, ready to attack. *Amazing.*

As I continued walking, every plant and insect became bioluminescent in the slight darkness that the wet, hollowed-out rock corridor provided. With each step, I realized I was not going to fall. I just focused on the magenta and white, candy-cane-striped tube plants and the wet flame, cinnamon-colored hummingbirds.

The waterfall went on forever to the left and the stone wall forever to the right until we finally reached more green and stable ground. We were descending down a hill through a windy, overgrown trail with stone steps that were buried in the dirt. I was in front and the first to see what we were descending into.

CHAPTER 10

Ancient ruins from centuries ago appeared in the mist. This civilization belonged to the heavens—the cloud realm—surrounded by thin air and an outer layer of surrounding mountaintops that concealed and protected. Yema looked at us. "Children, we are here!"

William was in a tyrannical rage, saying over and over again, "Well, finally, well finally!" Once he saw the view, his eyes grew wide. *"This is amazing!"*

Van had already run ahead and it looked like he was talking to a llama in front of a small cliff-side structure. There were llamas everywhere. Yema's face was bright and glowing. He wore an expression of accomplishment and relief.

As we descended deeper into this village of the sky, I noticed one large building in a shape of a triangle with hundreds of stairs and rooms made of ancient stone with holes for windows to look out onto the horizon. Surrounding this main structure were stone trails and steps that led to various other structures. I studied the sun. It was overhead but tilted slightly west. Maybe it was early afternoon? We followed our great and wise Yema in excitement and wonder. What new things were we about to discover?

We stopped to rest in an ancient garden. The light was magical. An oblong stone pool filled with water was surrounded by many delicate snapdragon blooms. They hung over the branches of neatly arranged mountain laurel bushes that symmetrically lined the edges of the pool. The grass was soft and springy underfoot. Yema pointed in the direction of a gazebo-like structure. It was constructed of layers of stone discs. It was just big enough to fit us all. It seemed to be an altar of sorts. Yema sat on one step and we sat around him. He put his finger down on the grass and asked us to look. All the small leaves curled into his finger once he touched them.

"This is sleeping grass," he said, with a childlike smile.

We all marveled as we put our fingers to the grass. We watched as our touch transformed the perky, upright grass into narcoleptic, green blades that drooped and appeared to be at rest.

We did not realize Yema had wandered off as we were amusing ourselves with our godlike abilities concerning inches of grass. He was walking toward us. He unrolled his shirt and handed us what looked like small, red passion fruits. Again, his smile was huge and contagious.

"These only grow here," he said. He pointed to a group of lotus-shaped flowers over to the right. They were as big as my head and glowing neon yellow with purple and pink petals that were moving in circles. I could hear the flowers vibrating and living—almost like the sound of bees. We peeled into the small fruits. Inside, they were filled with glowing purple and green seeds hovering in a bright pink jelly. After consuming this alien fruit, I felt a tingling shiver come straight from the base of my body. I shuddered with joy. I was not the only one feeling this new excitement. We lay on the stairs, eating these delectable yummy fruits, giddy with laughter and sounds of exaltation.

Looking up after minutes of nonstop giggling—feet appeared surrounded by red and turquoise feathers, strands of beads, seeds and nuts. I looked up a few more inches and then a few more. It was the birdman from the jungle village, Don Paddamouth!

"How did you get here? How is Jess?" I asked.

"I walk pretty fast. Your friend is fighting still. She is not free yet. There is a great darkness attached to her. My people are doing everything to bring her the light."

I nodded my head to express my gratitude but also felt like saying, "Try harder." I knew, though, that these people understood more than any Western doctor. This was not a typical malady. I just then realized we were all lying on the stairs, worshiping at his presence. He looked more wise and magical than I had remembered him.

He continued to tell us, "Your witch, she is the worst of all brujas. This is a battle that we will fight in the land of the spirits because that is where they are hurting her. I fight again tonight with my friends for her soul. You fight your witch here and we fight her here." He put his hands on his heart.

Yema chimed in. "As you might have guessed, you are in one of the holiest places on the living plane." He took his broad hand to his chest, palm facing up and sliced it through the air motioning out to the horizon. "We are surrounded by a perfect circle of erect earth. I am referring to this circle of mountains. Beyond this circle, which we cannot see from here, lies yet another circle of erected earth. Circles are protective. Even a mental circle drawn energetically holds a sacred or intended space. Mother Earth erected her stone to hold this space. This holy land is circled twice. Beneath us lies a deep, fiery volcano that has erupted at least once in the past, centuries ago. It will erupt again one day, but no one knows when.

"The wind comes in having been purified from the giant lung of Pachamama, which you saw on your way here—the great falls of Paddamouth's ancestors. He is your sacred blood that will unlock things no one else knows except for his people. His ancient relatives were all men and women of this civilization.

The greedy men of 'scholarly education' came to claim many of their lower lands, as well as much of their cultural heritage and religious artifacts to 'share' with the world. They brought disease and many of his people died. The remaining few went into the lower jungle and never spoke of their origin again.

Yema looked at me and just then, Paddamouth took his gaze away from the horizon and pierced his macaw turquoise and red, flaked, lava eyes directly into mine. It felt as though he were massaging my brain matter and running his energy through my mind. He was easing my fears and doubt while raising my vibration. I felt lighter and clearer in thought. It was as if all of the cells and atoms that composed my form were more organized and in tune with an elevated energy we could not see but, rather, could only feel when connected to a higher power.

Paddamouth spoke. "Pick any cloud in the sky. Now focus your energy like a laser beam and break it up with your intention and mind. Thank it for moving."

I chose a smallish, fluffy cloud. I thought it could be an easy one to move and it reminded me of James as a little boy. The cloud was the shape of what I imagined his innocent energy to look like or feel like. It was soft, airy and warm with playful, delicate wisps. I saw a beam of light come from my imagination and permeate the pure whiteness of my little James cloud.

Thank you for moving, little James, I thought. The cloud began to break apart and disperse into the blue sky. So I tried a larger one to see if this was not just a coincidence. *Clouds always move and small clouds are more likely to dissipate and move more frequently,* I thought. To my enjoyment and surprise, my larger, denser cloud moved just as quickly and easily. Then I noticed that many clouds were dispersing and moving fast, as if there was an incoming storm, yet the sky was a light blue. It was just me and my friends staring into the sky and moving clouds.

Paddamouth then began to walk down the stairs. "What we think is real. Each thought is more powerful than our hands. Our hands can only touch things in front of us. Our thoughts can touch the clouds; the farthest reaches of the universe; and, more importantly, our souls."

He touched each plant as he passed it. I was starting to understand that everything I thought was possible was really possible. I had always been afraid that I was going crazy or that my imagination was taking me away to a land that only I wanted to be real. I was beginning to understand the power of knowing and the power of calling upon my inner resources. Feeding my thoughts with light and positivity, instead of doubt and fear, allowed me to move clouds. I was starting to see what was really possible for us all.

"Come on. He wants us to follow," Yema said.

We did and with duly deserved excitement. We followed through the never-ending trails until we stopped. We were at an entrance of one of the smaller buildings. We were directed into the cool darkness of its damp interior.

I tried to see if anything was on the walls, but it was just raw, aged stone. As far as I could tell, there was only one way to proceed—through a dark corridor leading to … more darkness. We heard the screech of a macaw and then there was a dim turquoise light as we started to walk up a narrow staircase. The turquoise light became stronger, whiter and brighter.

I heard rushing water. We all met, eyes to eyes, with what I thought was a macaw. On closer inspection, I could not mistake the haunting, round symmetry of its eyes and sharp vertical beak. It was a turquoise owl! The bird was as huge as a macaw and more colorful than even Paddamouth.

"It's a macaowl!" Van exclaimed.

I let out a chuckle.

"Spot on, mate! You called it," Yema said.

The macaowl's eyes were glowing spheres of light and his beak was pink. His front chest feathers were flame orange, emerald green and iridescent grape. His feet were cute, like puppy paws, covered in fluffy fur feathers—like a baby owl's claws. Yet the macaowl seemed to have been dipped in metallic molten liquid. He shone bright like a reflective mirror. He looked at us and didn't eat us. I took this as a good sign.

We walked onto the roof. There was a small, round room on top. Once inside, we could see carvings of snakes, condors, hummingbirds and pumas on the walls. The room was just a cylindrical tube. There was a shaft of crystal clear water spurting out of a hole from above. *Where is the water coming from? The heavens?*

Yema translated once again from Paddamouth's native tongue. "Welcome to the fountain of truth. Or really, the water of your thoughts. Just like with the clouds, your mind can communicate with all water in the universe. My people know that the water from this fountain is from somewhere deep in our cosmos. It came to us in the form of an iced meteor. From the moment of its arrival, the water from this part of the world is the strongest on the planet for psychic to physical communication. This water is sensitive and expressive. The meteor's message is forever ingrained in this stone and where this water lives. The message is pure love and communication. On this planet, there is 70 percent water and 30 percent land. Humans are made up of 70 percent water and 30 percent mass. We have a connection to the water inside of us and outside of us, as we are water.

"Here in this cold cave, it is always the right temperature for crystalizing flowing water. So now I ask you to cup your hands and let the water fill them. Think a thought true to your intention, focus it into the water and then throw it into the breeze."

Yema walked up first. He cupped his hands and let the water fill them, closed his eyes and threw the water into the air. We all watched, including the macaowl. The water slowed and crystallized, hovering in the air. The crystals were big and vibrant like snowflakes. They were quickly changing form—into suns, women and tigers, exploding with rays of light. Each shape-shift told its own unique story.

William, not too impressed, said, "Wow, it's a snowmaker," and rolled his eyes.

"You next, mate," Yema said. "Make some snow."

William very matter-of-factly let some water fill into his hands and threw it at the air with a huff. There were no cool tiger crystals. The snowflakes that formed just seemed to be blobs with sad faces.

"If you really tried you could make something out of them," said Don Paddamouth in broken English.

William rolled his eyes again.

Out of the darkness, Van came wandering. He gathered his water and did as those before him. He smiled warmly at Don Paddamouth before gently escorting his water toward the upward airstream. His crystals were bold and clear. They grew larger and more animated until each vanished. Dessert flowers, crocodiles and mountains were being formed from his thoughts.

I was next and excited. My thought that I was focusing on the water was happiness. I threw my water into the air. The snowflakes took the shape of animals and creatures I had never seen before, ever-changing. Then at the last moment James's eyes crystalized. They quickly, changed to his face. He looked royal.

Paddamouth was last. His crystals took flight and amassed into the shape of a condor that was flying gracefully and hugely through the air, weaving between us almost furiously. In and out, it weaved past our bodies in the damp darkness of the stone room.

The macaowl drank the water, came to each of us and let the water drip from his mouth into ours. It looked like feeding time and we were his babies. The water tasted like ice and felt beyond refreshing. Our insides were now baptized and cleansed. I felt like a clear, sharp, thoughtful person who could be understood by any form of life in the universe. I felt myself to be without mental shackles. My mind was now going to make up its own language and thought process. It had nothing to do with thinking thoughts in any known language. I was guiding all the cells, atoms and water in my body to have one unified message of—dare I say?—love.

We spent one more night in the holy mountaintop city. Paddamouth had brought some medicine tea. He offered and I drank the terrible, bitter stuff while gagging and gulping. When it was finally down, it all came back up. As I was purging, I saw and heard Van vomiting a river to the left of me. Paddamouth was calm. Yema and William seemed to be dreaming. I watched as they swung back and forth in the breeze. Their bodies lay in hammocks suspended in-between the stone walls of the ancient city. Their inner worlds snuggled up in their hearts and heads. It looked like Paddamouth and I were about to go on a journey.

The minute I closed my eyes, the spirit of the tea came to me—Ayahuasca herself. Two larger-than-life white anacondas appeared—one going upriver and one going downriver of the Rio Negro. Their bodies were the whole length of the river, never ending. My spirit was floating above them where their pyramid-shaped heads met. At the same time their heads were in the river, they were in my hands. When I opened my hands, two snake mouths opened. I knew, if I touched someone with these serpentine hands, strong truth would course through them—like the love of a great teacher who had no time for doubt and only worked with the ready and willing.

I saw Paddamouth at the river's edge. He was standing by a tree. I saw violet lights dancing in the darkness of the sky and in the river. I knew what to do. I climbed down the tree next to Paddamouth. I slid down its river roots. I saw the violet lights dancing in the water. I felt Jess fighting. I felt her soul near

Paddamouth. I understood that he was going to her and I was going my separate way. I kept going until the trunk of the tree let me pass inside of its bark. The minute I melted into the tree, I was falling at a rapid speed going down a deep tunnel. When I looked up, I saw one hundred tree trunks. No! A billion tree trunks! Actually, there were infinite tree trunks! I somehow found one that I liked and opened its door.

When I entered, I remembered where I was. I was under the tree where I'd met Lydia when we were children at school. I was holding my marble, but the mean girls were not there. And neither was Lydia. I started to look around. I understood something. Ayahuasca was showing me the different areas where I used to play as a child. There was the big tree. The shade of its many branches and the cool, dark dirt where the acorns and twigs lived was a secret and calm area. Then there was the pool with the chlorinated water. The water made me happy, but it was there to show me the difference between natural running water and what happens when humanity plays with nature. I kept walking and saw the old house. I saw the old woman with her overgrown garden and rotten crab apple trees. There were lots of worms and the smell of wet decay in the air. Squishy, over wet grass sunk in-between my toes. That area had excited me with its wildness and scared me with its death. Today, what really got my attention and what always had as a child was the vegetable garden. I would spend countless hours playing with the snakes and watching the Japanese beetles' molten blacks and greens shine and flash in the sunlight, like beautiful minerals.

I saw a beautiful garter snake. He was brown with green vertical stripes. His energy was rooted, calm and earthy. He was fun and slow. Playful even. I would say, his energy wasn't very "snaky" at all. He said hello. I then looked to the Japanese beetles. They were changing form rapidly. From their Japanese beetle forms, they became Egyptian sphinxlike scarabs and then transformed back into a beautiful Japanese beetles. *So very interesting*, I thought as I marveled at their ability to work with a very intense science, math like geometry. I noticed it was, indeed, powerful. I looked deep into one of the largest, most spectacular beetle's rainbow-green eyes. Instantaneously, I was off into another world. I realized he was a gatekeeper.

Off I went through portals of energy. I was moving through tunnels of river energy with golden browns and yellows. I could see particles flowing in the sunlit water. I then arrived in darkness and came to yet another insect. He seemed to be covered in peach fuzz and was made of static. He was small, green, yellow and brown with big blind eyes. He was the keeper of the library.

He let me in. And once he did, I started to cry. Words couldn't explain the emotions of love that were overwhelming me. It was him! It was my teacher!

Our love was so strong. I felt like I was being blown away. My tears and sadness came fast and rushing. My soul was being touched in such a loving way. It hurt to know how much love I had not known as a human and how long it had been since I had been able to experience this love. It felt like coming home after billions of years and a million lifetimes. He had come to me once before in a dream. Now, I knew it was him! I asked him his name.

"Sarvin," he said.

I did not ask if he was my teacher as I had been taught to do when meeting spirit.

I already knew. He was a part of me in my spirit and heart. He was not human. He was too sublime to be. Where a face should be was a very long shape of light that moved, ebbed and flowed. When he had visited me in my dream, he had been wrapped up in a shell of a very old man. The energy he was couldn't appear to be human, but he did it so he could be seen by me. I understand now that donning this disguise was very difficult for him—that it was almost not allowed.

He had a little helper—a very small, studious woman. She spoke for him when physical minds were too present. When we'd met last, she'd told me that I had to leave, singing and laughing while I ran down the stairs. That would keep dark energies from feeling or seeing us meeting. It was very important. Here in the library, the meeting was not as stressful.

Sarvin had told me a secret that time in my dream. He had taken great lengths to come to me. Now I knew. Of course, I had forgotten that secret, despite his grand efforts and my trying so hard to remember. I only remembered how we'd met in the dream and the love I had for him.

Now being here with him again, I wanted so badly to know the secret and to never forget. He was going to show me. We were off! Just me and Sarvin. There was so much white and open space, followed by speed, circling and moving in ways that I cannot fathom. The first thing I was noticing was that I had no legs. Because I had no legs or anything physical at all, I could only feel my thoughts. My physical being at best was orb like, but really it was more nonexistent. My dear, dear Sarvin had brought me to where we'd first worked together. I started to cry again. I missed this so much. But we were here for me to remember.

I became his student again and enjoyed this at such deep levels as I focused. We were in the white air of majestic, snowcapped mountaintops. We were playing. We were air energy. Sarvin threw images into my mind as he guided me. He was pushing my energy and testing it so I could learn how to move. I soon realized this was a very special place. This was where a temple would be billions of years from now. Although time was not like that here, I understood what he meant. I saw the temple's energy. I felt the temple. And I understood that, even though I had never met a human nor been a human—*yet!*—I was just me. I still could comprehend that beings, not like me, would live here. The secret was here.

I heard a voice. I wasn't sure if it belonged to the spirit of Ayahuasca, Sarvin, or God himself. The voice told me the women were entering.

Sarvin was gone. My heart sank.

Hmmm. The women? I thought.

I was then brought to the great American West. I was on a large plateau made of reddish, glowing rock and dust. It was a golden hour. The winds were magical and slightly similar to those in the snowcapped mountains I had just visited. A spotted doe pelt and honeycombs were being shown to me. A thick, horizontal band of white light appeared from the horizon and came toward me. In the light were a tribe of Native American women wearing feathers and fur blowing in the mountain air.

One came forward. It was my mom! My heart lifted.

"Why does James have a red light and where did it go, Serene?" she asked.

"Mom!" was all I could say before she disappeared.

I missed my mom and then Jess came to mind again.

A rattlesnake appeared and he rattled his tail at me. I joined him for a ride. He brought me to Jess on the jungle floor inside a hut. Many *curanderos* and *curanderas*, male and female healers, surrounded her. She was alive still but not well.

"Fuck," I whispered.

DAY BREAKS

I knew where we were going and I couldn't believe it. I had been listening to my mom and the women. Their message was strong inside of me and I already felt their thoughts guiding me. We were going back to the United States. I was scared.

Paddamouth and Yema were off having a serious talk. Yema came over and confirmed my inkling. We would take off in three days. We were going back home—not to New York, but to the West.

"Well, this makes no sense. Will we be safe?" William asked.

Van started laughing. "Mate, we ain't safe here. Pull your big girl pants up, why don't ya?"

Paddamouth looked at me as he spoke out to the cliff winds. "You must fight and she must learn. This is where her spirit guides need her to go so she can learn how to fight her. They see what we cannot and that is why we must have faith and listen. They are spirit and see the dark one's realm and know Serene's energy. They can guide her to strength and her life's path.

"No one is safe from death. All paths lead to where true life begins—at death with the spirits," he concluded.

Yema continued. "She is gaining strength every minute. She works in the strongest realm, that of energy and spirit. Our bones and blood mean nothing to her. We need to keep vigilant and strong."

I could see the fear like taffy pulling and stretching in the whites of his eyes. I watched as his smooth, chocolaty skin became sticky and salty.

CHAPTER 11

THE GREAT AMERICAN WEST

The dirt roads weaved through the mountains. It looked like what I imagined the surface of Mars to be like. We were in rugged desert terrain. All one could see were reddish hills, giant rocks, mighty dust and a sparse sprinkling of small, sun-singed vegetation. I thought of my dreaming journey just days ago, on top of the magical, ancient, twice-circled city in South America. I thought of the native Incas who built it and inhabited it. My mind followed a line of energy. I thought of the natives of this red land and the Native American women who had come to visit me. Everyone had a bloodline and everyone was tied to an Indian tribal life.

Soon we started to see some strange trees with big, circular clumps of bristols on top. They were everywhere. The sun was starting to set. My favorite time of day was here, dusk! As we went deeper into this strange, barren land—secreted light sparkled like a disco, on the spikes of cacti. The hills themselves were covered with what seemed to be bright, golden-yellow dust and vibrant, emerald-green dust. In some areas you could still see the rusty orange of the rocks. Right against all of that was the sundown sky. It was blue, purple, orange and pink—creating the full color spectrum in one grand view.

We ended up in a courtyard. A dry and weathered old man offered us little red juicy plums from the depths of his sweat-lined and upturned cowboy hat. I immediately grabbed one. I was so thirsty, I just wanted the juice of the plum. It was strangely quiet. We walked over to an adjacent courtyard with sails of fabric situated tautly above, they provided some shade from the strong sun.

There were many tables and different "chill-out" areas. A garden of interesting little creatures made from iron, rusted from the elements was not too far off in the distance to the right. I found a bathroom, relieved myself and then washed my hands and face. The water felt so good. I let my hands fill and kept drinking from them until my tongue and lips felt like they possessed more water than salt and felt pink and not white.

When I went back outside, the sun was even stronger than it had been moments before. Everything looked sharper and flatter because of the lack of moisture in the air. I thought to myself, *This must be what things look like with no atmosphere.* I also thought that I quite liked the perception of matter here inside the moisture-rich atmosphere of Earth. I appreciated the reflective and diffusing qualities of water. I realized how lucky we are to be on a water-rich planet.

Could you imagine a world where we could not swim? Or a world where we were unable to breathe? How about a world where we couldn't eat any of the fruits and vegetables that grew in immense variety on Earth? What if there was only one vegetable that was edible or only one fruit that could provide energy? We all could have easily been born onto a planet on which we were the food, hunted to death. Yet we fit so perfectly at the top of our beautifully strange and complex ecosystem. I realized this was a simple truth I take for granted—I am glad I am not a tasty platypus, living in a honey badger den or that I was not born on a dying planet eating rotting food and drinking toxic water.

Yema was lying in a hammock. Van was off by our car taking a hot, steaming whiz. Ahhh, lovely. I began to wonder where William was. I tugged on Yema's hammock. He smiled from under the brim of his hat.

"We are going in soon," he said.

"Where?"

He pointed over to a large white dome.

Soon enough, we were called to walk in. Inside the dome was a circular, wooden room with a staircase that was really more of a ladder coming from the center of a low ceiling. We all walked up. On the second floor of the dome was a shrine. Wooden beams were bending toward a circular window in the exact center of the room, at the highest point of the arched ceiling. Dust particles were dancing in the air.

I saw William outside. "William!"

"Hey crazy," he said with a huge smile as he walked over to the ladder to come inside.

We all lay down on blankets. Van took a blanket from the corner of the room and rolled it out opposite from mine across the room. We both smiled at each other.

Two badass cowgirl women wearing denim cutoff sleeves, cowboy hats and prayer beads sat in front of nine white quartz crystal bowls. Their tanned desert arms started playing or, rather, tuning the bowls with huge sticks. One of them started to explain everything around us.

"My name is Sylvie and this is my sister Suki. This is the Integratron. It was conceived and built by George van Tassel, an aeronautical engineer and test pilot who worked for Lockheed. He was also one of the leaders in the UFO movement, who held annual 'spacecraft conventions' nearby, at Giant Rock. Van Tassel said UFO channelings and ideas from scientists such as

Nikola Tesla led to the unique architecture of the Integratron. He spent eighteen years constructing the building. He died a couple months before its completion. It was being built to expand the minds and assist in growth of spirituality in humans. We will never know its true potential, but what we have here is what we are working with."

I think my mouth was open. I was spacing out from trying to take too much information in. She stopped explaining and began to play the quartz crystal bowls. The sound was round in my ear and all over my body.

Suki then explained that she was going to tune our chakras. I looked over at William. His facial expression was deadpan. I wasn't quite sure what she meant about tuning our chakras.

Then, just like that, Suki started to explain the chakras. "We all have seven major chakras—starting from the crown; moving down through the third eye, throat, heart, solar plexus, sacral; and ending at the root. These are spiritual energy points founded in the early traditions of Hinduism, Buddhism and Jainism. The word *chakra* is the Sanskrit word for *wheel*," she finished.

I thought the explanation seemed very fitting because everything was turning into a visual landscape of circles. I could feel the circular energy inside of me and around me. First, we were in a dome and the center top was a circular cement window. The quartz crystal bowls were round. The floor we were all lying on was round. Then it made sense that we had these round flows of energy living within and around us. The sound was also creating round vibrations and these vibrating sound circles were aligning the flow of my inner circles, or wheels. It brought me back again to the ancient city in the heavens surrounded by two circles of mountains. I really felt their protective energy and started to have a better understanding of their sacredness in this world and within our bodies.

Suki then explained that the Integratron's wooden beams went thirty feet below the earth's surface directly into an underground river. She called this area a metaphysical soup. The river carried ancient energy that only the Native American Indians knew about. It was the blood of our earth. Being near this blood, you could hear her and you could feel your own "earthiness" in your body. Just then, I could feel the minerals in my body that were also made of her sand. I could feel my body's saltwater and thought of her oceans. I felt connected to Earth like she was human and I was a planet.

Suki began a guided meditation. "Feel the spin, dream, thread of energy connecting your root to the core of our planet. Send her what no longer serves you. She will consume and compost your unneeded energy into new life. She will birth these old energies as abundance and spring energies for the world. She cradles our dying bodies and absorbs them. She miraculously transforms them into new life. Think of her trees and plants that take in our toxic carbon dioxide and fill our lungs with life-giving oxygen. Every breath we take in is an exhale of a tree," Suki finished.

I thought how far away we had gotten from the simple joys of just being alive. We had forgotten how to enjoy being connected to what truly serves our beings. Money could not give us breath or life. Our phones were not trees that could build shelter for us. Power over people was not clean water to drink. Numbers on a screen were not beautifully ripened, juicy summertime peaches. We gave too much power to things that gave nothing in return.

Sylvie and Suki were now *really* playing the quartz bowls. The sound was intense. Strangely enough, I could hear breathing in my right ear, as if someone was two inches away. Yet no one was there. I knew this breathing well from spending so much time with him. It was Van. Everyone could hear the opposite person from them at the far end of the room, like the corner arches in New York City's Grand Central Station located outside of the Oyster Bar.

What struck me was how soft, calm and grounding Van's breath was and the trust it was conjuring inside of me—deep inside. I felt a tremble. *What the hell is that?* I could not believe that I could actually feel a very focused and real thick band of vibrating energy. It was going across the tips of my toes to the tops of my feet, stopping where my ankles began. This happened as the sisters hit very specific notes. As they played different singular notes, different singular bands of energy very clearly moved upward from my feet to my head. Once the seventh note was played, the last band left through the top of my head. The sisters then started to play a song with many different tones. I was now feeling the energy and vibrations throughout my entire body moving all around. I felt like I was a giant quartz crystal filled with a giant energy.

I was in a clean, altered state of bliss. I felt wholly euphoric. The bowls went on and continued to carry me on a journey. I fell into a vibrant meditation or dreamlike state. I saw white and glowing fluorescent, pastel wisps swing into jellyfish-like shapes. Triangles came together in the center of my forehead, pushing through a portal or a new tunnel of vision.

Then, as that show ended, another one soon began. All the colors left and it was silent darkness again. My body was at the top of the dome, on the roof of the Integratron. I did not open my eyes. I just knew wholeheartedly that I was at the top, still floating and vibrating. The strange thing I should mention was that I did not necessarily feel like I was lying, sitting, or standing. I was just simply at the top of the dome with no sense of skin.

Eyes closed, I was looking at the movie screen in my mind's eye to see what was now playing. There was a dusty orangish-red mountain landscape. To the left was much vastness and in front of me was a view of many mountaintops. To the slight right, there were two peaks that were more prominent and higher than the rest. I felt the sun on my spirit and kept looking. I saw flashes of darkness. The darkness soon was revealed to be a large crevice. It felt cavernous. There was a huge stone cut into two large pieces, forming a massive gash. It kept coming into my mind's eye over and over again, in strange flashes. It wasn't my image. Don't ask me how I knew that, but I did.

When I woke up, I was alone in the dome. I thought it strange that not even Yema was there. I walked slowly down the ladder and through to the first floor. I opened the door to the dry and sunny outside. My eyes were adjusting to the stark change of light. There was the old man with the sandy, sweaty leather cowboy hat and leathery skin. He tilted his hat back; his eyes were piercing blue—almost freakishly blue. I thanked him and walked rapidly toward the chill-out area and parking lot to see if I could find my friends. I was almost in a panic. I felt like everyone had left me behind and I was going to die of thirst and dehydration. It felt like my skin was melting off.

William was sitting in the back seat of a convertible white Mustang, top down. Yema was at the wheel and Van was sitting shotgun. I got in and sat next to William. We drove down a dirt road that opened up into a mountainous vista. Soon, the road vanished before our eyes. We stopped in front of a big rock. There were other groups of people hovering around the rock. "Well, this is it," Yema said.

Hmm, I thought. *This is Giant Rock?* I somehow expected it to be as grand and tall as one of the steepest mountains in the background. I began to inspect the rock. Why was it was called "Giant Rock?" It didn't look *that* impressive. I walked around and saw a large dark crevice. Here the Giant Rock had almost split in two. This was the image that had kept flashing in my mind's eye not too long ago at the Integratron. I entered as far as I could manage, fitting my body inside. I touched the cold, rough stone with both of my hands, running them up and down its surface.

I knew the stone right away. It was granite. In fact, I was born in "the granite state" and had hiked through its white mountains as a child—the Appalachian mountain range. Needless to say, I love the feeling of granite. It was home in my hands.

I walked back toward the sunlight and the strange people

hovering and milling about. One kid with dirt on his face pointed a BB gun at me. I saw that some of these kids were using Giant Rock for target practice. I am not sure how much skill they would ever develop with such a large target, and so close.

A man came out of a beaten-up trailer. He wore a dirty white T-shirt. His oily white knuckles squeezed a can of beer. I caught a whiff of cheap cigarettes, greasy skillet and burnt rubber, all rolled into one. There was a woman in the window of the trailer looking out into the distance. She had big blonde hair and caked-on baby-blue eye shadow. Another man exited the trailer wearing a simple affect of complacency. I walked back to our Mustang. The wind was picking up as the day was being dragged down into the earth once again by the falling sun. My dress was flying up and my hair was slicing into my left eyeball. We put the roof up on the car and drove in the direction we had come from. I wondered why I had been shown the crevice of Giant Rock back at the Integratron. I also wondered why there was no presence of honoring something with sacred energy or a revered Native American Indian site.

We moved into the beginnings of a beautiful desert evening. Yema bestowed upon us some knowledge. "Giant Rock is made of granite. This is actually the same stone that the ancient city in the clouds is carved from. Did you know that granite is 70 percent quartz crystal? The land surrounding Giant Rock has been held as a holy ground by the Hopi Indians for centuries. It is also thought to be the world's largest freestanding boulder. Hopi shamans have known since before 1920 that the fate of the twenty-first century could be foretold at Giant Rock. If the rock split in half, the Earth Mother was disillusioned with humanity and would not accept the prayers given on behalf of humankind. However, if the rock split on either side, relieving pressure on the earth's tectonic plates, then humanity's prayers would be answered and a new era would be revealed."

Although Giant Rock had not moved in a million years, the next morning the crevice completely split and broke away,

157

exposing a gleaming white granite interior. Leaving three quarters standing. The prophecy had been fulfilled. Mother Earth was on our side.

I knew I had more business before leaving the West. The women were calling. I knew what items I had to procure. One item was a spotted doe pelt. *How do I get one without a doe's life being the price?* The honeycomb I found rather easily at an organic market.

We all started a hike the next day, per my request. I was being led by the women, like a tug at my heart and brain. Every time we got somewhere and I didn't know what to do, I looked for a sign and always found one.

We hiked only for a day. My women were nice and easy on us. I had a feeling they did not want to keep me here too long, for fear of the Countess finding me. We got to where we were supposed to be. Then they told me that only I needed to ascend. I told the fellas to "beat it." They laughed. I saw Yema grab a mapacho cigar and light it. Van was writing his name in the dirt with his urine. *Why is he always pissing?* William was drinking water and swatting bugs with a look of disdain on his sand-covered face.

I followed my intuition and continued up the side of a red and orange rock plateau. Toward the end, I had to throw my pack up and scale a small rock face. I did this by stretching my right leg past my head as I hung on for dear life to catapult my body over the edge to a huge, elevated piece of red earth. The plateau had a bird's vantage point, with a circumference of about two miles.

I knew the guys were nearby, but I felt like I was the only person on Earth. The waning sunlight faded into the indents and crevices of the mountains, massaging their boldness and bowing to their valleys. The sky was turning darker shades of blue off to the right and I saw dark grey spots appear in the new clouds rolling in. *Ahhhh, a storm!* I felt excitement as I took my seat. Then I quickly stood up.

I remembered that I needed to gather some things. I only had my honeycomb, which I dug out of the top part of my turtle-green backpack. I walked around to look for something to be my doe pelt. There was nothing of course. How and where would I find a doe pelt on the top of a mesa? I felt disappointed in myself that I was not prepared. As I was wallowing in my shame, I noticed a massive bird's nest and thought, *How did I only notice this now? Wow!*

I went over and searched the inside with my eyes. It was an old nest. There were no eggs, no mama and no sign of it having been used in recent days. I noticed some strange things woven into it. Oh my God! It was a very small piece of a spotted doe pelt lying inside of the nest, sort of snuggled into the base. I was flabbergasted.

I held the pelt to my chest and closed my eyes. I knew this was mine, a gift. I saw a very beautiful and large eagle feather. I took this as well and thanked the eagle for it. I walked back to where I was going to sit and meditate, as I was being called to do. I saw a tiny speck of green. Just then, a big juicy raindrop fell from the sky right onto that tiny spec of green. At the moment it became wet, it shined yellow and then blue and then green. It was a shard of labradorite. I gathered these gifts from the women, took a seat, Indian style and flicked the air off of my body with the eagle feather. I placed the doe pelt, honeycomb and labradorite around me while reaching to their energies and actively melding them with my own.

I then placed my forehead to the earth. When I was sitting upright again, I closed my eyes and began to breathe. I had been trying with my meditations to connect to everything and anything that I was supposed to. I would search for the loving energy of my mom, ask for messages from my spirit guides and ask God what questions to ask. Truth be told, I knew I was not reaching any new depths in my practice.

I cleared my mind and focused. I sat for a long time. I felt the women. I felt my new gifts. Thunder cracked, the sky opened and a sheet of water fell through and rushed to the ground. All of the dust was transformed into mud in an instant. I held my focus. I was finally going somewhere mentally. I held my spotted doe pelt. I could hear drums. I could maybe see something?

Then a jolt struck me. Actually it was lightning and it struck just inches from me.

I jumped up and quickly gathered my things. I looked to the sky and had a very bad feeling in my gut. I felt panic from the women. I felt her. I felt her coming for me. My breath was growing shallow. I was all alone. I was vulnerable like I had been told not to be. I started to run to the edge of the plateau—to the spot where I had climbed up before. My nerves were firing off. I was losing feeling in my hands and fumbling. I got down despite it being slippery and having anything sturdy to grab ahold of. Once I hit the lower level at the beginning of the trail, I started to run. I was making progress. I thought maybe I was almost back to where I had left the gang. But I wasn't sure.

Out of nowhere, a huge black bird with a red neck flew at me from a tree. Was it fleeing from the storm, or was it the Countess? I lost my footing and fell a couple of feet down a steep sharp rock—*Slice!*—I screamed bloody murder. "Fuck!" I had cut my leg badly.

I looked down to inspect my wound. I was bleeding a lot. I scrunched up my nose at seeing little rocks and dirt caught up in the meat of my gooey flesh. I was feeling nauseous. I knew now was not a good time to inspect what was happening. I kept looking for the guys. I thought they should be right around here because this was where I had left them. I continued on a few more switchbacks down the trail. "Yema!" "William!" "Van!" I was howling their names over and over again. I was straining my ears to hear anything in return.

I needed to touch stone—not actual stone. I needed emotional stone and there was only the opposite on my path—air, water, nerves and the impending doom that the Countess was coming for me. I needed my gang. And then … *Thud!*

Something hit me from behind. I looked back and saw nothing. I kept going, running faster now but in more pain. I couldn't bend my right knee because, every time I did, it tore some new flesh open. I felt hot heat form and blood scream down my shin. *"Yema!"*

Thud! I was slammed on my back to the hardened muddy earth. *What the hell?*

I looked to my right and left and saw nothing. At that moment, my head was unable to move any longer, as it was being pulled back and right out of my neck. I could feel the pain of my hair being torn out of my scalp. My eyes were rolling right and left in my head to try and catch a glimpse of anything that would help me to see what was happening and free myself. I only saw the sky diving down, storming through the dirt while water filled my eyes. I felt my scalp pull in another direction. I struggled to grab my head to keep another clump of my hair from being completely torn out!

I used my left hand to try and steady myself and get back onto my feet. Just as I did, *whhaafttt*, I was knocked on my back again. I felt teeth going through my shoulder blade and heard the sound of flesh tearing through snarls and growling. I saw a wet, crunched-up black snout and venomous yellow eyes in the midst of silvery-grey fur inches away from my own eyes. I smelled his animal carcass breath—a wolf!

If I was seeing this one that meant there was another one because I felt its teeth trying to tear me in two, from behind. I let out a bloodcurdling scream. Part of my flesh was just then being ripped completely free from my back muscle and skin. I found the nearest rock I could with my fingers in the wet dirt. It took all of my waning strength to wrap my hand around the rock and hold it. I finally did and I was ready to smash the head of anything near me.

The women came. They were walking toward me. Each woman's head almost touched the sky. I saw that the feathers they were wearing were exactly like the eagle feather that I had found in the nest earlier. I heard shells and stones clink together in the air. The wolves immediately recognized the protectress's presence. They stood still with respect before they whimpered off. Stevie Nicks was playing in my head. I felt like butchered meat. My mother stepped forward as her Native American self.

"Serene, she's here. You need to leave now. Go somewhere happy and far. Stay away from James. We do not like what is happening with him. Heed my words and know we are doing what we can to protect you. But she is strong. Put the honey on your wounds. I love you." She said this as I was reaching to her.

Tears were bursting out of my eyes and rushing out of my face. I wanted my mom now more than anything. I needed my mom. I missed her so much. I screamed in the air, squeezing little mounds of dirt in my hands that I was scraping up with my broken fingernails. "I can't do this anymore! I give up!" I was screaming into the air. I lay there crying for maybe two minutes or two hours. It didn't matter how long I was there for. Nothing mattered. I was done.

At some point, I saw Van running toward me. My adrenaline levels were crashing and at just that moment when I could not take another moment of consciousness, Van's arms reached around my limp body and my whole being collapsed into him—hard. My eyes closed.

CHAPTER 12

INDIA

After two days of rest (and many stitches) we resumed our gypsy lifestyle. For my part, though, I looked more like a pirate who had fallen off of a ship and into a crocodile's mouth. I was all bandaged up, with an arm in a sling. *What had all that been for? What had I learned? That my life was borrowed time and no matter where I went or what I did, she would come for me? Why had the women and my mother guided me there?* I was weighed down by an overbearing sense of doom and utter helplessness. My mind was retracing what had happened over and over again.

We did exactly what my mom had said to do. I told the guys that we had to go to somewhere happy. They didn't disagree with me, especially because I was all banged up. I think they just were in the habit of trying to make me feel better with the word *yes*. So we went far away, to the land of "happy." It was also the land of intoxicating sensory overload—where dank, sweet smells; dirty, perfumed, diesel, human-stained air; and deep, saturated colors lived unabashedly.

India was her name. Her visual intensity coupled with her

sometimes putrid smells made me feel periodically unwell and I did not even have a case of the "Delhi belly" yet. We were traversing her streets by motor-carts, broken-down cars, trains and buses to get to our destination.

My wounds were finding it hard to heal, as I was constantly being jostled during our travels. My body needed stillness, but that was not an option. It took us some days before we finally set eyes on a white temple in the foothills of the Himalaya Mountains. It seemed a most sacred place. The temple was set back on its own, on very high ground. Not many people chose to live in or even knew how to breathe the thin mountain air here. It was shaded from time, but you could see that much care had gone into preserving its integrity. There were many staircases leading in. Once you entered, you could not admire anything more at first glance other than the intricate hand-carved stonework of its delicate skeletal system.

There was just the right amount of overhead skylight to illuminate a glowing rose quartz carving of a Buddha that took shape in the center of the room. You could feel a giant surge of energy from the massive size of the crystal. To think, just a chip of quartz is put into every watch to make it tick. Imagine what this crystal's energy was doing to us right now? The monks wore peach- and pink-colored robes. They were chanting, "Ohm mani padme hume." Maybe there were one hundred of them surrounding the rose quartz Buddha.

I turned to Yema. "What does their chanting mean?"

"It means the jewel of enlightenment sitting on a lotus flower. It is chanted for Quan Yin, a compassionate bodhisattva."

"What is a bodhisattva?"

"One who seeks awakening. The bodhisattvas make a vow to keep incarnating and helping all those who suffer until suffering is no longer. Their promise is a sacred and arduous gift. Their enlightened souls will never rest until we all rest."

The sound of the monks' chanting brought tears to my eyes. My vision suddenly went black. I saw a starlight flicker in the immediate darkness; around it, a swirl of vivid violet energy glowed. I began to talk to this light in my head. I told it, *You can do it. You are beautiful. I am excited to see what you become.*

When my vision came back to what was happening in the room, I couldn't help but notice that everything appeared round, including time, just like a chakra. Something was happening here in these mountains. I felt something for sure. It was as if the monks were working on something for all of us.

I was overwhelmed with curiosity and wonder. Something was starting to make sense. That thin thread of understanding that I was holding onto just opened up more questions. Why was I talking to this violet light? What was the violet light?

Just as these questions were swirling around in my head, we were all invited into a giant white tent by a holy man dressed in flowing white linen. Inside you could see that the tent itself was made of leather. It was white on the outside and a natural vegetable pink color on the inside. It was cool to the touch but warm in feeling. Dhoop resin incense was burning in a gold, lotus-shaped bowl. There was a round linen couch in the center of the tent. The matt covered floors had fresh pillows scattered about. Beautifully woven quilts in dusted hues were piled effortlessly around. A man and woman entered dressed in head-to-toe white dresses and turbans. They also wore pink and yellow marigold flower necklaces and crystal prayer beads wrapped around their wrists. We could still hear the faint drone-like, beautifully calm chanting of the monks from afar.

The ones in white sat and closed their eyes. Then they invited us toward them.

"Serene."

Hmm. How does he know my name?

I went to him.

He took my hand and placed it in his. "I know your name because I am your teacher," he said aloud to me while looking directly into my eyes. Another mind reader! "You can call me

Dechen. Focus on your rise and fall. It is not what is happening to us. It is what is happening for us."

I furrowed my brow and tried to keep an open mind. *Umm, okay,* I thought to myself, thinking of the wolves attacking me; never being able to see the man I might be in love with; and being hunted to death by a strong, dark force known as the Countess.

Yema was called to sit by the woman. She told him that she would be his teacher and that her name was Prisha. We were divided as such. Van sat next to me as he was called to do so by Dechen. William was on team Prisha. We were all given a full linen collection of robes, dresses, pants and shirts to attire ourselves with. At first I thought it was a bit cultish. I really didn't want to wear the same thing that everyone else was wearing. It made me feel like I was back in Catholic school or just living in a small minded, prefabricated town, drenched in depressing, ill-fitting clothes that were all bought online. Then I noticed we at least had some options. They were white, off-white, dirty-grey-rose and grey. I chose a short, white dress.

Dinner was served inside the temple. The interior was dramatic. Floodlights were shooting upward, illuminating the details of the space. The shadows of the hand-carved details and the grand hollowness of the room were accentuated. I felt like we were dining in a museum, when it was closed at night. Yet this was a temple—much more than a grand room created only for display. I could feel the ritualistic opulence from a time before the words Jesus Christ had ever been spoken. For the close of the evening, we all went for a guided night walk around the grounds.

Prisha was very eager for all of us to come. She was almost skipping ahead, leading the way. She shined her lantern in the direction of what appeared to be a massive, white, glowing sphere. "You see, you have all come at just the right time. Here is a very rare flower. We call this Brahma's flower, or the King of Himalaya's flower. Look above." She motioned with her finger as she spoke these words.

We looked up into the sky. The moon was full and massive. It seemed almost too low, casting a blue light on everything in sight. The surrounding universe shined laser pricks of starlight into our eyes. I looked again at the flower—an apparition.

Prisha began. "It blooms only once in its lifetime and only under a full moon at around midnight."

I took another look and smelled the rare flower's perfume. We watched it stretch its petals backward. One fell off and the one next to that one began rapidly wilting. Its beauty was enhanced by witnessing it express the full arc of life and death all in one singular moment I thought of James ... yet again.

I thought of his duality in sweetness and sadness and how beautifully he seemed to feel the world around him. I thought, *What I feel for him is life and death.*

Good God! Would I ever see him again? Was he the one? My soul mate? I felt in all of my being that he was. I wanted to smell him, like I could smell this flower. I wanted him to look at me the way he had at the pools. I wanted him to touch my face the way he had done. I wanted us to lie next to each other, feeling our bodies fitting together so perfectly, escaping the emptiness and this tortuous human existence for nights and years. I wanted the two of us to face the darkness together, forever. I wanted us to exist in the remaining time of our lives in a state of elated oneness—our love never waning. Never separated. Never causing pain to each other. Was that too much to ask for?

I decided that I would write him. My mother's warning was still with me. *Wouldn't any mother warn her daughter from having her heart broken? Is that not the risk of loving?* Although I know that is not what she meant. There was something she knew. *What was it?* It doesn't matter anyhow, because I can't help myself. The Brahma's bloom inspired me with its beauty. *Why hasn't he contacted me?* I reminded myself I had no phone and was on the run.

I wanted to email him or find a way to stalk him on social media. Although, I didn't have his email, I was sure I could find it somewhere online. He was in a band after all. I found a very old computer that was still running on dial-up in the temple's "office." I let my fingers meld with the clunky, inverted surfaces of the ancient keyboard. I felt a waft enter the room followed by a mephitic cloud that hung over me. I resisted it until I could no longer. It was seeping into my pores. I knew immediately that I could not send a signal digitally. That was definitely a way to call the Countess in. Social media was her domain for certain. I knew even an email could be traced by one of her "helpers." The only way I could think to contact him was the old-fashioned way—through the mail. While googling I managed to find a New York City address attached to his name. *This must be it.*

I gathered my courage and started my letter. I had to see him. I asked all the usuals and wrote way too many drafts. *I practically don't know how to use a pen and paper anymore.*

But I finally did it and I invited him to come see me. Now all I had to do was wait an excruciatingly long time for the letter to reach him and then wait another increment of excruciatingly long time for his answer.

HIMALAYAN DAWN

Bells were ringing over and over. I looked out my stone cut window toward the mountains. I saw a golden rooftop that belonged to an open-air pavilion. There was just a hint of sun dancing in the black air. *It must be 5:00 a.m..*

A temple attendee came to my room holding a cup of hot tea, with a flower resting on top. She stood smiling in my doorway, not leaving or speaking. I put on a long, white linen dress and drank half of my tea. I then followed this young girl to the very same open-air pavilion I had just been looking at. There were beautiful mats on the ground and a shrine with fresh cut flowers. The petals from last night's Brahma's flower blooming were scattered around a small statue of Krishna carved from amethyst. Van was the last to join. We started our morning meditation.

"Stack your spine. Let it reach down into the core of the Earth. Repeat in your head, 'Let go,'" Dechen instructed us.

I struggled to achieve a state of peacefulness. Random thoughts flitted into my mind as per usual. *What are we going to eat later? What was I supposed to learn from my Native American women? Will we one day finally be able to stop running? When will I hear from James? Will Jess pull through? When will my shoulder stop hurting? When am I going to die? When will I have to face the Countess again?*

This was what my meditations were always like. The only time I had felt that I was falling into a deep connection was on the mesa in the West, right before getting torn apart by a pack of wolves.

Meditations were hard for me. I knew that my white tiger guide had told me it was one of the things I must learn to do. If only I could get out of them what I was supposed to.

I was walking in the gardens with my teacher. I watched as the water was flowing from a stone fountain. Dragonflies were mating in the sky, one on top of each other, flying in unison. Water lilies floated in a pond, providing a resting ground for any creature it could carry: mainly insects, salamanders and frogs. I opened a dialogue with him.

"How can I learn to meditate better? I feel like I am still missing what I am meant to gain from my practice."

"Patience, child. Self-love. Let's see what you have accomplished. Your body has healed and your mind has quieted. The darkness has stayed away. These are all benefits to you and those you love."

"I am still confused as to why I was attacked by the wolves. My mother's spirit and the Native American spirits guided me into an attack. I still can't figure out why they would do that."

"Do you remember what I told you the day you arrived?"

"No."

"It's not what is happening to you. It's what is happening for you."

"Ahh, yes. I remember now. What does that mean?"

"The wolves were an initiation. Think, what other animals have been in your spiritual life?"

"There was the cuttlefish that consumed me and gave birth to me. Then there was the white tiger that scared me. He required me to ask for his help with truth in my heart. Most recently, there was the pack of wolves that attacked me with their fangs and claws and wished me dead."

"These animals are your guides. They are your initiations into different levels of awareness. You have succeeded thus far in gaining their uniquely designed benefit. The cuttlefish initiated your spiritual rebirth. The tiger initiated your inner truth to be known and your courage to blossom. This was to show yourself first and maybe to the world next what and who you truly are, not what outside forces have limited you to be or believed you to be.

"The wolves initiated your strength and resilience. Their gifts and lessons were given to show you how strong you are and how you can heal from deep wounds, be they physical or emotional. I know *I am in awe* of how strong and resilient you are. Know this for yourself, child. Make no mistake. These animals are as much your teachers as they are your allies. Know that what you have learned, whether their means were gentle or aggressive, that is how they best thought to teach you. Also know they walk with you even now as we speak."

I closed my eyes and felt a sense of relief and deep gratitude for having shared my burden with Dechen and for his loving wisdom. I felt a shudder of knowing that what he said was true. At that, I gave him a hug and felt an even deeper, sense of relief.

Prisha was playing an ancient Indian instrument called a harmonium. It looked like a miniature piano in a wooden box. Dechen had us begin to chant "Ohm" three times, each one in a different way. I felt like these three "Ohms" sung by all of us was connecting us to a vibration and energy in the room. Then we began to chant. We did this ritual of chanting, meditation and yoga practice every day.

On my last "Ohm" I thought of my letter to James. I wondered how much time had passed since I'd sent it. Had it been over a week? Had he gotten it?

I found a groundskeeper and asked if I had gotten any mail. The answer was what I thought it might be, *no*. I knew logically it was too soon to expect anything, but I was still sad and even felt a slight tinge of rejection that I had not gotten a response from him yet. My heart fluttered at the anticipation of his response. *When will it come?* I made a pact with myself that I would wait another full week before asking again, so as not to drive myself mad. I immediately questioned whether I would be able to honor said pact.

Not much veered from our teachings, except for today. My body was practically healed. I thought it was a miracle, considering the condition I was in when I arrived and the amount of stitches it took to put me back together again. Just as I was loving my ritual of simplicity, Dechen explained that now was the time of change and growth. "Like in nature, your body has healed and mended. Now it must grow." We took a walk in the garden.

"Serene, I am concerned with your focus. I am sensing that there is something holding you back from yourself. How do you feel your progress is going?"

"To be honest, I feel a bit like a sham. I am having a hard time connecting or feeling a shift of consciousness. I feel like I am supposed to be good at this and all I feel is that I am terrible at this. I feel shameful that I have not been able to do what I have been told I should be able to do. Overall, I feel bad about my meditating abilities."

"This feeling 'badly' is why I suspect you are not letting go. It is exactly what is standing in your way."

"I'm not following."

"I feel your struggle is with having faith in yourself."

The moment his last words hit the air, I felt overwhelmed. A tear shot out of my eye and I felt as if my whole being was crushing inward. I started to cry because it was so much more than having faith. I only just realized, at this very moment, that I didn't think I was capable of achieving what maybe had not been achievable for others or that I deserved any of this "special" attention. Dechen wrapped his loving, strong arms around me, and shrouded me in fatherly love. He wiped the hair out of my eyes so lovingly and tenderly. I felt safe enough to continue to be honest.

"I feel like there is something wrong with me—like I am not good enough. I just can't imagine being special enough to help myself, never mind anyone else."

"Let's soften. Can you agree that every living thing is sacred and here for a reason?"

"Yes, I do believe that."

"Why are you choosing not to embrace your birthright of a sacred life's purpose?"

"I'm not *not choosing*. I just don't think I am worthy of this special purpose or maybe even my life for that matter."

After those last self-hating words came out of me, I crumbled again—because that was what was truly in my heart. I did not feel worthy of my life or of anyone's love. This true belief and pain was from a place within, within, within—so hidden and so dark—a place I'd always tried to mask and ignore. This place was my own personal darkness, where my fear of rejection and abandonment lived and thrived—a place where I tried to prove to myself over and over again the "truth" of my unlovability in others' actions. If they did not love me, I must be unlovable. If they were angry with me, I must have done something wrong. This was my place of sadness and true mania. Instead of helping myself see that I was worthy of love, I was trying to prove to myself what I felt other people thought of me. How ludicrous and how insane. I was letting other wounded individuals separate me from myself. I was allowing and even inviting their self-hate and anger to reside within me, which was not allowing me to live *my* life. My deep truth was that I did not deserve real spiritual love. I was abandoning myself every time I thought these thoughts. What was crazy was that I had no idea I believed this about myself—not until this very moment. No wonder why I was so connected to the Countess.

Dechen wrapped his arms around me once again and cradled my head in his arms, helping me to rock back and forth ever so slightly. I felt comforted.

"Let's meet tomorrow by the river, tonight we will give you a floral bath and feed you well. Your bed will be made with extra love and care."

"Thank you, Dechen," I said through my tears.

When I got to my bed after my bath, I saw a hand-carved rose quartz Quan Yin statue on my night-stand. Pink blooms were scattered on my pillows. A warm, glowing fire was dancing on my wall and a cup of steaming rose tea was sitting on my night-stand.

The next day, I awoke feeling like I had been run over by a herd of something big and furry. I felt sad and lost. I walked to the river to meet Dechen. I saw him standing, wrapped in linen robes and draped in rose quartz beads. He was illuminated in the sun like a Buddha at the moment of an enlightened death. He turned to look at me with a big smile and he began to walk down the river, taking his steps slowly and with care. I watched as the smooth river pebbles rocked his feet up and down or side to side. I followed my teacher.

It felt great to have the water rush through my toes and the sunlight wash over my tired body. Dechen kept walking, looking back every so often to make sure I was still in tow. When he stopped, so did I. I saw a larger-than-life, maybe eight-foot-tall woman. Her large, young breasts bounced as she walked toward me. Her hips and backside were curved and strong. All of her commanding form was draped in a shimmering yellow silk. It flowered and flowed around her strong young body. I heard the word, *Oshun*.

I saw a large conch shell float toward me from an unseen sea. I looked to my right and saw another beautiful woman with deep, buttery, warm eyes. This goddess seemed to be flowing, as if perpetually repoured from the turquoise blue waves of compassion that washed around her body. *Jemanja*.

I heard rushing and out of nowhere, I saw a waterfall crashing down from the sky. Another taller-than-life, strong and smooth, cocoa-shimmering female form appeared. Her warmth was emanating from her beautiful smile and large intuitive eyes. Her every movement was exciting to watch. She was completely bare except for hand-strung aquamarine crystals that showered over her head and draped over her breasts—dancing in the light. *Osara*.

Next to the river's water, I watched the sky transform into a light rainbow. The sun—a juicy apricot. I saw her serpentine form as mist swimming and slithering in the air. Her face was covered in rhodochrosite beads. She could not see with her eyes—even though her vision was stronger than the others. She was a serpent at the moment of shedding her skin. Blind, she was using her severe instincts and heart to guide us into the unseen, into the next phase. *Ewa*.

They all looked at me. Their drums played and their full beautiful mouths released songs that brought the sadness up from the bottom of every river that flowed within me. I let the music and their power raise the waters from up inside of me. The full movement of my pain was able to finally complete its arc, expressing the totality of its dance that I was always working so hard to stop.

When I felt anger and sadness, I tried to ignore it—as I was taught to do. I thought this was strength. I never allowed it to complete its dance or full movement within my soul. I was trapping this pain and keeping it in a cyclical existence. It could only repeat and repeat in its futile efforts of trying to be freed from my control. I could only release it by acknowledging it, by allowing its life to be completed, by learning what it had come to teach.

In these waters, I finally realized I only needed to acknowledge what was within and let it finish its dance to be released. My body began to move and sway from side to side. My hips circling, Samba de Roda drums were banging up from deep below. Hebola, hebola, the lushness of my swaying and circling hips bringing gratitude for my female form. The Orishas were now dancing alongside me, supporting my soul's solo. We danced hard, water falling from our lips, cascading off our hips. Sweat, salt and tears came. Our tribal rooted, birthing, quaking movements filled the world with our unseen scent. Sensuality set the sun. I thanked these goddesses for their wisdom and strength and for showing me what it was to be a powerful woman of the water—how to let my energy express fully through me.

Real strength was the ability to fully express your soul and your truth. Energy was movement and needed to be expressed; whether it was love or hate, it was all sacred and each variance of emotion existed for our benefit.

I am worthy of love. All creatures are worthy of love. It is our birthright.

My full soul had finally entered my being for the first time in my life.

"Thank you, *Oshun!*"

"Thank you, *Jemanja!*"

"Thank you, *Osara!*"

"Thank you, *Ewa!*"

CHAPTER 13

THE NEXT DAY

In the back of the garden, there was a door nestled into a mountain of ivy. We entered after walking for twenty minutes through a maze of many doors, with many turns. I was beginning to feel dizzy. The air was thinning. It seemed like the hallways were becoming narrower and the space between the ceilings and floors less and less.

The only light was coming from oil lanterns nestled in the cold stone walls. We were in the heart of the temple: it was a warmly lit room, in the shape of an octagon. The floor was herringbone. The eight directions of the ceiling were made of triangle-shaped wooden panels placed on an upward angle. They all met at a point in the center of the ceiling. The room emanated visual and physical heat.

Dechen sat in a yogi position. I did the same. He started to chant and sing. I followed each verse, repeating after him. We did this for hours. Then he pulled a bowl filled with water out of one of the wooden panels. We washed our face, hands and feet. Dechen explained that the water was from Mt. Everest. In it lived a special kind of mountain moss that was good for creation and for cell rejuvenation. I thought of my amethyst and how it had been brought to the pinnacle of Everest. We were near her now. After all, the mountain range of the Himalayas was her home. He then went to another panel and pulled out a black silk quilt. He unwrapped the quilt very carefully and ritualistically. He asked me to continue the chant he had just taught me.

"Lokah-samastah-sukhino-bhavantu" Sanskrit for "May all beings be happy and free."

I closed my eyes and started my meditation. Much like all the other times I meditated thoughts drifted in. However, for the first time since the wolves, I was able to clear my mind. After breathing in through my nose and out through my mouth a few times, I felt a different sensation, one I had not felt before. I felt a state of connection to an energy source. My being was vibrating. I felt pressure pushing into every surface on my body. I felt a rod from the crown of my head to the tail of my seated spine energetically grow. It surged deep into the Earth's core and extended into the far reaches of the cosmos above. Then, all at once, I didn't have to *try* to sit straight (or to do anything). All feeling fell away. I was locked in. My skin disappeared. My legs and arms were gone. I started to see things—and not with my eyes.

I heard faint whispers from Dechen. I could not hear what he was saying, but I saw a definitive color flush through my mind's eye after each whisper, until the color permeated everything.

First, it was a vibrant, juicy, glowing, jumping red. I felt heat and sensuality. I smelled ripened plums and tasted ruby black cherries bursting on my tongue, trickling into the back of my throat. Sour tang flexed the insides of my cheeks.

Second was an orange fireball that was prickly and spiny, tickling and piercing my skin, almost mischievously. I tasted wet, sweet blood orange. I felt tangerine juice pouring onto my lips.

Third was a blinding, bright, happy, sunny yellow light that appeared to be almost white at times. I felt light. I felt air and sand in-between my toes and the smell of hay in my nose. I tasted a combination of banana and a giant Italian lemon; it was sweet and mellow. I felt the texture of white birthday cake in my hands, frosting squishing between my fingers.

Fourth was a lime, citrine, green, gummy filled with sugar that appeared neon at times. I kept swallowing green algae and aloe down my throat. I saw fig trees and new green coconuts. The smell of a jungle filled my lungs with moist, heavy, lush oxygen.

Fifth was turquoise like the most tempting Croatian sea. I saw mountain water traveling into tributaries. Butterflies and dragonflies flipped their wings directly into the sun to shine their blue, green and everything in-between colors into the retina of my eyes.

Sixth was a deep, iris, grape jelly that glowed and vibrated more strongly than the others. It smelled of light prisms and felt filled with possibility. Every color was at its darkest hue, cool and heavy like antimatter.

The last color I saw was a light violet with a tint of red, vibrant, blushing blood. It smelled of tangy fruit. I saw glimpses of the most beautiful passion fruit flowers growing on a massive strange vine, reaching green tendrils moving ever so steadily upward, bursting even more alien blooms into the unknown. My third eye, a huge lotus unfurling explosions escaped from my crown into a spectacular everlasting view of the expanse that exists between celestial bodies.

I heard a bell chime and I opened my eyes. I first saw Dechen sitting in his yogi position, vibrating and glowing from the ebbing lantern light. Then I saw a thing that I could not believe. Starting from the base of my body, hovering in front of me was a vertical rainbow of crystals suspended in midair.

A bright rhodochrosite was in front of my root chakra. A carnelian in front of my sacral chakra. A citron quartz in front of my solar plexus chakra. A green dioptase in front of my heart chakra. An aquamarine in front of my throat chakra. An amethyst in front of my third eye chakra. A celestial fluorite in front of my crown chakra. They were all buzzing inches away from the front of my body like small, fluttering hummingbirds. Yet these crystals had no wings. I realized I too was floating. My head was almost touching the top of the ceiling. Looking down, it was beautiful to see two human forms illuminated in the darkness by the small glow of an oil lamp—two souls hidden in the deep secretive cavern of a temple with a floating color spectrum of crystals in-between them. This was what true beauty was. I knew this could only happen in such a place with only two souls—never in the view of people who did not want to see this.

As I enjoyed this rare experience from above, Dechen asked that I come back into my body. He asked me to feel each toe, each limb, each muscle, each eyelash, each cell, each molecule, each atom within my human form. I somehow did what he asked of me. As the crystals floated between us, he asked something that I thought to be even more of an impossibility.

"Now, my child, ask every fiber of your being to align with your chakras. Feel them and know them alongside the chakras of all life, whether it be mammal, plant, oceanic, or life that you are currently unaware of. Align your chakras to the universe and every dimension and non-dimension in each multiverse. Once you have made a celestial alignment, you will know what to do," he guided.

As I was focusing all of my energy, a dark rainbow appeared in velveteen darkness. It was being poured over the earth. Krishna, Kahli, Ganesha, Matangi and Lakshmi were letting me ride with them through portals and dimensions that surround our Earth. I was traveling through time and space, being pulled through the cosmos. A voice came to me and said, "Welcome to the Akashic Records." There was a different spectrum of emotion and energy for every color of the chakras. I also felt them absorbing into my mind and spirit. In the heart of the temple in the same room with Dechen, the floating crystals were being absorbed by my human form. One by one, they were downloaded into me from the Akashic library.

This is insane, I thought. But when I came to, my body was shaking and yes, I felt different. The crystals were gone or, rather, inside of me. I could feel them. Violet light was dancing in the air. It started to throb, ebb and expand. I was excited, I could see and feel my excitement was helping it grow and delight in existence.

I was filled with the light and color from the crystals. I could feel their vibration inside of me. I was like a new human, buzzing with pure energy: without mass. Maybe I could move faster through space. I was different. I felt a slight glimmer of hope. Maybe I would be able to defeat the Countess.

Dechen was rolling around the floor of the temple, belly laughing. "Serene! Oh that was just perfect. You are a good student," he said as he laughed some more.

What I had just experienced was beyond my wildest dreams. Then I wondered, *What are the Akashic Records? What is this violet light? Why am I developing a bond with it?* These were three questions I would soon ask Dechen, after I absorbed the magical madness of what had just happened.

The next day, William was off having his own adventures. He, being a solo creature, was wandering around the grounds alone. He was always just about to leave the realm of the ashram during his little hikes. Yet he never quite made it outside of the ashram's grounds. The jungle beyond the gardens and lawns would entice anyone to do so. They are alluring, dangerous and filled with treasures.

One morning, while everyone else was practicing yoga, William found himself out in the hazy mist of the early sun. Immediately, he knew it was going to be one hell of a hot day.

He put on his black speedo and found himself alone in peace by the grand stone pool. Jungle trees and manicured bushes were cleverly placed. You could smell the sweet incense of dhoop sticks burning in the air. It smelled of Lakshmi making love. He dove in and swam a few laps back and forth. He then pulled a ripped-up black Metallica T-shirt over his head and slid into his soiled black plastic crocs. That was his new favorite shoe. I had no idea why. Off he went, exploring. He was again at the edge of the ashram's property. His gaze was directed at a clearing where there was a small hut.

A young man was working and joyfully talking to a baby monkey. William, dripping wet from his swim, stood silently watching him. The young man had a beautifully prominent nose that spoke of his good looks and sensitivity. He had almond-shaped eyes. His skin was ever so milky, with levels of bluish, warm, toffee tones. William looked at him as if he was in the middle of great worship. Then a look of surprise and perhaps a feeling of embarrassment quickly came over him. He did not look comfortable in the body of a man who worships. This very moment shook his core and created a sense of wonderment.

How could a stranger captivate him in such an unfamiliar way? Then he thought of when he had spent time alone as a young man on his father's farm back in Ohio—how he would take in the structure of the old barn. He liked to run his fingers over its insides. Its walls were made from wooden planks that were halved and vertically cut trees. He could feel information in the grooves of the bark and marvel at the beauty and strength of each twined tree. He would often find himself at the ends of his days, climbing the old silo. He would sit on top just so he could look over the farm and wrap his gaze over his beloved wooden barn. He now sensed the correlation watching this young man tend to his ancestral land. There was something simple, noble and loving that he could relate to.

BACK AT THE TEMPLE

Prisha had just finished a morning session of yoga. Yema was walking by and Prisha invited him to join her. They walked for a while and found a place to enjoy a sweet sun tea and conversation by a rushing river. Yema picked up a fossilized shell and handed it to her. They went back for a lunch of dosa, a crepe-like "pancake" of fermented batter and dal (a yellow lentil soup).

The next evening, Dechen and I continued our work. I explained to him that I had some questions to ask. He said we could talk later. We went through the bowels of the temple again. Starting at the dark outer layer, we peeled away the mass of the cold shadows with each step, until we reached its warm inner heart.

We sat in silent meditation as our one candle flickered, providing heat and illumination. I sat in the center and waited for Dechen to direct me. I dared not ask him why I had to wait so long for instructions. I knew everything my teacher did was with purpose.

I decided that, until I knew what I was meant to learn, I would learn to be patient. So I did and maybe an hour passed. I felt the sensation of being locked into the universe once again. I had no human form the moment the vibrations and pressure were felt. My soul was once again free from the physical restrictions of my body. I began to float around the room. It felt like a safe place for my soul to be free and leave my body unattended. I felt hidden and knew this was a sacred space held by many.

I looked at the surrounding walls. They formed the wooden octagon shape of the room that I already knew I was in. Upon further inspection, I noticed that there were eight flat panels that connected and formed the wall's entirety. Strangely, I now began to associate these panels with different feelings and emotions. The first panel felt wise and had a fatherly energy. The one directly behind me pulled my attention to it. I felt a gentle feminine energy. The one to the right was also feminine but like that of a dear aunt or close friend. I quickly associated very specific ideas about each panel as all of the information flooded into me. Then, as I floated around, something from below called to my soul. It was intense, and my body was telling me to return my soul to it.

I entered my human vessel and started to writhe like an animal ready to copulate with its mate. Waves of heat were bending my vision. All the blood in my body was rushing to the surface of my skin. One panel in particular was pulling at the inside of my organs. I stood up and walked to that panel and laid my hands on it, obeying my urges. I wanted to understand what was causing me to feel this way. I knew it was James on the other side of this panel. I could feel his male energy and his deep, dark channeling eyes and flesh.

I heard Dechen's voice. "Child, do not let your body blind your soul."

I instantly saw it was Van on the other side of this wall. I felt sickened with shock and guilt. *Van?* Why would I feel this connection to Van? And how could I confuse his energy with James's? They were so different! Van was always goofy and unabashedly open with his need to give and receive love. He was like a handsome lion who knew he was the only one around. James was so mysterious and deep. He was secretive and very selective about how he chose to express his love. How could I confuse the two?

The next day I could feel a change in the air. There was a slight breeze, a sense of a new season. It felt dreamy and introspective. William was back at his watching post, by a great big tree on the edge of the property looking at the same young man from the other day. Today, the young man was working in his family's field, harvesting the same crop that probably had grown for centuries on this fertile land. William could not take his eyes off of the young man. He just stood there hiding in the brush like a shy, bashful giant. After maybe thirty minutes of William being lost in his own imagination, he saw that the young man was walking toward him. He was still very far away. He put his hand in the air and motioned for William to follow him. William looked behind him to see if there was someone else standing out of his field of view. There was no one.

The young man started to walk into the jungle toward the right of the field. William hastily walked around the field through the jungle, stepping on bulbous, slippery roots. He was trying to navigate his footing until he got onto what seemed to be a pretty well-manicured trail. He thought this must be where the young man had gone out. William followed the trail deeper and deeper through the jungle, batting away bugs and recognizing a familiar sense of fear that was welling up inside of him. He heard water running and saw the beginning of a babbling brook that quickly turned into a giant rushing light blue river. Upstream, he saw the young man. He had stopped. Not until he saw William did he continue walking alongside the river on the giant sandstones. William kept on. He was almost running at this point. He did not see the young man again for a while. He slowed his pace, finally stopping. Sweat was running down his forehead and chest. He was looking in every direction. There was no sign of the young man. He stood there like a tree growing from stone. He looked steady and strong, but inside, he was shaking.

He was lost. At that moment, he felt pure radiant heat behind him. He turned and saw the young man. He smiled. His teeth were perfect, his lips, broad and smooth. The whites of his eyes were strikingly clear and clean. He handed William a hawk feather, while grabbing his other hand. William was in shock when he looked down. The young man was naked. William's big, strong hand brushed against the warm softness of his behind. There was so much heat emanating from his skin. William felt lit on fire and was lost in complete exultation. The young man sensed William's fear and devotion. He was taking joy in how much William seemed to be enamored with him at this very moment. This was his first time.

They spent the afternoon swimming, feeling their body parts float while gently being played with by the rushing water. Sitting on a huge wet granite boulder, William put his legs around the young man's waist. He used the rocks behind them to anchor their connected bodies. Still in the powerful current of the water, eventually he let go. They were being carried downriver by the current. They used the smooth rocks like waterslides to slow the ride. Both wore ease-filled grins.

I had not honored my pact about checking for a letter from James. But today was the day I was officially allowed to ask the groundskeeper again if I had received any mail. I went to the temple's office to find the nice old man.

But before I could ask, he spoke. "I'm sorry, miss. There is still no mail for you."

"Are you sure? I'm sorry, but do you mind checking again? Maybe there was an afternoon delivery?" I asked, with a sweet smile and a high voice.

He went into the office and came out with something in his hand. My heart was fluttering with excitement. He unfurled his fingers as my brow furled inward. It was a small, yellow flower.

"No letter, but this little flower came for you," he said with a compassionate smile.

My face must have looked as disappointed as I felt, because his face was overcome with concern. I felt foolish and silly. I resigned to give myself one more week before asking again.

Once again, I was back in the heart of the temple with Dechen. I asked him if now was a good time to discuss the questions I had. He shook his head gently and then gestured with his hand for me to close my eyes and begin my meditation.

I was going down to the root of the Earth through my spinal cord as the crown of my head was extending to the cosmos above.

My body was moving quickly with the Earth, the sun, our solar system and our galaxy. I felt the movement of the Milky Way in the fibers of my bones and on the surface of my skin. I continued my meditation. I saw large crystals moving around on an axis. I saw gardens with running water. Then I was back in the heart of the temple in the wooden, octagon-shaped room.

My eyes were open and Dechen was there. I also saw Lakshmi standing eighty feet tall to my right and Krishna standing ninety feet tall to my left. I stood up to salute the cosmos. I saw a long rose crystal blushing with light and pulsing with sensuous blood flying off of its surface. There were veins of light slicing through the air. It grew and I grew with it. A word fell from my mouth: "Krreeeeemmmm."

Like a dance, my body lifted up and dove through the air and then sat down, Indian style. My arms were out to the side. My hands were touching my forehead. The crown of my head was resting on my hands. I felt locked into this position. I saw a triangle crystal floating with wisps of purple flying off of it. Another word fell from my mouth: "Kraaaaammmm."

I stood up and dove backward through the air, arching my back. My hands reached the ground and grabbed the back of my ankles. I then saw a large sphere crystal with wisps of many colors flying off its surface. The last movement and the last word: "Aum."

I looked to all of the panels in the room. I saw my friends and family behind the panels. We were communicating with words, thoughts, colors and emotions. Yet we were not speaking. We were, instead, showing each other pictures, sounding out words into our thoughts and sending feelings to each other. Dechen wore a smile and Krishna was playing a song with his flute. Lakshmi was shifting into many different likenesses of her goddess forms—her skin tone ever changing from fleshy blues and greens to whites and pinks.

Dechen shared his joy. I tried to hide my feelings and desires from Van, James and myself. I still had not processed what I'd felt when I had been drawn to Van when I had thought he was James. I thought better to block any strong feelings until I understood what they meant. It was up to all of us to decide what we wanted to share and what we wanted to keep to ourselves. I saw William's heart was elated. It was a new expression for him. I had never seen him so happy or felt his energy so much in the ether of creation and love.

I came to and expected the dream to dissipate. Dechen was communicating directly into and through my mind. *We could give this gift of communication to any soul we choose. We could open humankind to receive a sixth sense and help our fellow beings evolve, as we were meant to, as creatures of pure love and light. We strive for these things because that is where we are from—and where we were going. We are spiritual beings living a human existence. Think of the possibilities.*

DAWN

I heard the prayer bowls signal in their long golden tone. I looked out my window and saw the tree line of the Himalaya Mountains. I thought of how Jess would have loved this view and said a prayer for her. Then I thought, *Today is the day!* It had been a week since I last asked about a letter from James. I felt good about today. I had not asked since receiving my yellow flower of pity. I felt a goal had surely been accomplished and I should be rewarded in some way. The air was thick and sweet and the mist was heavy and full. The dragonflies' and butterflies' excitement were on grand display. The light of the first sun's rays moved up the temple, like lovers' hands, smooth, steady and strong. The temple seemed whiter than ever. I felt energy and joy in my stomach. It was definitely a good day.

The beautiful girl who brought my morning tea entered. I asked her if she could check if any letters had come for me. I was

187

too embarrassed to ask the groundskeeper again. She left and promised she would.

Soon after, Yema came by and let me know that we were moving onward with our journey. We were heading to Vrindavan to celebrate spring and the festival of colors known as Holi. I waited in my room for the girl to return. *What if James hasn't sent the letter? How will I get it if we leave?* Then I wondered if he had ever gotten my letter. *What if his band was on the road or he just didn't check his mail? Who did these days?* As my brain grinded away, the passing minutes painfully took their time to materialize and then evaporate.

I waited for the temple girl's return. I tried to breathe and relax. Finally, I heard a knock. I opened the door. It was her. "No letter for you, miss Serene."

My heart sank. I asked her if she could forward any mail to our next destination.

I took her details so that I could give her our new address once we were again settled. She politely agreed. I could see my reflection in her face. It was a look of empathy. I knew I was acting desperate the moment I saw that look staring back at me. Truth be told, I felt desperate to feel his love in any way possible. Every day, being torn away from it was becoming more and more painful. The truth of probability set in. Each day that we were not connected propelled me into the possible truth that I would never see him again. There seemed to be no more pacts left to make with myself. It had been almost two months since we arrived at the temple. That has to be enough time for a full correspondence, even in these remote mountains. My heart was sinking ever deeper. The answers to the questions I did not want to ask were flooding in and drowning any hope I could possibly have left to hang onto. *He does not care. He does not feel the same way I do. There is someone else.*

Yema, William, Van and myself all lined up outside of the temple to say our goodbyes to Prisha and Dechen. I still had my questions but finally I understood—Dechen showed me how to communicate through my thoughts. He was motivating me to practice this skill, as my questions were still burning inside of me. There was no time left. I breathed deeply and opened a sacred space as a line of connection, with no ego or realization of myself as Serene. I was speaking through my higher self—the part of me that knew Sarvin and the Native American women, the part of me that has spiritual animal friends.

Spirit to spirit, I asked Dechen, *What are the Akashic Records?* I showed him the picture of the library I had been taken to. I sounded out the sounds in front of his mind and swirled them a bit to activate their vibration: *Akashic Records.*

Dechen's answer quickly came to me in my mind. He showed me the light of my soul and then a book. The book's pages turned and there were many different people leading different lives. The pages were being shown to me as they quickly fluttered by. The book then stopped and it was open to a page that showed me the present moment. I was lined up with my friends on a driveway saying goodbye to Dechen and Prisha. The book's pages continued to move again, now slowly and passing over chunks of pages at a time. I saw other lives that looked very unfamiliar. Of course! It was the future. I then saw thousands, no millions, or an infinite number of books. There were bookshelves from which other soul lights were extracting books to study their pages. The Akashic Records were the records of all life everywhere and all life to come.

It was a spiritual library where we could go to learn in the soul world. There, we could learn about our past and present lives when we were not in a physical incarnation. I was blown away! What did any teaching before this mean? We were not taught in the West about multiple lives. The information was a shudder through my soul. I had heard about past lives but really only thought science could explain what happens at death or that maybe we do go to heaven. My only hope was that I would not simply cease to exist.

The Akashic Records had just blown the doors wide open. What a beautiful gift to know that these lives we lived were not only what mattered. This vision was showing me that Earth was a classroom. Here in this life, living could be very painful at times. I saw now that was only for the reason of learning. There were lessons we agreed we needed to learn before we incarnated. The pain was only our teacher. It happened for us—not to us! I finally understood the first words Dechen had spoken to me the day we arrived. In the spirit world, we lived! That was who we were! Spirit! We were always spirit and sometimes human!

I used my newfound gift of mental communication. I thanked Dechen by sending him a picture of hands pressed together. Then I showed him the violet light that I had been conversing with.

He showed me the amethyst that I was carrying with me in my pocket—the one that Gertrude had given me. There were many violet lights glowing all around us. I understood now. These were souls. The violet lights were soul energy. They were somehow connected to the amethyst.

I got another vision in my mind's eye. It was the Earth forming and my crystal forming deep within her. In the beginning, the birth of Earth's core was purple and glowing. *The purple light was soul energy; it was Akashic energy. My crystal was part of the earth's soul! Wow! My mind was now officially blown away.*

I searched with my fingers in my pocket. I held a part of Earth's soul up to the light. I saw it with new eyes. The sun shined so tenderly on it. Then images all flashed together simultaneously in my mind. The violet lights in the creation space (my amethyst, the earth's violet light, my own violet light and the Akashic Records) were all one in the same! The violet light was pure Akashic energy and we were all connected through it.

I kissed my amethyst. Dechen walked over and gave it a kiss too. He showed me a huge smile and we embraced. Prisha and Yema let their bodies take time in saying goodbye as their embrace lingered long and deeply. The look they exchanged told me they needed more time together and would probably be reunited soon.

I felt like Dechen was a long-lost father. After we hugged each other, I handed him a necklace. I had made it the night before with beads that I had been finding throughout the temple. It seemed to me that each bead had a story and was from a different period of time. He took my gift in one of his big, tanned hands. He placed his other free hand on the side of my face and kissed my forehead.

"Thank you," was all I could say.

He again gave me a huge smile and let out a belly roll laugh and simply said, "You are a good student, my child."

CHAPTER 14

Three old American cars drove up. They looked like they were Chryslers from the 1950s. We coupled up and took off.

The roads began to become more congested and soon there were rickshaws, cows, tourists, goats and bicycles. Sometimes the roads were just dirt or mud and other times they were paved. The town was alive. Piles of wood and old women wearing beautifully colored saris lined the streets. They were selling colored powder in every vibrant hue imaginable. The smells were pungent and intoxicating. The scents of marigolds, orange palash and violet-colored dhak and tesu (also known as flame of the forest) were all entering my olfactory system at a swift pace. The smells of sweet fried things and aromatic spices also took residence in my nose.

We neared our new home. You could not tell anything about it from its entrance. It was dull and plain, just two cement walls painted in cardboard-orange. The wrought iron gate was white. Upon entering a beautiful alabaster miniature Taj Mahal appeared. Once inside, we were served cool, refreshing drinks by an older gentleman dressed crisply in white waiters' clothes. The sun was setting. We had dinner while drinking and absorbing our new atmosphere.

I set to my first task of writing a letter to the temple girl to let her know the address where James's letter could be forwarded.

"Yema, can you send this letter with our address back to the Temple?"

"Sure, but why do you need to send them our address?"

"I wrote James, the guy from the night at Arenal. I am still waiting for a response. I am guessing mail must take a long time to get to the temple."

"Yes it can. How long ago did you send your letter?"

"I guess a couple months ago." I looked down at my feet because I was embarrassed at the amount of time that had passed.

"Serene, I say this with love. He would have gotten the letter and been able to send you one in reply by now."

"I know," I said in a soft whisper.

"You should not waste your time on this man. You have more important things to concern yourself with. I warn you against giving your energy away to someone who does not appreciate it."

At these last words, I felt my innards crushing and I wanted to scream. What Yema had said was true and his words sliced into my skin. I felt sad that James did not think I was worthy of his time. It must be true because I had not heard from him. Yema saw my inner destruction.

"Serene, are you okay?"

"Yeah."

Van piped up, "Oi, what are you all on about?"

I looked at Yema. He understood I wanted privacy in this matter. My ego was wounded enough.

"Nothing, mate. How goes it?" he said.

"What's that smell? Are they burning us to the ground tonight?" Van said with a chuckle.

Yema explained that the night before Holi, celebrators burned the traditional Holika bonfires.

"Well, let's get out there and see the sights!" Van exclaimed.

William was walking by and declined the offer, saying he needed some rest.

Van made a frown like a child. "All right, mate. Feel betta."

So it was just me, Yema and Van. We set out to see the fires of the Holika under the bright full moon of spring.

My first thoughts were woven together by fear. There was something about multiple bonfires with crowds of excited people in foreign lands that made me think of the end of the world. Maybe because this was humanity at its most primal. Maybe it was the way the fire was flickering and manipulating the light over the strange faces of the crowd. It was like looking into the eyes of ghouls. The horns of the goats and bulls became more pointed and purposeful. All of the imagery before me was taking shape into a Hieronymus Bosch painting. In reality, nothing was further from the truth. We soon felt the gaiety and levity of the evening quickly unraveling like a birthday gift. It was as if everyone was a young child waiting for something big to happen—a spring Christmas.

We combed the streets. My eyes were wide open. I was trying to take everything in. Yema shot a glance toward an old woman with a five o'clock shadow accompanied by a rather healthy and stately mole sprouting from her bulbous nose. He nudged Van and said, "She told me you gave her some good loving last night." He smiled and laughed at his own joke.

"I aim to please," Van said jokingly.

Yema pointed at a cucumber and said, "That's the biggest cucumber I have ever seen."

Van added, "That's what she said last night, mate!"

They both let out some residual laughs as we continued on.

I grabbed both Van and Yema's arms. I could see bright, flashing lights and heard what sounded like a party. After entering a courtyard, we found ourselves surrounded by columns. Above our heads lived the full round moon, white like a bride, illuminating the marble with her loving glow. A few people had tambourines; others were singing, drumming, dancing and laughing.

I had found an elevated platform that was wildly decorated. One would expect to see a statue of Vishnu or a celebrated Guru siting there. It was a scared place. Yet, for some reason, I really wanted to sit up there—like a child with no inhibitions or understanding of right from wrong. I climbed up and sat between two elephants carved from marble. Their majestic trunks dancing upward through the sky, looking more like the fluid necks of regal swans and less like earthly trunks.

I sat on a purple and silk pillow that was placed on top of an alabaster lotus. I took some nearby strung together necklaces made of many marigolds, violets and pink palashes. I placed them around my neck. Above me were silver bells hanging from flowering vines. In front of me were many gold bowls filled with mixtures of oil, amethyst crystals and loose rosebuds. I closed my eyes for a minute. When I opened them, I saw Van climbing up next to me. I moved over so he could share some of my pillow. I placed one necklace around his head, dipped my hands in the oil and rubbed it on his face and arms. We sat there quietly, like good performance artists at the MOMA or Yoko and John during a sit-in for peace.

Van took my right hand and we both took our remaining free hands and turned them up to the sky. When we opened our eyes again, it was because of the many flashes that were going off from people's cameras and phones. We looked at each other and laughed.

I saw anger move over a reveler's face like a waning moon. After all, this was like putting on the Pope's robe for Ash Wednesday in a crowded St. Peter's Cathedral while he was away. Van hopped down, grabbed my waist and placed me on the floor. I grabbed his hand and we started to run. Through the crowd we went, trying to get lost, or at least not to be around angry, non-celebratory folks.

We actually made it out of the temple unscathed. We only then realized that we'd lost Yema.

"Fancy a drink, dawl? I'm parched and could be down for a bite," Van asked while looking at me.

I nodded yes. I thought, *Hell, it is a celebration after all.*

We continued on our path through the evening. The fires seemed to have burned off the humidity while cooking strange, thick smells of curry, flowers, manure, burned grass, diesel gas and animal stench. Everyone on the street either had a smile or was laughing, talking, or just taking it all in. Restaurants, teahouses, temples and bars were filling up and pouring out into the streets.

A finely dressed man with a brightly colored, sequined, embossed, flame orange scarf and white gloves welcomed us into his establishment. He spoke in English but with a distinctly proud and playful Indian accent. Every sentence he spoke was like a song. Van and I looked at each other. I walked in first. There were two men wearing white linen shirts and gold turbans standing next to large topiaries. They pulled apart two heavy velvet drapes. Leading us through a large corridor, at the end, a gold door stood engraved with Lord Shiva dancing on it. We heard music. The door opened and—*boom*—Bollywood!

There was a full production of Indian singing and dancing to club music. I felt my body move and release my sadness about not hearing back from James. It felt good to dance! To the right of the room, there were about thirty women dressed in bright, bangorama, glittering sari mania. They were singing and dancing with their delicately hennaed and gold betrothed hands, wearing heavy black kohl eyeliner around their feline-shaped eyes.

The star of the show was a stunningly beautiful woman with light green eyes wearing a red sari, dripping in gold. She was adorned by a traditional headpiece, earrings, finger rings, toe rings and bracelets all the way up her arms. Her voice was like a swan. The sitars were playing. All the women had sultry eyes and playful, coquettish smiles. We were in the thick of the crowd. Onlookers were being offered cocktails by a waiter with a monkey on his shoulder. We ordered our second bevy. The dancers dispersed into the audience and began to grab the hands of random men. By the time I turned around, Van was already attached to and dancing with a tourist-eyed, sari-wearing woman.

She was singing and smiling and before we both knew it, another eye was staring at us. One of her breasts was freed, now bopping to the music and her song. Van was mesmerized.

It wasn't long before other men came near. She smiled and pretended to act alarmed. Laughing, she ran into the crowd and behind the stage. Van smiled, I was laughing and watching as all the men dispersed looking for the lady and her breast. Van and I were on the dance floor trying to dance like Bollywood actors.

I think the drinks were taking effect. Really, we were just moving around in a ridiculous manner—sort of like serpents who just had a stroke. I was even trying to crouch down like a tigress and fell on my bum. Van quickly grabbed my hands and threw me up in the air. I landed on my feet just in time for a flying roach to hit me in the face. I screamed and began to run around in circles. Van laughed so hard he had to lean over to catch his breath.

We left the club covered in our own sweat. There was the thinnest layer of incense with the smell of bonfires in our hair. We walked down a massive amount of stone steps that led directly into the Ganges River. There were a few other lingerers like us, sitting on the steps. The sky was light pink and the full moon was bigger than I have ever seen before. It made the moment seem more magical, like we were on an alien planet looking at an alien moon.

I felt a rugged hand close over the right side of my face. I turned into it and saw Van's eyes very close to my own. For a split second, I saw every pore in his skin until it was just a sea of light green, black pupils, and honey brown, thick short lashes. His hand moved down to the back of my neck as I watched his mouth. I wasn't sure what was even happening. *And boom!* Powder in the face, just like that! We were beaming blue. The sun was up and we had just been Holied!

It was a small child who granted us our first Holi powder dusting. He was shrieking with joy throwing his blue colored powder on anyone sitting on the steps. He was having the time of his life. Another little kid snuck up behind him and threw pink powder on the blue giver. He was shocked for a moment that someone had actually Holied *him*. He shrieked again with joy and laughter. The two boys quickly became a motley pair. They moved to the next group of people, who they turned purple with their combined colors and efforts.

"Shall we, Smurfette?" Van asked. He had his hand out.

We ran home, trying to give the other kids good, fun, moving targets. By the time we got to the house, we were covered in powdered rainbows, like two doughnuts.

When we walked in the doors, I felt a pang of shame and guilt. I don't know why. I said good night. As I walked up the stairs to my bedroom, I saw Van get a blanket and sleep on the couch. James's face flashed through my mind's eye and I continued up the stairs to my bedroom and lay down to sleep.

SOMEWHERE IN PERU

Jess was lying in a small hut, writhing in pain, with Sammy by her side. Don Paddamouth rushed in and called to the tribe. The Shipibo women and men were running inside of the hut chanting icaros. They were sweeping the air with their champaca's, making wind and shaking their seeds vigorously, causing vibrations. Coaxing the spirits out of the room while extracting the viortes from her body with their mouths. They were all working humbly and with all their abilities focused—no ego, no pride, just work. Jess was moaning. She let out a small scream as one healer sucked a very strong viorte out of her. It was a stubborn one, strongly latched to something horrible from inside of her. Sammy had to hold her steady as they operated. One of the Shipibo's icaros sounded out.

"Take this darkness out, oh black magic of Earth, absorb this darkness. Oh white magic, teach me who she is. Oh green magic, help her heal. Oh red magic, take the Countess to your blood room where we can change her." She sang these words in her native tongue over and over again, shaking her seeds.

VRINDAVAN

The next morning was filled with hustle and bustle. The teakettle was going off and something was sizzling in a pan. There were giggles and chatter. I didn't get too much sleep and felt dazed. Yema gave me a look. I walked out of the room and stared at a fountain of Lord Shiva dancing and decimating what lay in his path so that new life can begin fresh and anew.

The house was gathering once again. I didn't know how much more moving around I could handle. I also felt hopeless, as no letter had come from James and we were moving camp once again. Would the temple girl be able to track me down even if a letter did come? I wanted to see him and touch him so badly. This letter was my only thread to connect me to him and I could not let it go. My obsessing was giving life to new energies within—anxiety, panic and fear. As these emotions grew in power over me, I could strangely feel the Countess's tether grow stronger toward me. My feelings of emptiness and rejection from James, my confusion and guilty feelings about Van and my shame for putting yet another friend of mine in her way were all pulling me closer to her.

She was ushering in on a river of deep darkness that I had been trying to control. It was my most guarded and secret fear. I was crouched down as a little girl with her back to me, lost in the dark narrows of my mind, soul and heart. I was feeling again that I was not worthy of real love, that I was not special enough for a spiritual and sacred bond. This was what I was dreaming of and aching for. My soul recognized this deep, deep, deep inside. As my conscious self was crashing into this reality, I felt totaled. It was here—my pain and fear of abandonment—deep inside of my chest. The Countess was feeding off of my wounded emptiness during the moments this ultimate fear of mine was festering up. I could feel her hands wrapping around my neck, crushing my trachea just like she did at Lydia's funeral.

My fear of being unloved allowed her to not love me. My abandonment of myself let anything reside in that emptiness. My own fear gave her clearance. She came in on my own self-loathing. My true inner belief that I was not worthy of love meant I was not worthy of life. She rode that inner truth like a tsunami wave into my soul. Life was love and love was life. But I couldn't seem to feel it.

Just then, a lucid vision appeared to me. She was tending to her aches and sores, feeding on souls and flesh. I could hear their screams and cries of sadness. I felt the coolness of the stone basement in her behemoth castle. I could smell the must and bacteria from the depths. The stone hadn't seen a ray of light for centuries. That kind of stone scared me. It was the kind of place where you could catch a cold that got inside the marrow of your bones. It only left when you were happy again. Happiness was the only thing that could break that frigid darkness from settling into your blood forever. Her trick was to never let the people she managed to catch have enough time to look back or to look ahead. She kept them in constant fear—a primal cage of present being that did not allow them to be aware of hope.

William had been talking to me for at least five minutes already. I had just been staring at him while I sank into this troubling thought. I needed to learn more about her. *Who is the*

Countess? She is not human. I need to find out what exactly she is. How am I meant to fight her if I do not know what she is?

He finally chimed in at a louder octave. "Hellooo? Is anybody listening to me?" he asked.

"Oh sorry. What were you saying?" I asked.

He rolled his eyes and walked out the front door. We all lined up once again to be taken to the nearest airport in groups of twos.

"Where are we even going?" I asked.

He laughed.

"Girl. I knew you didn't hear a thing all morning. What is up?" William asked.

"Everything."

I decided right then and there to really devote myself to listening to William. "How about you? How's things?" I asked with a direct intention of being present for my friend.

"I haven't told anyone this, but I met someone at the ashram," William started in.

I gasped. "Oh *my* god! No way. You?"

"Ahahah, don't look so shocked. Yes, me."

"Okay! Now I want to know everything."

"Well, there isn't much to tell because I don't even know his name. I just know that I would like to see him again."

"I have a feeling you will. Let's ask Yema if we can locate him," I said with a smile.

William looked sad at my reply. I could tell his heart was longing and he didn't have faith that he and his young lover would reunite. The throws of emotion and love were all over his being like a blanket soaked in a still river.

CHAPTER 15

MARRAKECH

We arrived in the afternoon. We all got into a 1979 Mercedes-Benz that had Arabic decals on the back windshield. We drove past the Koutoubia Mosque and watched a crescent moon appear in the late day sky above a line of palm trees. We entered the square on foot.

"Why are we in Marrakech?" I asked Yema.

"Like anything in life, I follow Gertrude's orders," he said with a laugh. "There is something here for us. So that's why we must come," he added.

I nodded and understood.

There were snake charmers and old women wearing robes, head scarves and leather babushka slippers. Each piece of clothing offered an ensemble of pastels in mint, dusty peach, violet, or deep blue. They were all selling something, be it handwoven bags or lizards. Some were sitting on floral printed bedsheets splayed out on the ground. Others sat in plastic chairs next to large bags of dried green weeds, which were actually henna, not weeds. They were offering their services to the tourists.

There were carts and stands selling fresh-squeezed orange juice and a myriad of dried fruit, merchandized in an alluring way. Dates, apricots, figs, peaches and other fruits I had never seen before were all neatly lined up, displaying their best side. We walked toward the back left point of the square, the entrance to the old medina, which was also known as the Grand Bazaar. Not one square inch of storefront space went unused. There was so much to look at and take in. The thick, sweet smell of orange blossom and freshly brewed mint tea was in the air, mixing with a faint odor of humans, drying camel skins and spices.

To the right they were selling teapots—not just one kind of teapot or one kind of glass to drink the tea from. It was more like thousands. They all looked like a genie had lived inside them. This was the case with every store in the bazaar. If a seller sold rugs, there would not be one square inch of wall or floor not covered with a rug. Bundles of them would be overflowing out of closets and layers of them on the floors would be piled so high that they would create walls and labyrinths inside the smallest of spaces. All materials reached to the heavens of Allah.

We passed a café. Yema pointed to the rooftop terrace and said that it had been bombed last year by terrorists. Four people had been killed. Even though this had happened, I did not feel unsafe. I just felt dizzy with all of the visual information and winding tunnels of the bazaar. It was like living inside of a massive animal. I was the invading bacteria and everything else belonged to the colorful, shaggy, mystical beast.

We were all tired, but so used to moving and settling into new digs none of us complained anymore.

The bazaar became more like a dreamscape as my weariness took shape and my eyes got heavy. A boy grabbed my hand and said, "Come with me. I'll take you where you need to go." I replied, "No, thank you." Yet he continued to follow us. I lagged behind as the others were moving faster and getting lost in the crowd. Yema kept turning around and looking back to make sure we were all accounted for.

The next moment came upon me with speed and thievery. I told the little boy once more in a stern and perturbed tone of voice, "No, thank you!" as he tugged harder at my arm,

Then the thievery came.

I looked at him and was stunned to see James staring back at me with hurt, tearful eyes. The next moment, I was in a dark alley right off of the main bustling thoroughfare. I was surrounded by three women wearing full long black burkas. I could only see hints of their dark kohl eyes. They were filled with venom and bitterness. One had her hand on my mouth. They were whispering some chant in Arabic. It almost had a melody to it. I felt they were cursing me somehow. Before they pushed me back into the street, all three whispered, "She is coming for you."

It was as if time had not moved. I was walking once again in front of a store that I had passed before. Yema turned his head to look back at me. I only looked at him and said nothing because I was confused. I just kept walking—and then the boy! I saw him to my right in the crowd coming toward me again. I was about to push him away from me, but I stopped. He just looked right past me while walking toward an old man selling djellabas, long hooded robes. I felt like I was going mad. The bazaar could do that to a foreigner. But this was too much. We kept walking.

Two minutes later, we went down another street and came to an unassuming door. But as was true of anywhere in this city, you never knew what was waiting for you behind a plain door.

Once the door opened, we walked into a Moroccan paradise. The first thing my eyes were drawn to was the turquoise pool of water. Surrounding the pool were tiles in an array of colors and columns holding up the surrounding walls—to keep this secret garden just that, a secret. The archways were grand. Each was a half circle divided and swooping up to a precise tip. There were pomegranate, fig and palm trees, all decked out with exotic birds of various jewel tones. There were fountains imbedded into the walls, surrounded by grand cacti and bowls filled with the all-encompassing, hypnotic orange blossom water. The girls who worked here were beautiful and happy. They wore a plum-colored uniform with loosely tied head scarves. This was where we would call home, at least for now.

The next day, we walked through the streets, turning left and then right. The color drenched, shaggy-beast bazaar was forever eye-expanding. Its spirit frequently shifting as we passed. We were in a neighborhood that was the "Brooklyn" part of the old medina. It was where the young, cool kids hung out, wearing Dior Homme spectacles, talking about Western culture. It was also more remote and inexpensive. We kept walking, which brought us to a narrow, dirt pathway separating the riads into two sides. We made another turn and let the dirt carry our feet along a road that was not even there. A huge hole covered with loose wooden planks to walk on was replaced by dirt. Truth be told, I felt like I was scaling a mountain. The hole looked deep and dark. Just then, my foot slipped off one of the wooden boards. I grabbed ahold of Van's T-shirt to steady myself as I watched a stone fall into the darkness.

A door opened and we were in an artifact heaven. There were cool marble floors, a massive open blue sky above and a second-floor balcony that one could look down from. Five men ushered us to a table while pouring mint tea. Yema was talking to the eldest in Arabic. I was floored by how amazing the rugs were. All were hand-loomed by the Berber women of the Atlas Mountains.

One of the elder men invited William to see some pottery in the riad next door. William accepted the invitation. Once inside, he was very happy he did. He was impressed with his surroundings. One thing that always held true about William was that he told you how he felt, one way or another—never a grey area. "This is fantastic!" he exclaimed. He was also pleased by the feeling of brotherly love that came together. This brotherhood curated and cultivated this very fine-tuned vision of amazing artifacts and history through art. The older man was dressed in a well-tailored, dark grey wool djellaba with a perfectly quaffed hood. His eyes were steel and his skin a soft caramel. The short hair on his head and his manicured facial hair matched his clothing and eyes. He brought William through and showed him one piece after another. William was thoroughly enjoying this. The gentleman offered his hand. "My name is Qamar. Nice to meet you. About how long are you staying for?"

William replied by stating his name and added, "I don't really know how long we have here. We are all traveling together and we never have very much time."

Qamar's eyes widened and almost looked as if they had a swift and severe case of cataract. "You must come tonight then." He handed William a folded-up piece of paper. "You will find it rather easily."

William was intrigued. He took the piece of paper. As we were all leaving this magnificent home, we added carpets and ceramics to an order that we all thought we would never be able to own or put into a home. It did not matter. They were too beautiful to leave behind. The investment in the idea of one day having a home to enjoy them in, seemed satisfying enough. It is always important to invest in your dreams.

Later that night, William excused himself early from dinner. He left the rest of us in the emerald oasis of Le Jardin, a beautiful, open-air restaurant. The medina at night could be intimidating and scary to some. The only women out at night were tourists. The dark streets were occupied mostly by young boys who tried to make you lose your way. They then showed you the way home and shook you down for as many dirhams as possible. But as in any city, it's important to keep your wits about you. William always had that. He was always in control. He found the location in no time.

Of course, it was a plain door and once opened, you were inside of a magical riad. Turquoise and white Arabic tiles surrounded the fountains and trees. A massive pool that had been carved from fleshy white marble was lit by oil lanterns. There were two young boys dressed in the same djellaba that Qamar had been wearing earlier. They were finely tailored and made from steel grey wool. The boys handed William a similar djellaba to darn then ushered him down a marble staircase that led to a cistern city of water. In the tranquil darkness, he watched the white light play and dance on the pale marble walls. The walkways navigated through a large pool of water. You could see the light dancing inside the water. It looked like something was swimming inside. Small fish maybe? There were four massive crystal clusters as tall as trees in each corner of the room.

In the center of the room stood around thirty men. All of their hoods were up. You could only see their chiseled jaws. William was oddly excited and thought once again that he loved this environment. It was cool and dry. He felt physically and visually comfortable.

"William, please meet everyone." Qamar did the introductions.

Yet William heard nothing, for he saw a young man who looked a very great deal like his lover from the ashram. He was in the midst of experiencing a strong sense of déjà vu. His heart and soul skipped a breath and a life. He laid his eyes on another man in the group. He instantly knew he was on this Earth to find this man and to love him. He felt pure recognition and knowingness of both men. William had to learn what these two men's names were. The one who so reminded him of his recent lost lover was Abdullah. The other—the man with the soul that was surely meant to find his—was named Asad.

The ceremony was beginning. The eldest, Asad, walked to the center of the room and lit five white candles, one red candle and an amber candle. He disrobed. His thighs were very sculpted and muscular. His hip bones and stomach were strong and smooth. He had short, black, thick hair that was combed back. He was a man who worked the land, a man who took care of his family, a man who stood up for his people and did the right thing. He also had a sensitivity and sensuality that suited his rugged features. His face was broad yet angular and defined. His eyes were large dark deep pools of intensity. A slight low chanting became audible. The reflecting light in the waters moved faster and soon came out to slither around their feet. They were beautiful, pearlized water snakes with steel eyes and soft flowing energy. The trees grew larger overhead, hugging and keeping the group of men together during this discrete nesting. In the trees, the figs glowed. The chameleons lost their anonymity as they too gave off a bioluminescence. The four crystals that were the gateways of the room's corners morphed into opaline labradorite stones. Labradorite was used to connect with spirit and to protect.

Asad then grabbed William's hand. William was now standing in the center. The four labradorite stones morphed back into the massive, clear quartz crystals, save for one that turned dark green and grew even larger in size. It was dioptase—a crystal that is good to heal heart wounds of any lifetime and open a divine direction to your soul mate. Another turned into a massive ruby crystal cluster. Ruby is to bring love and abundance. A third one was now rhodochrosite, a pink crystal that was shaped in massive cubes known to bring deep, compassionate, lasting love and comfort to the soul. The fourth was now a black Tibetan quartz. One of the oldest crystals on the planet, it has the ability to clean and charge the chakras, as well as give information from the universe. Once all four crystals morphed into their new likeness, young Abdullah came forward. His appearance seemed to be even more aligned to that of the young Indian man. William now looked at him and knew—they all three were part of the same soul. Abdullah unrobed while simultaneously taking off William's robe.

Asad took William's beautiful jaw in one hand and directed

his lips to his. They began to entwine their strong muscular tongues, fighting for space in each other's mouths. Abdullah was being grabbed by Asad's left hand and William's right hand. Together both of their hands separated his smoothness with their equal intent to have him at the same time. Their love created a thick, sweet smell. They all shuddered over and over again— their beings rolling into and out of one another as their energies entwined like roots from a tree. Disjointed, imperfect timing was creating an ancient harmony blessing this holy trinity with a pattern of silent sound. They were born into this moment and life, purely to have their bodies, minds and souls ignite. This moment was a metaphysical key. They did not know it. Yet they were in the process of unlocking a deeper learning of spirit, science and thought in the sanctuary of their love and the protection of this coven.

In the morning, they all smoked *shisha*, ate scones with honey and drank multiple pots of fresh, sweetened mint tea.

BACK IN COSTA RICA

The moonlight was shining on Gertrude's old beautiful face. Her curtains were dancing in the calm night breeze. There was a grasshopper perched on her teakwood bed frame. Howler monkey eyes were watching her from the trees. They were not howling their frightening night winds yet. It was too early in the evening. Gertrude's eyes were twitching and her body started to stretch and writhe in different ways.

She was dreaming—she was walking around the grounds at this very moment, while at the same time her body was lying in bed. She saw the howler monkeys in the trees watching her sleeping body as she watched herself. She asked the wind what she was meant to see tonight. Her soul floated up and toward the sky. As she continued upward, she noticed strings of dark purple energy coming from Earth. They were flowing into a single river of energy. Her soul fought to fly higher so she could see where the energy was going and where exactly on Earth it was coming from. She fought, expending an incredible amount of energy just to gain a few inches upward. Finally, her accumulated efforts paid off. She finally got high enough to see. The dark threads of energy that seemed to be coming from Earth's crust were actually not coming from the planet at all. The threads were attached to people.

Gertrude forced her focus down. She saw a couple fighting, a drunken man at a bar screaming, a homeless man passed out. He was covered in his own sickness with his pants and underwear at his ankles, dying of a heroin overdose. She saw a child getting hit, a woman in Africa receiving a female circumcision, a young boy being circumcised, a man eating a steak that came from an animal that had been abused, a person filled with anxiety walking around his home trying to sleep, a jealous wife, a friend gossiping on social media about another friend, a man taking his anger out on his girlfriend. She searched and saw that each of these people had his or her own unique thread coming from his or her body, flowing into this river of energy that was being sucked out of them.

Where was the energy going? She had to know. She fought tooth and nail to get higher. She focused her soul to see above. She gained some more height and continued to watch. The river of energy was leading her deep into a plushy, sinking feeling of darkness. She followed and felt almost suffocated from the density. There was a feeling of awful gunk filling up inside of her. The feeling was that of a kind of pain—a kind that you would never rid yourself of. It was that kind of perpetual sickening worry that spawns deep cancers in the human body—an emotion so sick it manifests into a physical death. The darkness was heavy and filled with despair and sorrow. She felt her courage diminish. She felt her energy shrink. Before she could visibly witness the destination of this muck and mire, she had a realization that she was too far in it to see it and too sad to try and go on. She was crying and weak. She wanted to vomit but could not. Her soul was beginning to taint and to lessen. The more moments in the mire, the more life and destruction that was being diminished from her spirit and from the light she carried into her physical body from our creation source.

Gertrude was now fighting to go back to Earth with the little energy she had left. She knew that she would cease to exist if she did not return to her body *now*. She felt a pull behind her. She did not want to look back. She did not want to give this pain and darkness the satisfaction of seeing the sickness in her eyes. It would know that it had caused it and that would give it more power over her.

Yet Gertrude could not fight it. She was too weak. Her head twisted in a slow and tortuous way. She saw two glistening rotted-out balls of pustule-filled pupils and a jigsaw of mangled metallic teeth framed by two mounds of horizontal flesh, puffed and cracked. They were placed together as lips. A pile of stolen, dead remains, all smashed together created a body. She now saw what all of this darkness truly was. It was the Countess. She was human loathing. She was human fear. We fed and fed and fed her so well. She was the size of a small moon—a barren black hole of a moon made of hate and pain. We had created her. We did not even have the ability or awareness to know it.

Gertrude knew she would not be able to save herself from this deep sadness and darkness that was the Countess. She only knew to do one thing. She called to Earth. She called to our planet and to her body still lying in her bed. Gertrude remembered that, as she was leaving Earth's atmosphere, she had seen a thin layer of glowing rose auric protection surrounding Earth. She was in a fight to save her life and her soul. Earth showed this to her now so she could use this information to survive.

Gertrude acknowledged the source and energy of our planet. She called on it directly for help. It was working. Earth called

211

back Gertrude's soul to her and to her body. That was Earth's sacred pact and bond to us. We were her children. She protected us. Yet she was also visibly weak. As Gertrude floated back to her body, she saw that there were tears in Earth's protective layer of love. The Countess was not only feeding off of humanity, she was feeding off of our planet.

When Gertrude was back in her body, she quickly opened her eyes. She was covered in sweat and back in her bed. The moon's light was behind a tree; the howler monkeys were going buck wild, screeching their thick, ghastly winds directly into Gertrude's face. They were only inches away, teeth glaring, saliva glistening. She swatted at the monkeys. She ran to turn on the lights and shut the shutters and ran back to her bed. She sat in silent, horrified astonishment.

BACK IN MARRAKECH

Three bells rang. Then came the call to prayer.

William decided that he would stay here in Morocco. It was also clear to us, for some odd reason, that this was where he was meant to be, regardless of the Countess or anything else going on in the world. This was William's calling: to work and be here with these men. These were his soul mates. This was his path. This was his home. Yema explained that he received an urgent message from Gertrude. It was okay for William to stay, but the rest of us must go back to Costa Rica immediately. Again James popped in my head—*a message*: I wish I would have received a goddamned message from him. Despite mortal wounds to my ego, I went and asked Yema if anything had come for me one last time before we moved again.

"No, sweet Serene, nothing has come for you. I urge you to move on from this person. He is not good for you. You need to focus. He is taking away from you, instead of giving to you. Your work here is important. He, right now, is issuing you reason to doubt. Don't you see that he is not safe? He is harmful, Serene."

"I know what you are saying is right, Yema. I can't help how I feel. It's not what I wish I felt. I wish he would just show me a sign that he cared for me. I wish that more than anything in the world right now. I felt our connection. I cannot just throw that to the wind. I still feel the connection now."

"Is it a connection of trust and love or your fear of not connecting to trust and love? You need to connect with yourself and with the source."

I knew what Yema was saying was right. I also knew I could not explain this connection I felt with James. It was so deep and strong. It was what dreams were made of, what pure ecstasy felt like. I knew it was best to not bring him up again. It would not be in my power to keep his name off my lips. Some outside force would have to help me with that. I couldn't manage that on my own.

"What about Jess? Have you heard anything?" I asked, moving the conversation along, hoping for any positive news.

"No, nothing. But no news is good news in this case."

"God, I hope she pulls through soon. I can't imagine what she is going through."

"She will, Serene! Remember, you did not do this to her. The Countess did."

"I guess, but it feels a lot like the other way around."

"It will be good for us to be back home in Costa Rica. I am sure things will come together."

My mind went back to James again. The last time I had seen him had been in Costa Rica. Just then, a thread of hope tied around that thought. *Maybe he will be there again? After all, his friend had a place there.*

CHAPTER 16

COSTA RICA

We returned and it was as if nothing had changed. The smell of jungle flowers and rain was in the air. The trees were throbbing with life. The road was muddy and holding onto each tire of our jeep for as long as it could. There were water runoffs from nearby rivers and waterfalls, decimating the way.

Gertrude was wearing a floor-length orange dress and a pink turban with a giant turquoise necklace. She seemed preoccupied, which was not like her. Despite her visually wandering mind, she kissed us with her red lips, smiling. Gertrude asked us to sit. I could see the urgency in her countenance.

"Jess is not doing well. The Shipibo tribe has been falling ill. The whole village is under stress. Don Paddamouth said she had to be placed deep in the jungle away from people. He said the things that come for her at night are strong and dark.

"They are letting her live for now because they are looking to attach to us. However, I have asked that she be sent to us. No soul can last in the darkness that she has been facing for this amount of time. We must try to heal her here. The Countess will most certainly follow her energy in. I am very concerned. I know now what the Countess is. Please listen carefully.

"We, humanity, have created her. She is a manifestation of our anger, hatred, fears, shame, guilt, worry, jealousy, pain, suffering and sorrow. She is this dark energy, which we give her. These are the energies she claims from us to build her existence. She is so in tune with our suffering that, like a manipulative lover, she feeds it back to us—perpetuating a codependent, symbiotic relationship. We have created the Countess from our constant spewing of base, negative emotions. Energy can be neither created nor destroyed, only repurposed. The Countess is our creation; she is our repurposed, toxic energy.

"I saw that Earth is being harmed. She is keeping us from our divine creativity, love, compassion, intelligence, peace and, ultimately, from the natural trajectory of our species. We humans are sacrificing our birthright to evolve. We are going to kill ourselves and our planet simply by allowing our own creations of fear and pain to take control."

She continued, "My guides have shown me how, in the beginning, before she had a name, she came to be. Our negative emotions were just helpless bits of fleshy, gooey masses like cancers that materialized in Earth's ethos, as well as deep in our organs. Our Earth sent these cancerous sicknesses out of her atmosphere into outer orbit, in order to protect herself and her beings. As our fear and emotional maladies increased, so did these gruesome, sick masses. There were finally enough of these masses floating around in our solar system that it was inevitable that two of them would collide. That is exactly what happened.

"Instead of colliding and then separating, from force, they stuck together. Their oozing, sick goo acted like glue. This happened enough times that even larger masses formed. These larger formations desired to grow. They formed with each other over and over again, clumping into an obesity of gruesomeness.

When this mass was truly powerful, it wanted more and wanted to feed directly from its source. It was hungry constantly, never satiated. It was addicted to the chemicals our brains produced: adrenaline, testosterone and cortisol. It wanted power.

"Instinctually, the mass that would become the Countess gave us whatever we needed in order for us to produce these cocktails of chemicals. She could then feed from us at will. We gave her so much nourishment. She gave us physical pleasure and a false sense of power, only to take it away. When taken away, it caused us worry and anxiety. She purposefully fractured the connection to ourselves. Now we have an entity fueled by an entire species, energetically connected to us and our planet. Our energy, like an umbilical cord, attaches us to her, like mother and child but with no way to severe the cord or be free.

"We humans shed our lives and give our energy so frequently and freely to her that we do not do much else. We are not living to our potential. She wants to perpetuate our continued rage, insecurities and self-loathing so she can prosper and feed. My children, we have enslaved ourselves to a monster. She rules us without our even knowing. Her name is human fear. Her name is the Countess.

"*We are* the Countess. We are one and the same. We have forgotten our history. Native cultures who hold the knowledge and inner wisdom of our Mother Earth and our truth have been overrun by the desire for power. Our ancient knowledge is a connection to our strength as spiritual beings. When we forget where we come from, we forget that we are interconnected to all life and death," Gertrude finished.

We all sat there frozen.

"Gertrude, I'm scared." I said.

Gertrude was still and quiet for a long time. I saw a tear escape from her eye. As she wiped it away with her hand, her rings clanked together. She looked at me and simply said, "I am too." She came over to me and wrapped her arms around me, hugging me tight. "More will be revealed soon. Our infinite wisdom will come to light." She said this in a whisper. Her words gave me a chill because I could tell she was talking more to herself than to me.

"Will there be enough time?" I asked.

"Yes, because we will create that time," she said with certainty.

"When will Jess arrive?"

"It could be a week or two. They can't take her on a plane. She has to travel by land and sea. It's the only way to keep her safe."

"We have very little time," I said with a quiver in my throat.

"No matter what happens, I will stand by your side, Serene. Do not fear death."

At that, I knew it was hopeless. Gertrude did not think we would survive. I could not breathe and tried to gasp for air.

"She's hyperventilating!" Van yelled.

Gertrude wrapped her arms around me and cradled my body. She was singing me a song in Portuguese. I began to breathe again, but only slightly.

THE NEXT DAY

I took a walk on the beach by myself. I didn't know what else to do. I wandered and tried to piece information together. How was I supposed to defeat the Countess? There was no clear answer. The sky was overcast. I looked up into the palm trees. I saw a glow around all of the leaves. I looked down to the right of the beach and saw a horse coming from the ravine. He too had a glow around him. I watched as the pelicans flew in an open triangle formation overhead. They possessed a unified glow in the shape of an arrowhead, which was connecting and surrounding them.

As they each dove directly into the waves to hunt for their evening meal, their communal glow separated from asserted force and surrounded each bird independently. *Wow*, I thought. *This light is crazy magical.* I smiled, being very grateful for this new "glow sight." I took this moment as respite from fear.

I thought of Jess and what a long journey she had ahead. I said a prayer for her soul and whispered "sorry" into the ocean breeze. I thought of Lydia and how her golden hair used to illuminate in the sunlight.

A tear ran down my face. I clenched my fingernails deep into the palms of my hands, hoping to make them bleed. I looked up into the sky and thought, *The Countess is up there draining us at this very moment.*

It was all too much to bear. I had more appreciation for what I had always felt about unseen energies. I had no idea how powerfully we could manifest such energies into the physical realm. However, I was overcome with so much sadness because we used our power of creation to our own demise. As my brain was trying to untangle a mess of emotions and thoughts, I saw two people far off in the distance.

They were walking toward me. As they got closer, I noticed that they were a couple. I could see that they were holding hands. I looked at the sky again and noticed it was still gloomy. I watched the palm trees swaying in the wind. The ocean was dark and the waves choppy. I looked up again and saw that the couple was embraced in a long kiss. I continued to walk down the beach. The sand was cold and wet and felt squishy between my toes.

Just as I was about to pass them, the couple stopped kissing, turned their heads away from each other and looked in my direction. Right then, I felt a tightening around my heart that quickly grew into a viselike pain. My body went into shock. *It was James's face.* It was James's body. It was his lips that had just been kissing Abbey. A screeching was coming from deep inside of my cavity. A nest of baby birds had croaked and left an awful sadness of death that was seeping through my being.

I wanted to die, to run and hide. I did not want them to witness the pain and utter shock that they had just caused me. I needed to protect my dying self. Yet there was nowhere to run and no immediate cover to take. I looked at a nearby palm tree. I begged it, to run over and cover me. I begged the waves to take me out to sea. I begged the biggest cloud up above to drop down and smother me. I could not believe what I was still seeing. I wanted to tear my skin off and scream. Instead, I tried to turn around and walk at a normal pace to escape my present moment of torment and utter betrayal. Yet, despite my best efforts, my head and body would not move. I only kept looking at James in horror.

He looked up. Our eyes met. I was waiting for any kind of acknowledgement. Yet, there was nothing. It was as if he was staring right through me like I was air or, worse, nothing and no one he had ever known.

Just then, my soul cringed and my stomach felt like it was filled with broken razor blades covered in poison swishing around my innards. I just stood there as they walked by me. I stood there for what seemed like forever, just trying to understand something or anything at all. Everything was lost on me from that moment on.

THE NEXT DAY

I poured myself a cup of coffee and cried into my cup. I put my sunglasses on in case anyone was around and covered my coffee with my shirt so my tears would not continue to pollute the brew. I thought, *What's the point? I have nothing left to give.* I felt thrown away. Worse, I was forgotten in plain sight. It was as if he had never known me. The way he had taken away the simple acknowledgement of my being alive and that I was a human with emotions was like a dagger in my chest. He was my happy place. I was sitting still but kept feeling like I was falling.

I only have the Countess. That was all I had left, along with this emptiness and rancid sickness inside that had once been my heart. How could I fight her now if all I wanted to do was die?

CHAPTER 17

MOROCCO

Back in the dusty streets of Marrakech, William was walking down a centuries-old road. The sun sometimes hit the hood of his grey robe as it escaped through the missing wooden planks from the overhead covering. He walked by freshly dyed alpaca yarn hanging from doors and gates. They were the deepest reds and brightest oranges. He paused to feel the heat from the just boiled yarn. He watched as the yarn reached its lowest hanging point and released the excess liquid color onto the streets below—a dance between fibers absorbing and gravity calling. William was heading back to the gardens of the coven. When he arrived, the old doors were opened by the young students. He was ushered to a table. Asad came over and took the back of William's head into his two hands, pressed the nape of his neck into his chest as he breathed in his scent and let out a deep relaxing sigh. Qamar, the elder, walked over and joined them.

"We have a very important ceremony this evening as you

know. The blue moon is upon us. It has great wisdom. It is a time of universal connection and messages from long ago."

William was listening while his eyes scanned the room for Abdullah and his hand searched for Asad's. He sipped his mint tea and asked a young boy for another scone and some figs.

NIGHT BREAKS

The large ceremonial candles were lit. The large crystals were cleansed with Tibetan song bowls. Ridding them of any stagnant energy and charging them with new energy. The men of the coven were slowly descending into the beautiful bowels of the ancient travertine cistern. They were being called to temple rituals. This evening was, in fact, already different from any other ritual event. Younger men were opening the stone floor above so that the night stars and sky could be a part of what was about to happen. Asad led the chanting.

The labradorite stones glowed and the silver serpent fish swam through the opalescent waters of the cistern. William felt something in the air. The stone smelled thick and rich, not in its usual fragrant way of minerality and waning sunlight. The water was crystal clear and the fish more sublime. The love he had for Asad and Abdullah felt more potent than ever. The coven had been uncovering many scientific theories of late, through ceremonial rituals and communing with the cosmos. But this one felt "bigger." The fervor in the air was palatable. The sound of three large gongs went off. Asad was still reading and chanting aloud from a very old book. He was pointing to the heavens above.

It is easy to forget that stars owe their light to the energy released by nuclear fusion reactions at their cores. These are the very same reactions that create chemical elements like carbon or iron. At the stars' cores, bathed in temperatures of over ten million degrees celsius, hydrogen and then helium nuclei fused to form heavier elements—a reaction known as nucleosynthesis.

During a supernova, when a massive star explodes at the end of its life, the resulting high-energy environment enables the creation of some of the heaviest elements, including iron and nickel. The explosion also disperses the different elements across the universe, scattering the stardust—the building blocks of all planets and life, including Earth.

"We are all made of stardust," William whispered.

"Yes," Asad replied. "Tonight, we will communicate with the stars. There is a message for us to receive and pass on. They hold the wisdom of our past, present and future. We must learn not with our words but through the wisdom of the atomic and subatomic particles that we share. The force present tonight will cause quantum channeling between us and the stars. We are called here to learn on a stardust level."

The men joined hands and simultaneously the greyish-blue moon floated into position. The chanting grew louder; the wind blew out the candles. The stars' lights became as bright as the moon's. It filled the room, blinding the men. Their eyes went cataract white and the four points, being the gateway crystals, vibrated audibly. The fish also came to a halt as their eyes turned into still-as-stone moonstones.

The men bathed in the starlight, glowing and vibrating. As quickly as it arrived it was gone—the light sucked back into the heavens. The stars twinkled as they always did. The moon continued on its path past the opening in the ceiling of the subbasement cistern. The men were huddled on the floor shaking and vibrating.

Abdullah was the first to speak. "I can feel the higher vibration moving through my being."

"Me too," said another brother.

"Is this science or is this God?" another asked, but it felt like he was talking to no one.

William said nothing but was intensely looking at the skin on his arm and touching his fingers.

"I know what they want me to know," said another.

Asad stood and asked that they all join hands. They did and—all let go immediately. They were transmitting information from the universe and receiving information through physical contact. What each man now knew was too much to hold twice fold.

"I know where each element of my body was made. I can see the supernovas and nebulas from where the elements in my body were forged. I know that one of the atoms in my arm was once part of a meteor. An atom in my foot was from a species that existed twenty-five million years ago—from a planet many galaxies away. I have never felt more connected. I am listening to atoms. An atom's lifespan is the same as the universe."

Abdullah finished his exclamation of new hyperawareness.

"*We are* all planes of time. There really is no time. It is all existence. I saw the darkness. Did you see the darkness coming for us? The stars raised our vibration. Why did the stars pull us through a vibration so strong and so soon? Men, touch no one and let us together figure out what we shall do with this information," Qamar guided.

William agreed. Then he booked a ticket to Costa Rica.

BACK IN COSTA RICA

I was sitting in the house trying to keep cool.

"Serene!"

I heard my name and it sounded like ... "William?!"

I feebly stood up to give him a hug. He usually hugged me and lifted me into the air. Instead, he backed away. I thought, *What is wrong with me?* Did I smell? My only solace was that his grey woolen robe seemed itchy. I didn't really want to touch it in the hot, humid air.

We all sat down for cool drinks. The feeling in the house was somber and laced with tension.

William and I soon had a moment alone, as Van and Yema tried to escape the gloom and went somewhere else. He asked, what was the matter with me?

"James," I replied. As soon as I uttered that word, the water works came.

William's face was cold. William was never good with consoling. He just said, "He's a stupid dick."

"Who's a stupid dick?' Van asked as he walked back into the room, opening a can of beer. He guzzled it down while taking off his shirt.

"No one," I said and gave William a keep-it-under-wraps look.

"Fancy a swim, dawl? Looks like you both need one," Van asked while his head was turned away.

"No, you go ahead," I replied. "I want to catch up with William."

Gertrude came over with some lavender lemonade, spilling some on the floor before she placed the pitcher on the table. William told us both what had happened only a night ago in Morocco.

"We were welcoming in the blue moon when we received a high vibration. It was a gift from the stars. I also received a message that darkness was coming for us. I know it is the Countess. I was told to stay with my brothers. I came directly here instead. I hate to do this, but I have to be the bearer of bad news." He looked at me.

My ears perked up intently, listening to his next words. "I'm sorry Serene, but you are not the 'chosen one.' The information I am receiving is telling me that you cannot help us. I came here to stop you from trying. What's worse, if you choose the path to try and stop her, it will be the opposite of what you or any of us wants. The Countess will win, the darkness will take over and you will die. I'm sorry to tell you this, but it's clearly there in the stars. I just can't see you get hurt—not after all we have been through," he finished with a defeated, sad look plastered across his face.

Gertrude sat quietly, taking in what William had just said. I couldn't really tell what she was thinking and her silence was piercing the back of my spine and my inner ear. Finally, she spoke. "You are right, William. The darkness is the Countess and she is more powerful than we had ever imagined. How exactly are the stars communicating this information about our Serene to you?"

"We were pulled through what felt like an unseen portal. We began to vibrate. The stars downloaded us with a higher vibration and an ability to see and know the interconnectedness of everything. I just know. If I touch something, I know where all of it came from. If an atom was from across the universe or from our planet, I know the difference. They showed us the darkness and the Countess. They showed Serene trying to fight her and they showed not only her death but also the death of everything. The stars are trying to help. I came here to help," William said.

"Yes, of course you did. That I do not doubt," Gertrude said with a look of deep concern, her foot tapping the floor.

I just stood there for moments trying to understand what this meant. I felt relieved. I felt hopeless. There was no plan. Just then, a rippling wave of feeling extremely foolish washed over me. I noticed that there was a part of me that had actually thought that maybe I had a chance to help save the world from the Countess. I felt sad that I was going to let down all of my teachers. I felt sad that, if I even tried to help, I would only be the problem.

"Now what?" I asked the air, Yema and Gertrude.

For the first time ever, Gertrude seemed without words and without an answer.

"Let's take a walk," William said.

I just followed like a puppy who had been shamed and scolded. What else was I going to do?

William and I went to the beach to watch the sunset together, in silence. I could tell he felt terrible. I was looking ahead at the ocean, watching the waves come in and out. I was numb, filled with droves of deafening hopelessness.

Like a cruel repeating nightmare, I saw James walking on the beach, yet again. It was like he was a ghost. My heart and soul were shattering and I felt like I was falling again. I prayed to God. *Take me now. Please let me not have to go on.* The pain was too much for me to bear. He didn't even look in my direction. He continued into the far-off distance.

William looked at me. Then he stood up and walked over to James. In horror, I watched and hoped William wasn't telling James what a mess I was. I, too, got up to leave—so I could stop what my eyes were seeing. But before I walked out toward Gertrude's house, I looked back and saw William lying down in the sand. James was nowhere to be seen. I walked back over to William.

"What did you say to James?" I asked in a shaky voice.

"All I can tell you is that something is wrong with him. I think you need to talk to him."

"Umm. He has a girlfriend and pretends to not know that I exist. I think maybe a conversation is out of the question. I am not in the business of forcing myself on people." I managed to get the last sentence out with only a slight quiver and a sniffle—as my eyes were watering. I just stared at the beautiful sunlight reflecting off the water and dug my fingernails deep into my hands again. I was trying to replace my emotional pain of soul rejection with physical pain. I knew that was the only thing that would stop me from a complete breakdown and public embarrassment. Pain for pain was the transaction and the commerce felt cheap.

The next day, I could not get out of bed. I woke up at 8:29 a.m. and watched the beautiful breeze coerce my linen curtains. They blew inside my room like white waves coming into the shallow from the depths of the sea. Logically, I knew that today was a beautiful day. I even logically knew that my life was a good one. Yet all information was unable to reach the fibers of my being. I could only lie here as I forced myself back to sleep. I woke up again at 10:30, feeling even more groggy and depressed. I decided, *Who cares? I'll just get up.*

I looked at myself in the mirror and saw my puffy eyes staring back at me. I felt a pang of nausea come over and then a feeling like my soul was being wrung out like a dirty washcloth. I convulsed with tears and moved from my bed to the floor.

My heart was continually breaking in so many ways. The lack of reason to exist and the feeling that I had let so many people down were combining to make me feel as if it was wasteful for me to breathe air.

The man I loved wanted nothing to do with me and all I could do was search for answers in my mind. I couldn't look at the ocean without thinking of him. I couldn't listen to music or see the color green without thinking of his eyes—the way they had once looked at me and how it would never happen again. *Why is he doing this? How can he be so callous? How can he have absolutely no empathy?* After a while, the tears dried because there were not any left.

I walked downstairs and plopped myself on the couch. I was waiting—waiting for the end of the day so I could sleep again and try not to feel what I was feeling—and hoping that God would answer my prayers. Then to my horror, as I was lying on the couch unshowered and feeling like a shell of a human, William walked in … with James. I shot William daggers from my eyes. James just sat next to me on the couch, looking straight ahead.

I was sure I smelled. I knew my eyes were red and swollen, as I had seen my reflection staring back at me at some point during the day (although time didn't matter to me anymore). It was one thing to be in pain but for him to see me like this and, worse, for him to know he had done this to me was unacceptable. I put on the coldest face I could muster and gathered my limbs inward, to the core of my body, to protect my vital organs. My heart was bled dry. I needed anything I had left inside of me to stay mine. We sat there in silence. I knew I would not be the first one to talk.

Sure enough he started. "Serene, this is so hard for me to explain."

"Try," I told him.

He looked at me. "Something has come over me since I have met you. All I can say is that I feel like something bad is going to happen to me. What is worse is that I know I am going to hurt you."

I breathed in anger and tried so hard for it not to be audible, but I couldn't keep anything in. Not even the sound of my breath. On the exhale, I exploded. "James! That is a lame excuse. You have control over yourself, your actions and how you treat the people in your life. It's okay that you don't like me. It's okay that you like Abbey … I get it. She is beautiful." My tears were fresh and wet again, welling up in the sockets of my eyes.

"She is not you," he said. I heard an emotion in his voice for the first time and my ears quivered, straining to hear more.

I looked at him. His eyes seemed soft and caring, almost confused even. I could sense his suffering as the sunlight filled the room. The pale stone travertine walls behind him were illuminated and I began to see the "glow" around him. It was the "glow" similar to the ones I had seen around the horse and pelicans when I first arrived back to Costa Rica. It was strange. His glow was defiantly different from all the others. Don't call me a "glow" expert just yet, though, as this has been something I was only starting to be able to see. But what I noticed was that his glow was not strong around his body. Instead, there was a glowing red orb floating around him. I saw a few purple specks of light flash. It was pretty and mesmerizing and I wondered why his was so strange and different.

I heard my mother's voice ring through my head. "Look at him."

Instantly I was compelled to take his hand—something my

ego would, normally, never have let me done. Something inside of me, an important voice, was telling me to set my pain aside. I listened to that voice. It all made sense the minute I took his hand and placed it in mine.

In the wooden heart of the Indian temple, I could never feel James. His soul never called to me—simply because his soul had no voice, no presence. I had wondered how could I love someone so much and not feel his pull. I thought of how he'd seemed almost like a ghost to me on the beach when he was walking far away in the mist and fog in early morning or at dusk. His aura wasn't even his.

I saw a flash of James as a little boy, crying and huddled over. I felt his pain. I felt his deafening detachment. I saw in the records of the universe of all living and nonliving entities that his soul, in this lifetime, was never meant to be his. I remembered the red flame that had left him the night his mother had died in the fire. It had left him and gone to the demons. They'd killed his mother to weaken him. They'd separated his soul from him that night. In my mind's eye, I saw the Countess above the demons. I saw that she was the one who had started the fire. She had separated his soul. *Did she know that I was going to fall in love with James? Was our love written in the stars but always doomed? Just like my life's mission?*

I placed his hand on the couch and looked at him. I saw energy strands from the red orb, which I now understood to be his soul. It was connected to his physical body and even a very faint glow resided in his chest. But his soul was not inside of him. The Countess had traumatized him; she had taken as much of his soul as she could without ending his life. She had let him have just enough to keep him here living in his body. *Is he half ghost? What does this really mean?*

"James, did you know this?" I asked.

"What?" he asked.

"That your soul is outside of you?" I said matter-of-factly.

"Serene, are you okay?"

"Yes, I am okay, and I am serious. Your soul is not yours."

"I do know something is wrong. And trust me, Serene. That is the only reason I was staying away from you. I have felt different after my mother died. But something changed in me that night with you at the pools. The only way I can describe it is that I felt something very deep for you and then something very dark attached itself to me. Ever since you left, something has been different and that something wants you. It wants me to hurt you. As much as I don't want to, I can't stop the darkness from coming over me. I'm trying to ignore whatever these voices are."

"James, I have never felt so connected to another human before I met you. What we have is a gift. I want to fight for what we have. I will help you in any way I can."

"Believe me, I think what we have is a gift too. That's why I have to stay away from you. I can't live with this pain and fear," he said.

"I'm not pain and fear," I retorted. "Why are you making me your pain and fear?" I begged. I looked away and felt the hopelessness set in again. I saw in my mind's eye the red orb getting stronger and James's body losing almost all of its light.

Before I knew it, there were hands around my neck. A terrible feeling entered the room. I heard a clash of thunder and the winter rains that come not only from above but sideways. Sheets of water were in full effect. I gasped for air. I tried to peel his hands away from my neck, but I couldn't. I tilted my head as far back as it could go. I wanted to see his eyes. I was looking up at him and he was looking down at me. I saw nothing but cold, callous, unfeeling rage in his eyes.

William, Gertrude and Yema rushed in. Yema and William were fighting with James to get him off of me. Gertrude went outside. She put her arms into the air and looked up into the eye of the storm. The rain was not hitting her. She was casting a small gleam of light around her and the grounds of the house.

James was finally peeled off of me. He looked like a beautiful animal that wanted to rip me apart with his hands. I swear, for a second, I could see his devotion to me and the look he had once given me. I knew it was sick to even let myself think that. I saw his pain and I saw "him" for a sliver of a second before he ran off into the storm.

Gertrude said what we all knew. "She will be coming sooner than expected."

The storm picked up. I looked out into the darkness, letting the murk and mire of the clouds fill my bones. The absence of the sun filled my heart. Two large shiny black spider crabs dripping with slick oil appeared. They had been waiting for me. I invited them into my soul and let my rage and anger take over the entirety of my essence in a most magnificent way—my head and chin down, my eyes leering up, my eyebrows cast in slant, my breath siphoned inward, my hate exuding outward.

Only then did I look at Gertrude. "Tell her to come. I will kill her."

Gertrude's face wore a look of deep concern. "Now is not the time to fight her."

"Oh this *is* the time. Either I'll kill her, or she can kill me. But, It has to end now!"

THE NEXT DAY

The storm continued. I walked out into it. I found myself again walking on the beach, alone. I walked in solitude, gathering all the darkness that would join me. I saw two sharks in the distance. I knew they were with me. I felt powerful and invincible. I felt beautifully shut down, numb, callous and ready to throw myself into a fight to the death. She had eaten my heart and strangled my soul. I wanted to see *her* suffer. I wanted to see *her* in pain. I wanted to see *her* bleed.

I heard William's words of caution play over in my head. "She will win. You will die."

I didn't care.

I saw him again, like a shade of himself floating toward me from down the beach. I didn't know what to expect—a version of the James I once knew or the rabid dark animal that wanted to rip me apart on every level, controlled by her.

Van and Yema came out of nowhere and ordered me back to the house where it was safe.

"Safe?" I laughed. I followed them back because I did not care—not about what I did or where I went.

I walked into the house, with Yema and Van in tow. I slammed the door. "I'm ready, Gertrude," I yelled into the air. "I am ready to do the work. I am ready to kill that fucking bitch!"

Gertrude was coming down the stairs ever so slowly and gingerly. It was annoying me that she was taking so much time. When she finally got to me, I thought she would never open her mouth. "Not like this, Serene," she said. "Don't you see? Right now, your pain and anger are only hers to turn on you. She is getting what she wants. She is playing to your emotions. This is exactly *not* how we will ever fight her and win. We have so little time. I need you to understand this. I'm sending you and Van to a special place. I'm hoping you will find some answers there."

"You still believe that I can fight her?" I asked like a small wounded child. I was embarrassed by my own question and scared to hear her answer.

"Nothing is certain. Nothing is ever certain. That fact alone is enough hope for us to continue on our path. If there is a sliver of a chance to save our souls, we must try," Gertrude said.

I looked down. These words were not enough. My anger turned inward. My self-loathing and fear took over. I felt so helpless. As soon as my anger transformed to sadness, I knew I could not fight the Countess.

I slept that night and could only dream about death and murder. I dreamed about the end of my own life. I awoke covered in personal disgust.

CHAPTER 18

Gertrude rushed me out of bed at sunrise. "There is no time! You and Van need to go now. Jess will be coming very soon—in a day or less. If the Countess comes before you return, there will be no hope. Go and rush back, Serene. Go now!"

Gertrude's big bracelets clinked and clanked together as she raised her arm to take a sip of something. She added, "What are you waiting for? *Go! Go!*"

When I went outside, I saw Van sitting on a black and silver motorcycle. "Hop on, dawl," he said, flashing a wide, childish smile from his sculpted, tanned face.

"Oh God," I said as I hopped on.

He handed me a helmet and after donning it, I reluctantly wrapped my arms around his stiff leather jacket. We were off.

I noticed a young girl on the side of a dirt road looking at Van. The look in her eyes made me take another look at him. I noticed through her eyes how attractive Van was. Not two minutes later, we were on a crazy, muddy jungle road, going too fast for sure. I had to hold on to Van even tighter.

I saw his eyes every so often in the reflection of his mirror. It was odd because there seemed to be so much between our gaze—two

233

helmet visors, wind, weather, speed and reflections. Yet our eyes sometimes met. There was a mist hanging in the air, shining rays of heavenly light through the jungle canopy. The earth was steamy and luscious. I smelled floral scents wrapped in green plant bursts, laced with wisps of ocean air. Life seemed more precious, I knew that mine could be taken away in a matter of hours.

When we stopped, we were at a trailhead. *Okay, a hike*, I thought. "I don't have hiking boots on. How long is the hike?" I asked.

Van was walking ahead. "Don't worry, dawl. I'll throw you over my shoulder if you can't walk it," was his reply.

"We are here!" Van said with a giddiness in his voice. The whites of his eyes were clear and his pupils big.

I looked around. There was nothing and we had not summited even a small hill. To be honest, I was confused.

He grabbed my hand and we walked around a giant boulder. "This way," he said. He put some sort of headband on me. I heard a switch turn on.

Oh man. We were going down into darkness. I demanded that Van at least tell me how long this trek was going to be. I had always been petrified of the dark. Silence. He just held my hand and guided me down multiple faces of dark, slippery rocks. I could only see two inches in front of my toes and I kept looking back to see if something was there. After way way way too much darkness, I was breathing shallow. Van instructed me to turn off my headlamp.

I scoffed as I laughed. "Hahaha."

He reached over to the top of my head. *Click*—it was off.

I was punching the air. "Van, you motherfffff—."

It was pitch-black. I heard nothing. I saw nothing. I only smelled dampness and wet stone.

"Van?" I asked in a shaky whisper.

Nothing.

"Van, please." I was fumbling to find the dumb switch on my headlamp.

As I started to panic and sweat, *wooooooosshshhhhhhhhh*, I felt a huge waft of air pass over me and—*boom!*—illumination. I could see. It was incredible. We were in a crystal cave! It wasn't just clear quartz but every color imaginable. The crystals were growing in huge massive clusters not only from the ground up. The walls and the ceiling of the cave were also covered in magnificent crystals.

Van was smiling and staring at me. "So, what do you think, dawl?" he asked.

I felt deafening energy. Each crystal had a different tone, sound, glow and hue. There was watermelon tourmaline, amethyst, topaz, citrine, aquamarine, stilbite, apophyllite, vanadinite, galena, dioptase, danburite, apatite and rose quartz.

Van had his hands on my shoulders. I turned to look at him. His hands moved to the sides of my neck as we looked into each other. I felt something. I wasn't sure if it was the crystals, the end of my life approaching, or Van. Then another *wwwwooooosshhhh*. Now that I could see, holy hell! A huge wingspan was wide open overhead. Twenty feet of wings were thrown out from each side of a massive body. It was a condor the size of a house.

I knew a little something about these magnificent birds. Yema had told us when we saw one back on our hike to the ancient city in the clouds, "When you see a condor, know there is always another one nearby."

From behind I heard a faint sound and then from overhead another *wooosshhh*. There she was, his mate. Condors live a little over half a century. At the tender age of ten, once they turn midnight black and shed their earthy brown plumage of youth, they choose a mate. Only one mate is chosen, for life. If one dies, the other commits suicide. Usually this is done by flying too high, until the oxygen is too thin to sip into its love-torn lungs. It ultimately suffocates itself by leaving the earth's atmosphere and losing consciousness. The bird falls from the edge of space and is impaled on earth's crust—all in the name of love.

I had thought James and I were each other's condors. How

could I have been so wrong? It made me so sad to think of the love we'd lost. I was drastically disappointed in our final outcome. The love of the condors and their loyalty demolished my heart. Their commitment represented what I had always yearned for and yet, somehow, had never been able to achieve. My fear of abandonment always came true. *What is wrong with me? Why does everyone eventually leave? Why do I pick people who only know how to leave?*

I felt around in my pocket. My amethyst was warm to the touch. Just then, I saw a large amethyst cluster right in front of me. I walked over to it and watched the light from my headlamp dance around its beautifully repeated pyramidal structures. Its many variances of purple changed into different shades and shapes of dancing light. I sat down, closed my eyes, placed my amethyst on my left thigh and then placed my hands on this large cave amethyst. I began to meditate, locking myself into an intense crystalized energy. This energy was flowing in from the center of the earth, directly through me. I immediately felt a deep connection to Earth. My root chakra was receiving primal energy. I could hear Her voice—yes, Earth's voice. It was low, feminine and still. Yet, its vibration was wide and broad, like a masculine energy. Her sound brought calm.

"Serene, sweet child, know that I am protecting you and all of my children with my love. I too am vulnerable. I too am suffering and being encompassed by the darkness that is the Countess. If we are connected, we will not cause harm by our creation."

"Creation." I said the word in unison with Earth. If we created the Countess with our negative thoughts and fears— with our low vibrational energy—maybe we could reverse our creation with a higher positive vibrational energy? Buddhist monks laughed to raise their vibrations. Happiness was a higher vibration. We needed to make a conscious decision to be happy, and to ultimately raise our vibration. We needed to raise all of humanity's vibration for it to work! "How can we make all of humanity decide to be happy?" I asked Earth.

"Through connection."

"I don't know how to do that."

I closed my eyes. Earth wanted to show me what was currently happening. There were many wars—some small and seemingly easy for humanity to ignore. Narcissists and the power hungry were given the responsibility to decide our futures. She was showing me all of her jungles and forests burning, all of her waters polluted with radiation. The darkness up ahead was growing and no protection from her was left. Then I was shown an image of scales tipping to one side. I understood what that meant. Once they tipped, you could not reverse the effects. Once they tipped, we lost. I saw the Giant Rock that was Her heart. She wanted to help us, but we were making it almost impossible. She then showed me the violet Akashic souls. I sent them love and saw how big they had grown. I was surprised and overwhelmed at their beauty. She showed me my own violet Akashic light living inside of me and her violet Akashic light inside her planetary core.

The amethysts, in her cave and on my lap, were vibrating. It was emanating heat and intense energy. I think I understood.

I cut myself on the amethyst crystal and let a few drops of my blood fall on the cave floor, my mother's skin. This was an offering to her—a way that I could thank her for communing with me and holding space for my body and life. When I grounded myself and opened my eyes, I asked Van if we could move this crystal. I knew we needed to get it to the ocean in the open. He said we could. It was the size of a small house. I looked at him with doubt and disbelief. "Don't worry, dawl. I know we are fighting the good fight. We will get some big boys with some big toys. I would move mountains for you." He said this and then gave me a cheeky wink.

When we got back, I ran and kept running until I got to the ocean. I dove in and let the cold saltwater wash over me. I felt a moment of relief and a thin, singular thread of "connection." It was enough. I held that thread and wrapped it around my finger and then my soul and then my heart. It was as if I had not felt this love for billions of years. This little thread was enough knowingness and sustainability for many lifetimes to come. I had placed myself in a desert of self-loathing. This angelic thread of consciousness, in contrast, was a supernova of bliss. I felt a break in my lower neck and saw a field of protection around my body.

Out of the ocean appeared Jemanja, Oshun, Osara and Ewa. I was so thankful to see them—how I needed their help.

In unison their crystalline voices sang as drums played:

> *Luar se Fez*
> *Um raio prateado*
> *Iluminano o Cèu*
> *E as e's Pumas do Mar*
>
> *Lindo claro*
> *A beira-mar*
> *Vejo mamae Yemanja*
>
> (Moonlight was made
> A silver ray
> Illuminating the sky
> And the foams of the Sea
>
> Beautiful light
> By the sea
> I see Mother Yemanja)

I looked down at my hips and watched as they swayed. I felt my body flowing to the music. The drums rose in volume and vibration. I felt immersed as a wave of deep sadness came over me. Their full lips ushered in words that I could not understand. Yet I knew what their words were weaving with my thread. A shadow lifted. I could see my anger and the anger and sorrow of others that I had let seep into my body and being. They were lifting up from me and evaporating like mist the moment Ewa looked in their direction. I then felt the music come over me again. I was taking control of my body and calling my spirit alone to reside inside of my form. I danced in the ocean, naked with the water goddess of the Orishas. I was crying tears of sadness that transformed into compassion and then deep gratitude. I cried and danced them into the sea until all of my sadness was gone.

I felt power. I ran my fingers over my hip bones, feeling their strength and severity. I marveled at the feeling of my muscles as I arched my back. Light seeped into my hair, tickled my mind. Illuminated. *I am strong.* The drums, the river song and the power of these goddesses further inspired my transformation. I finally knew what I was—a being deserving of my own love and protection. No one had the control to tell me my worth—not the Countess, not James. Only God and my soul could communicate my highest self and my truest nature. I stood in my own power for the very first time in my life.

I felt bliss and once again connected. I felt my auric egg strengthen with impenetrable white light, ten white cobras grew from my feet. Their scaled designs arched backward, their collars fanned, meeting their heads at the crown of mine—completely encasing my body in sapient serpentine protection. I was removed from human suffering and pain. I felt without a body and mind, having no connection to life through hard heavy elements. Light energy was moving through me. Each passing wave tickled the crystals in my chakras. They made different notes, sounding off in the air. I felt aligned, straightened out and compelled to help align and protect my Mother Earth and all of my brothers and sisters. I was floating in the light.

I suddenly understood: If I was meant to die, if I was meant to lose, let it be. I knew in my heart my truth was to fight. I heard William's words of caution. I chose to listen to the strongest intuition, the strongest message. That was to simply be me.

I ran to the house. I saw Don Paddamouth. I knew Jess was home. I hugged him and noticed right away that he had aged ten years. His eyes were sunken and dull; his skin had a yellowish matte appearance. I could feel the heaviness in his heart. Gertrude walked in; her jaw was visibly clenched. Nerves were like thin wisps of electricity in the air.

"Can I see her?" I asked Don Paddamouth and Gertrude.

"Yes, you should see her. Go to her," Gertrude said.

I went upstairs and saw Sammy holding Jess's hand. I gave him a hug and noticed he did not look so well either. I admired his loyalty for Jess.

I let my eyes drink in my friend. It was hard, like sipping something awful. I kept wanting to turn my head. I thought of Lydia. Then I remembered the look in James's eyes—how he'd wanted to hurt me and tear me apart.

I should have let him. I deserved it. I watched Jess's face writhe in pain. She was so thin, so frail. "Hi, Jess. You're home and safe," I whispered into her ear. I knew it was a lie. I also remembered that I had to send out positive thoughts and energy, to not get lost in the dark. It was so easy to get lost right now.

The Countess, I assured myself, was the killer, not me. Now was the moment to take action.

The sky was darkening and my throat was closing. I sensed that the Countess was moments away. I asked Van if the amethyst from the cave was here. He said it was. I asked if it could be placed in front of Gertrude's house—in the white sand facing the ocean.

I ran to Gertrude and Yema. "Can we get as many people as possible to come out to the beach for the coming sunset?"

Gertrude and Yema looked at me with pause to judge if I had gone mad. Yet, they both agreed to facilitate my wishes. I went up to Sammy and asked him to do the same. He agreed to rally as many people as he could.

I explained that I had a plan.

Don Paddamouth took Jess out to the beach and stayed with

her, fanning his champaca and singing his protective icaros. I ran inside to grab the healing vessels.

Van had somehow made good on his word. He'd managed to move the giant amethyst from the cave to where I was now standing on the beach.

I began to work.

I started to place the vessels, calling forth their respective energies to join us. White—the energy of the central sun, purification and clarity. Black—strength, power and the acceptance of our shadows. They are our teachers. Red—shamanic energy and Earth passion through the ancient knowledge of Pachamama and our sacred human past as tribal social organisms. Orange—the nomads, Berbers, ancient storytelling from the sands of Africa and the grounding of its Atlas Mountains. Yellow—the golden sun and giver of life, the Egyptian Neteru. We are gods. Green—the turquoise waters of the Orishas. Blue—Buddha, bodhisattvas, the end of suffering. Purple—enlightenment, spirit guides and astral energy. Pink—passionate love and compassion.

I began walking around the amethyst, placing large, clear quartz clusters down in the sand or in the water. I was creating my first circle of light. I then alternated spirit quartz, conichalcite and faden quartz in an outer circle. Next, I gathered the biggest and smallest branches of palo santo. I started five small fires. Circles, circles, circles—like I had learned at the ancient city. I made many sacred circles around the large amethyst. This was to hold the space for what I was about to call in.

I had other smaller crystals that I had been gathering along my travels, as well as shells, flowers, stones and feathers. I started to work speedily in a trance. I was moving my objects ever so slightly, running back and forth. I could feel when something was activated or an alignment was off. I listened and shifted them to where they needed to be in order to pick up the best energy.

Finally, everything felt in place. The sky was growing more sinister. As I worked, I struggled to pull sips of air into my lungs. Jess was crying and moaning ever louder. I saw people coming down from either side of the beach and through the jungle. Everyone from the town was there. Gertrude, Van, William and Yema were all present. I asked Yema to play the drums. I asked Don Paddamouth to sing his icaros as loud as he could and shake his champaca. I asked Gertrude to sing and shake her seeds. I began.

"I call in a sacred space, I speak to the winds of all directions. I call in energies of the highest divine light to allow messages to be received through love. I call in the central sun, the source of all life. I call in all spirit guides, angels, Mother Mary, Christ consciousness, the keepers of the jungle, the Shipibo, all animals, all plants, all trees. I call in Earth. I call in William and his coven aligned to all of the stars. I call in the sun and moon. I call to the crystals inside of my chakras, the divine knowledge of ancient ways and future ways uploaded and intertwined by the Akashic Records. I call in my teachers—Gertrude, Yema, Dondi, Don Paddamouth, Dechen and Quenia. I call in all sentient beings everywhere."

I stopped, I waited and I watched. The souls and spirits of all who I had just named revealed their presence.

I entered a meditative state, consciously raising the vibration of my energy. I looked to the people around me and asked that everyone who was joining do the same.

"Call on your strength. Call on your guides. Call on Earth and your ancestors," I yelled into the air. I was laughing on the inside and feeling euphoric. I did this purposely to raise my vibration. I then connected all of this blissful energy with all who had joined and sent them my gratitude. I was weaving my intention deep into the womb of the cosmos.

George's and Lydia's souls floating in the breeze. Quenia the samba bird was shaking her feathers. The Orishas were gathering waves of love behind them. I heard the crystal condors' wings. A moment later, I saw them circling the giant amethyst crystal grid, their feathers purposefully moving the texture of the sky.

I dropped to my knees. I pressed my head into the ground, sand in my eyes and in my hands. I called upon all of humanity's highest healed, the part of us we do not bring into our lives on Earth. I was calling to that part of everyone's soul that is always with God, the part that we must leave to return home to—the part that is too strong for our simple human forms to handle. This was the time for us to handle it.

I then sent all of this combined energy into the large amethyst, anchored in the sand, now being licked by the ocean as the tongues of the Orishas. We all watched in awe as the amethyst was activated. It was glowing so brightly that wisps of light flew off of its surface and danced into the air, creating an electric storm. Each lightning bolt touched the smaller crystals, shells and flowers, infusing them with divine light. I continued to watch as everything started to quiver. All material mass started to shift, coming in and out of focus. We were reaching multiple dimensions. I then searched for Gertrude and Don Paddamouth's eyes. I looked deeply into them, needing their support to utter these words:

"I call in my master teacher. I call in *the Countess.*"

The sky cracked with black lightning. Grey thunder rolled in. The darkness from above was swirling and gaining mass like a tornado encompassing all that I could see.

"Akashic creation energy, pull us through her power. Pull us through this portal of pain and learning. Pull us through to the other side," I yelled, while rolling my small amethyst in my hand. I covered it in my soul energy. Earth's core, was being covered simultaneously.

I continued watching the Countess's energy in the sky. She was growing, whipping up form. Using wind, rocks, dirt and anything that stood in her way to create herself. I could see what was now the shape of a mountain, worthy of the Himalaya's range. The "Countess mountain" continued to amass at rapid speed. She was loose and volatile. The moment a section came together, it fell apart, causing immediate destruction—rocks fell away, crashing to the ground. I watched as trees were being ripped out of the earth and thrown on top of her, animated by her will. They writhed like the snakes of Medusa. I watched as animals were skinned and smashed together, their raw muscles bleeding, her lips glossy with their sanguine lives.

Black shards of granite crumbled from her behemoth mass into the ocean, hitting people on their way down—all of this crumbling away in order to form the shape of her bosom and backside. Arms and legs took form as more of the mountain was thrashed aside, completing an arc of devastation. Dolphins were bludgeoned, coral reefs were shattering and people were maimed. All condemned to her form. I heard the screams of my friends. Jess's sweet voice was smothered in fear and I knew she was hovering near death. I heard Gertrude scream and Yema yell.

Everything was coming down on top of us. The sky was falling. The ocean was tumultuous and dirty.

I refocused. Through a deep, mind-melting meditation, I was able to move my energy and gather, once again, the battalion force of Akashic energy that I had called upon. I welled up a pure intention to transform the Countess. I welled up laughter, I welled up bliss and I welled up love and gratitude. I saw clearly in my mind's eye what was going to happen next. I screamed into the air:

"I call in human evolution!"

I once again wrapped my soul over my small amethyst. The action was different now and I knew what to do. I threw it at the heart of the mountain Countess. The sky continued to shake and shudder, its long clouds separated to reveal a violet light, utterly beautiful and heavenly, illuminating the universe.

This was the beginning of the end—the end of Earth, the end of us.

My small amethyst was now doing what it came to do. Everything was aflame in a heavenly Akashic glow. My face, eyes and body were covered. I couldn't see. All I could feel was stillness. I heard nothing.

Our existence and our planet were moving forward on a trajectory through multiple dimensions. This was a feeling I had surely never felt before. In my soul, I saw that we were being pushed through into a new dawn of humanity—a new dawn of enlightenment. Now we were almost at the other side of our new existence.

My sight was slowly coming back into focus. I saw the mountain was still glowing. Everything else had a shimmer, but it was no longer covered like the mountain.

Where had the Countess gone? Had that really happened?

I looked for Gertrude, Yema, anyone. I wanted to ask them what they had just experienced. Again, I looked for the Countess. I could not believe she was gone.

Still staring at the mountain, I was watching for signs of her. The mountain was no longer animated by her energy. Instead, it was peaceful and seemed that of the Earth that I knew. A sense of relief came to me as my body shook with tears. Yet my newfound clarity allowed me to see and know that, of course, this was too good to be true—too easy.

Just as this knowingness passed through me, I saw her walking from the deathly depths of the ocean. She was in the form of the Countess I had first met in the gallery. She stood six foot six inches tall. Her eyebrows were shooting violently inward, her forehead aggressively furrowed. Her breathing was swift and clean like a machine. She stopped like a blade slicing meat. She was standing tall and murderous, inches away from me. Her disdain for my existence was worn all over her face, with an extra layer of pure hatred for even having to wear it. I looked at her flesh.

A sickly cancer emerged held together by pure will, hatred

and disgust for human existence. She continued to walk toward me, screeching in a dark dialect, demanding my attention. I heard a crack. It was the sound of her arm breaking by her own hand. She did this with a look of hatred plastered on her face, no show of pain. I continued to look at the now bleeding, broken mass that had only moments ago been her assembled forearm. Seconds later, I felt a sharp pain in my own arm. I looked down in horror and saw bone popping out of my own skin at an obtuse angle. I looked up. Her head was gushing blood. Insects were crawling out of her brain. As I watched in disbelief and nauseous disgust, I felt a hot, warm gush escape my own scalp and run into my eyes.

She threw herself to the ground and actively dissipated her body in complete destruction. As she did, I watched and I did as she had done. I felt my body crash to the ground. All I could do was writhe in sheer pain. I could not breathe. I could only feel granules of sand scraping my raw flesh as my skin loosened. I was falling apart. This pain, this feeling of utter darkness was ripping through me, like an accelerated disease, disintegrating my bones, eating my flesh and polluting my blood. It was all happening so quickly. I couldn't control it. I couldn't stop it. I screamed with what was left of my mouth.

What is happening to me?

I saw the darkness in the sky once again with what was left of my eyes. The mountain was even more sinister and growing even larger. She took her own hands, wrapping them around her neck. Her face contorted as she strangled herself. My own air and connection to my life was ceasing. My entire trachea smashed.

Why? Why is it that what happens to her happens to me?

I felt my life force once again being ripped away by her will. I saw my body as a pool of bloody soup on the beach. The Countess's sloppy, flattened flesh was ferociously bleeding into the Earth. I floated up, away from my life. I saw Lydia and George; their faces were sad and defeated. They were floating along with me. I saw everyone on the beach suffering and heard sirens screaming into the space around them.

What happened to human evolution? Is this how we are meant to evolve? Are we meant to end so other life can exist?

I was trying to search for meaning and purpose. Defiled and deranged with anger, I writhed with no body. The Countess had done it again. The Countess had done this to my family, my friends and my kind.

No! No more pain and suffering!

I remembered what Gertrude and I had talked about. I remembered that we had to evoke light and positivity. That was our only weapon against the Countess.

Just then a voice came to me. "Boundaries. Guard the light."

I understood. I was not focusing on myself. I was focusing on her. I was giving away my power to her. *She* was commanding my existence and my future. I was simply not focusing on *my* path. I was focusing on hers. I needed to hold *my* space. I needed to guard *my* light first and foremost. I could not do anything for anyone without taking care of myself first.

Guard the light.

I focused on the light of my soul, the light of the crystals in my chakras. I immediately felt a wave of heavenly light, which was always there just waiting to be recognized and called upon. I only needed to acknowledge my light. Just then, a surge of organization moved through me. I was slowly returning to the messy remnants of my body. As I continued to focus on my light and the crystals within, I felt a wholeness of my body and soul return.

I was once again alive and complete. Then, something more.

I felt something trembling inside of me. My chakras were shaking like chandelier champacas. I looked at my feet, hands and arms. My flesh was not only reformed but was also illuminating with thin rainbow lights that traveled through my veins and glowed. It was just like how the cuttlefish's skin had glowed and moved. I could see and feel the crystals inside of me, multiplying in my blood and organs. The crystals were completing their own dance of perfect, sacred geometry, over and over again. They were transforming my physical body. I was blown away. I was being physically crystalized. I was no longer made of blood and bones.

I was only made of crystal and light! Each movement I made was expressing a myriad of possibilities. Each point on my crystalline surface, my "skin," was a line to an infinite amount of possibility—a multiverse of different realities and dimensions. Each line was an extremely expressive cuttlefish tentacle that spanned time and space—tentacles piercing into new beginnings and *connecting* to things I could not see.

I could hear minute sounds. *Are these the sounds of angels?* My vision was light. I could see through matter. I watched as atoms and molecules expressed their energy inside of everything from water to a grain of sand. I saw other colors that had no name. I saw bands of energy pulse and vibrate like clear rivers in open space.

What's more, I could feel love like I had never felt before—a love that I had been yearning for. There was no way to describe it other than divine love. This was my dream existence and I was experiencing it now. My gratitude was billowing out of my rhodochrosite heart and anthracite eyes.

As my new crystalized self, I continued to do what I had come here to do. I followed my path. Calling to my energy and guides, I asked to help heal her. Dondi appeared. Don Paddamouth and the Shipibo came. Everyone held hands as we started to chant and call upon our light. I started to work. The white cobras crystalized as well. Encasing me once again, growing from my feet upward, facing their heads outward, meeting at the crown of my head. Their collars flared in focus and concentration. I continued my work on a spiritual plane, yet it was also happening on the physical plane, right in front of me.

I called forth the snakes of truth that lived in the Rio Negro. They too were now made solely of crystal and light.

I was about to perform my first spiritual surgery. The Countess's body was now as whole as mine. I called forth her brain and heart. I watched as her head and chest split open. Both organs floated toward me. I took them in my hands and fastidiously examined them. I took time, slipping my Lemurian quartz fingers through the coral of her brain, watching as the thin membranes moved left or right; squeezing her heart a bit too tightly, taking joy while watching the veins expand and retract. I did this with a mischievous, childlike curiosity and abandon. I was going to help her, but I wanted it to be uncomfortable. I wanted her to know that she should allow her energy to be changed. I did this by asserting dominance.

I then gently washed them in the ocean in order to heal them. I watched as her brain matter turned from dull and grey to wilting milk. I watched her collapsed, dusty veins transform into throbbing, glistening, wet tributaries. I watched her heart turn from blood sausage, coagulated and black, to a ruddy, sanguine red. I then took her spine out from the nape of her neck—snapping it so I could extract and work with her DNA. I spun silken threads of golden nectar through the helix, string theory waves into the coils and woven thought and light into the pathways and the space in-between. I then asked the two snakes of truth to slither into the hole from which her spine was retracted. They sent their hard-hitting truth. They worked from the inside out. Allowing her to experience the perspective of a human. They shifted her perception so that she could feel *everything*.

I called forth my animal guides. I gave the wolves whatever matter needed to be pierced by their fangs. *The light gets in through the cracks.* I gave them her liver and some muscles.

The white tiger came. I gave him her heart to lick with his course tongue. I let him play with it in his mouth. This guided it to know that her life could end in a moment's notice. It transformed her heart from an abhorrent existence to gratitude.

Once I felt all of her mass and organs were aligned to a positive vibration, I placed everything back into her body. I watched her face soften as a look of curiosity moved across it.

"I thank you for teaching me and all of humanity that our soul energy, what we think and omit into the unseen, is more important and more real than what we can physically see. We are governed by the fear of not being loved and the moment of death. These truths are without physicality and the most powerful things known to humanity. It is time to understand them more. It is time to walk without shame or guilt and find joy and happiness in the breaths of powerlessness, being alone and letting go. I thank you, Countess, for allowing humanity to develop a counter energy to your powerful one. Because of your strength, we needed to be stronger. You provoked us to grow a thick, powerful positive skin. Your trying to end us only helped us reach our potential. Without you we may have never evolved. We thank you." I said these words while calling to the giant cuttlefish.

The Countess, much to her disliking, was being consumed by the massive cuttlefish as I once had been. I'd thought it to be an enlightening experience. I could tell from the look on her face that her opinion was not the same. She was being reborn. I could see a purple glow in the water as I watched her struggle. *Change is not always welcomed or easy.*

Once the cuttlefish's giant floral-shaped organ birthed the Countess, she was no longer with form. All that was left of the Countess was simply a sweet violet soul energy—now evaporating on the reflective scales of Ewa. I looked down at myself and the cuttlefish. Light and color danced within our shapes, allowing our texture and form to change. After moments of our light exuding, the cuttlefish spewed the last remnants of the Countess's energy into the great amethyst.

The amethyst immediately started to shake and vibrate while absorbing the afterbirth. The larger-than-life amethyst then broke away. No longer was it connected to the sand. We all watched it float into the sky. It throbbed and beat—a giant heart.

With every beat, it was calling in Akashic energy. It continued to beat and grow into a large glowing violet mass of purified energy, ebbing and expanding in space. At one last breath outward, it burst into juicy droplets that dispersed downward. Each droplet found a respective human head to hover gently above. The droplets then slowly floated down through each of our crowns to rest softly in-between our eyes. Most everyone, out of sheer curiosity, tilted his or her head back. It was a sight to be seen, as we were all looking at our special drops.

Moments later, after the drops had seeped into our minds, I heard chatter and felt a myriad of emotions. A strain of severe psychic pain was most present and came to the forefront. *Was it the Countess again?* As soon as I questioned this, I could tell immediately that it was not her. It was different: this pain was familiar somehow. I felt drawn to it. I watched as people were gathering at a specific spot on the beach. I wondered what they were looking at and why they were all going towards the same destination. I saw a body. Strangers had their arms stretched outward, obstructing my view. Some arms were over the person's head and some were touching the person's head. One girl laid her soft fingers on the person's shoulder. She shifted slightly and I saw an eye. I would know that eye anywhere. It was him. It was my James!

I was bearing witness to a group healing for the man I loved. I could feel what they were feeling and thinking. On this beach, his pain was deafening. Everyone else feeling less pain than him naturally felt compelled to stop and help, so they would not have to go on personally feeling his terrible suffering. I would say it was almost a selfish act. They were healing him not from a place of sheer philanthropy but from a place of sheer necessity. *They can heal! We all can feel and heal each other!*

Someone touched me. I heard their thoughts—although that seemed secondary. The real communication was an overall knowing of their feelings—a knowing of their fears, true intentions

251

and who they loved, all in one moment. We were communicating like Gertrude, Dechen and I did at times. Everyone had the "gift."

I felt the lessening of James's pain. I saw people move onto another person. This Costa Rican village was healing itself. They were starting with the people in the most pain and working their way to the ones suffering the least. This was a true purification of energy. This new connection was not allowing for individual suffering because we all shared it. No one could think while in great discomfort if he or she was not accustomed or immune to it. The most severe emotional pain happened slowly. You never noticed that you were dying because you were conditioned by small destabilizing increments that you learned to tolerate. Even when it was too much, you no longer had a measurement of severity. It all became one and the same as your tolerance grew.

Going from having little emotional pain to a severe boiling point of emotional pain was too much for anyone to bear. It had to be taken care of immediately.

Jess!

I ran to her. Sammy had his arms wrapped around her. Her face was soft and beautiful again. She too had been healed!

I walked over to James and searched his eyes. I looked for his glow. His red-flamed soul was once again his own. There it was residing within his human form. I put my hand out. He pulled himself up from the ground and wrapped his arms around me. His eyes were red and watering; finally, a pent-up burst of tears released. They fell down the heaven-sent terrain of his beautiful face.

He looked into me. *Is what was taken away truly here in front of me, returned?* He touched my face with the back of his hand, turned it around and slid it behind me. He was grabbing the back of my neck while guiding my face closer to meet his. Our faces were not even an inch away from each other. We gathered time and stopped it. We were home.

He pressed my body even closer into his. All of my feeling was lost. I was swimming. My imagined control over anything was permanently and forever lost. All time was gone. We were not just here but somewhere else too—somewhere far away. We could get there in a second if we needed too. His lips were full. Our tongues were electric eels, my mouth was full of him in so many ways. My ears were on fire. My head was lost in deep sparkly space. He took his flat, strong free hand and placed it at the base of my back while pushing my body into his.

I was insatiably wet inside of my mouth. A surge of adrenaline coursed through my body. I couldn't help it. I bit his soft skin. He let out a deep, thick, low breath. I wanted him. I could hear and feel how much of his body wanted me too. I watched as more tears ran down his face. My eyes joined his and released. I almost couldn't take the relief I was feeling.

"I love you, Serene. I have always loved you. I am so sorry for ever having hurt you. Can you forgive me?"

"I love you, too." Then I thought, *Can I forgive him?* As soon as this thought bubbled up, my emotions took over again.

I wanted to tear his flesh apart with my fingers while pressing into all of his skin. I could taste his heart and mind. They were soft and scared. His body was dominant, filled with raw energy and delicious bits of rage. I felt so drawn to all of him. It was unexplainable.

We went to my room and held each other. We rubbed our limbs like kindling to start a fire and then released each other because the energy was too much to handle. We didn't want to incinerate and die just yet. Our bodies hugged each other so tightly because the moment of release brought us back together again. Our natural bodies, as if living in a forest, felt so good together. We fit into each other perfectly, seamlessly, with no beginning and no end. We were one. It was intoxicating. Neither of us would ever just sleep again. I lifted the covers and looked at the glow coming from us. We were beautiful.

CHAPTER 19

The next morning we went downstairs for breakfast. I already knew how everyone was. I could feel them and their emotions. It was a strange new existence. The thing I could not believe about this opening of telepathic communication was that I had almost been there. Before all of this, I had been very sensitive. I think we are all sensitive. Some have an easier time of blocking their feelings, for better or worse. The unleashed Akashic energy had only slightly shifted something inside of me. Yet that slight change made all the difference. I was astonished that we were all so close to this gift of telepathy, truth and healing.

The best way I can describe it is that you only know how to get someplace if you have already been. Once you've made your way there, the path was always available to you. Even though it may have seemed out of reach, it would always be available. It had just taken humanity some time to figure out how to find the road—we had to create and face a world of darkness to access it.

Yema and Prisha were in the kitchen making cardamom coffee and laughing. An African warrior goddess was sitting at the table. Yema walked over and they passionately kissed. *Was that Dinka?*

I walked over to pour myself a cup of coffee. I looked at the coffee precariously. *I don't want to drink coffee? What does this mean?* I always wanted to drink coffee. I looked down at my hand and realized again, *I am no longer flesh and blood.*

I looked like me. At first glance, I could not tell any difference in my skin. If my eyes hovered for more than a moment, I would get lost staring at my own alien appendages. I would watch light dance and reflect in the absence of opaqueness, playing in the translucency of the gem silica that was now my predominant molecular makeup. I watched my "blood" or, rather, a violet, glowing stream rushing and flowing just beneath the surface of my crystal exterior. This violet life flow was a unique blend, consisting of the gift from the cuttlefish and my own Akashic energy. I saw thin rainbows residing in layers here and there. After moments of being lost in inner space, I began to think, *So what do I do about nourishment? Can I ever eat again? Can I drink water?*

Gertrude descended the staircase. She had on large, turquoise necklaces and huge silver and quartz crystal rings. She wore a soft grey cashmere sweater over a long, flowing blue dress covered with silk-painted lotuses. Another woman followed behind her. Hmmm. *Strange,* I thought, as I could tell she had come from Gertrude's bedroom. It was a woman I had not met before. She was mysterious and strong. Her hair was long and dyed black. She had old, strange tattoos on her hands that were bleeding into the crevices of her rich, tanned skin. She wore dark kohl eyeliner around her eyes, dots and lines around her cheeks. Her bone structure was angular and classical. The two women held hands. Before Gertrude could get any words out of her mouth, her dark companion kissed her on the lips and introduced herself as Karima. She and her white Berber linen swiftly left the room.

I only looked at Gertrude. She sent me a message that told me not to worry or pry because it would be rude. Funny, just that thought from her allowed me to respect her privacy and quelled my questions and nerves. I simply said, "She is beautiful," and added a smile as I looked at James and searched for his hand with my fingers.

"Well, my child. You did it. What's next?" Gertrude asked, even though she probably already knew what my answer was going to be—a question in fact:

"What about the Coun—"

Before I could finish, Gertrude interrupted. "Let's not speak her name anymore. You, my child, have done what we had only hoped for. You are the *human crystal!*

"Humanity is on a new path toward its intended spiritual and physical evolution. If our work continues, think of the possibilities. If we feel everyone's pain, we will have to heal all suffering before we can partake in this existence. With no pain and suffering, there will be no need for war. When we possess the ability to know all intentions there is no need to hide. Fear is lessening as we speak. Truth will set us free from these primitive emotions. Now the real growth and work can begin.

"We can co-create together with the energies that exist. We can set our energy, not for survival in a brutal world, but for the evolution of our species in a spiritual world. This freedom can give us tools to understand and think about ideas that were not possible before. As true consciousness opens, we must know and be responsible for the energy we create. It is the most sacred expression of our souls. The more we learn about our true responsibility to the energy we omit, the more powerful it will become. How we choose to cultivate and express our true soul energy is the thing that really matters when one lives. We all came here for a reason. Now the work begins, my child. And remember—pressure is a privilege."

CPSIA information can be obtained
at www.ICGtesting.com
Printed in the USA
BVHW08*0935270818
525723BV00006B/34/P